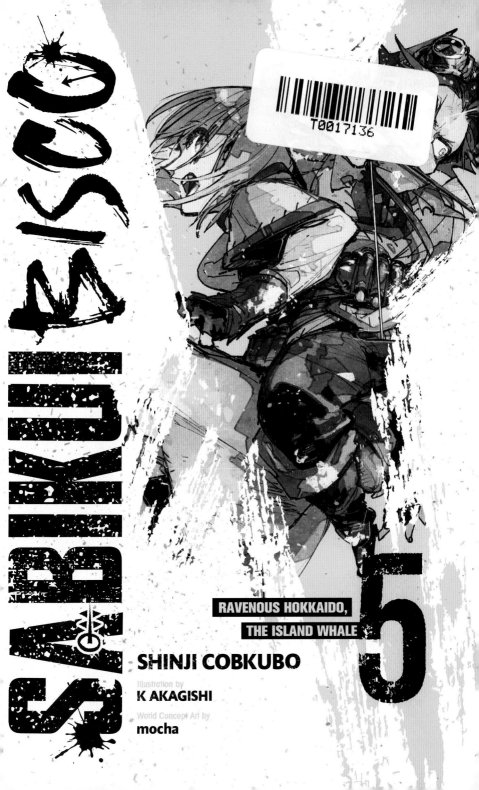

SABIKU

> When dawn arrives, and nature
> cries, we rise at earth's behest.
> And ev'ry night we sleep amidst
> the beating in its chest.

THE RUST WIND EATS AWAY AT THE WORLD

The sporko of the north are we,
devouts of beasts divine.
And servants to the life this
island's darkest bowels confine.

Let cries of ouya fill the air!
Proclaim our humble praise.
For naught but great Hokkaido's
mercy grants us peaceful days.

A BOY WITH A BOW MATCHES ITS FEROCITY

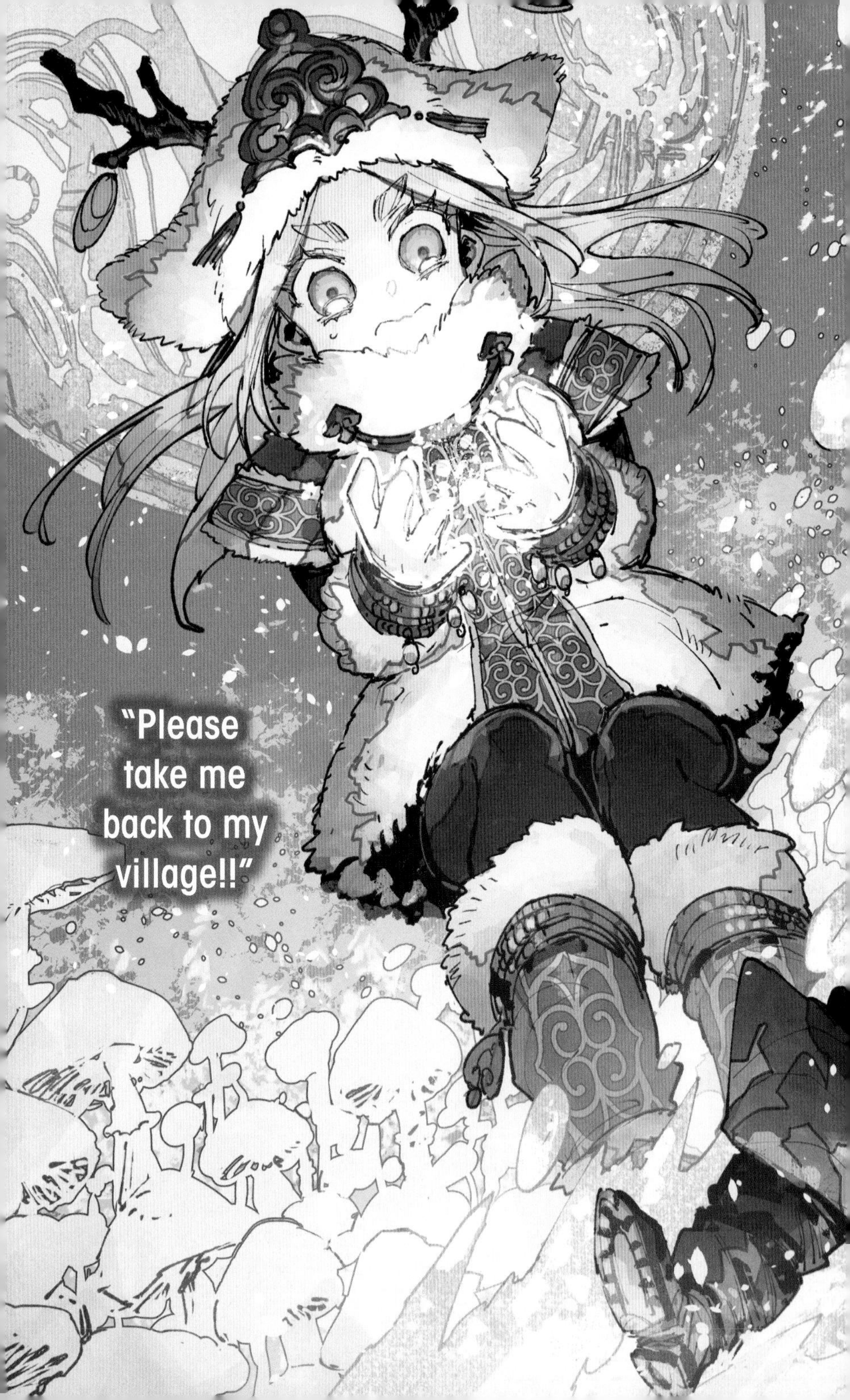
"Please take me back to my village!!"

"That was amazing, Bisco! I can't believe you're just a child!"
"I've always been Bisco Akaboshi, from the moment I was born!"

"This time, they shall be forced to know the tyranny and oppression we have endured."

SABIKUI BISCO 5

SHINJI COBKUBO

Illustration by
K AKAGISHI

World Concept Art by
mocha

Map Art by
hatena to kinoko

The Rust Wind eats away at the world. A boy with a bow matches its ferocity.

SABIKUI BISCO

5

Ravenous Hokkaido, the Island Whale

SHINJI COBKUBO

Illustration by
K Akagishi

World Concept Art by
mocha (@mocha708)

Map Art by
hatena to kinoko

YEN ON
NEW YORK

SABIKUI BISCO 5

Shinji Cobkubo

Translation by Jake Humphrey

This book is a work of fiction. Names, characters, places, and incidents are the product of
the author's imagination or are used fictitiously. Any resemblance to actual events, locales, or
persons, living or dead, is coincidental.

SABIKUI BISCO Vol. 5
©Shinji Cobkubo 2019
Edited by Dengeki Bunko
First published in Japan in 2019 by KADOKAWA CORPORATION, Tokyo.
English translation rights arranged with KADOKAWA CORPORATION, Tokyo through
TUTTLE-MORI AGENCY, INC., Tokyo.

English translation © 2023 by Yen Press, LLC

Yen On
150 West 30th Street, 19th Floor
New York, NY 10001

Visit us at yenpress.com † facebook.com/yenpress † twitter.com/yenpress
yenpress.tumblr.com † instagram.com/yenpress

First Yen On Edition: July 2023
Edited by Yen On Editorial: Payton Campbell
Designed by Yen Press Design: Wendy Chan

Yen On is an imprint of Yen Press, LLC.
The Yen On name and logo are trademarks of Yen Press, LLC.

The publisher is not responsible for websites (or their content) that are not owned by the
publisher.

Library of Congress Cataloging-in-Publication Data
Names: Cobkubo, Shinji, author. | Akagishi K, illustrator. | mocha, illustrator. |
   Humphrey, Jake, translator.
Title: Sabikui bisco / Shinji Cobkubo ; illustration by K Akagishi ; world concept art by mocha ;
   translation by Jake Humphrey.
Other titles: Sabikui bisco. English
Description: First Yen On edition. | New York, NY : Yen On, 2021- |
Identifiers: LCCN 2021046139 | ISBN 9781975336813 (v. 1 ; trade paperback) |
   ISBN 9781975336837 (v. 2 ; trade paperback) | ISBN 9781975336851 (v. 3 ; trade paperback) |
   ISBN 9781975336875 (v. 4 ; trade paperback) | ISBN 9781975336899 (v. 5 ; trade paperback)
Subjects: LCGFT: Science fiction.
Classification: LCC PL868.5.O65 S3413 2021 | DDC 895.63/6—dc23/eng/20211001
LC record available at https://lccn.loc.gov/2021046139

ISBNs: 978-1-9753-3689-9 (paperback)
        978-1-9753-3690-5 (ebook)

10 9 8 7 6 5 4 3 2 1

LSC-C

Printed in the United States of America

Ouya is the word of the land.

Happiness and anger, shock and prayer.

All dwell within this sound.

So let us come together and sing.

Ouya! Ouya!

—Festive song of the northern *sporko*

THE STORY SO FAR

How a girl became king and was consumed
by darkness:

Bisco Akaboshi, pride of the Mushroom
Keepers, infiltrated Six Realms Penitentiary
on the island of Kyushu alongside his partner,
Milo Nekoyanagi. There, they encountered
the Benibishi, a race of genetically engineered
plant people designed to serve humanity.
After rescuing their princess, a girl named
Shishi, Bisco and Milo agreed to help her
liberate the Benibishi from their persecution
and impending execution at the hands of the
mad prison warden, Satahabaki. Aided by the
mighty camellia, the three succeeded in
returning the warden to his senses, and
Shishi's indiscretions against the crown were
forgiven. With her succession rights restored,
it seemed at last that Human and Benibishi,
mushroom and flower, would be able to live in
peace and harmony. However...

*"The king must cast himself aside. Only for
the people shall his flowers bloom."*

Her father had let his love blind him to these
words, and so with sword in hand, Shishi
brought the old king's reign to a bloody and
dramatic end.

Land was eating land.

There was no other way to describe it. Cliff-faces rose and swelled unnaturally like the jaws of some giant beast, descending on towns and cities one after the other and wiping them off the map. Looking over their shoulders, fleeing citizens witnessed the very horizon lift into the air, blotting out the sun and casting a shade across the land.

It brought to mind the scene that a pitiful krill might see in its final moments before being swept into the gaping maw of a mutated blue whale, though such metaphors seemed woefully insufficient to describe the sheer scale of the cataclysm at hand. It defied imagination.

"Hurry, get to the chopper!"

"If that thing catches you, you're done for!"

The citizens of Kaso Prefecture scrambled, each fighting to be the first aboard the Kyushu allied forces' relief helicopters. The attack had come without warning, and even now the oncoming mouth stretched high overhead, casting the entire region in darkness while raining destruction in the form of undigested rock that came crashing down on the buildings below.

One fleeing woman fell to the ground as a falling boulder narrowly missed her.

"Help!! Somebody, help!" she cried out.

"Look out! Someone's fallen behind!" called another.

"We don't have time to go back," shouted a third. "The rocks are coming!"

Sure enough, a second boulder fell directly toward the fallen woman, the cold fist of nature on the verge of claiming its next victim.

Fwip! Gaboom!

A single arrow, like a streak of light, pierced the rock and blossomed into a red oyster mushroom, scattering the debris in all directions.

"...H-huh?!"

The woman, cowering in fright, slowly lifted her head, when all of a sudden she was whisked off by a figure with bright-red hair. This figure carried her in his arms while using superhuman strength to kick away falling rocks that couldn't be dodged.

"Eek! Wh-who are you...?!"

"Stop strugglin'! Unless you want me to drop ya!"

The figure leaped across building tops, his cloak fluttering in the wind, before landing heroically by the escape chopper...

...and falling flat on his face.

"Oh my! Are you okay? Someone call a paramedic!"

"Oh, piss off. I just didn't stick the landin', that's all!"

The figure leaped to his feet, his nose now as red as his hair, and handed the woman over to the allied forces, who helped her onto the craft.

"She's the last one!" he yelled. "Now get outta here before you all get squashed!"

Safely aboard the helicopter, the woman finally calmed down from her panic. She turned to the redhead and shouted, "Who are you? Hurry up and climb aboard! Where are your parents?"

"None o' your business!" he replied, wiping his bleeding nose and turning to leave. "Now stop askin' stupid questions and take off already! I'll cover you!"

"Don't be silly!" the woman cried. "You're certainly strong, but you're still just a child!"

"I ain't a kid!" he yelled back, his tiny fists shaking. "I'm a Mushroom Keeper!"

He spun around and shouted, his voice trembling. "I'm the Man-Eatin' Redcap, Bisco Akaboshi!! You sayin' I look like a kid?!"

The fire in his eyes was the same as ever, but there was no mistaking it...they were the eyes of a child. He was short, his face youthful, and even his voice had not yet broken. He was no taller than one-hundred-

and-forty centimeters, and that was generously including his spiky hair. At a guess, he looked to be roughly ten years old. His hunter's garb was tattered and baggy, and the cloak trailed along the floor. Plus, no matter how hard he scowled, he couldn't shake the look of some lovable little rascal from a child's cartoon.

Look *like a kid? You are one!*

Just as the woman was mulling over whether it was prudent to respond, the ground shook once more.

"He's started up again!" came a voice. "We need to leave now!"

"Hold on!" shouted another. "We can make room for a single child. Quickly, hop aboard!"

"Oh, can it, all of you! I told y'all, I ain't a goddamn kid!!"

The red-haired boy turned and faced the oncoming tsunami of land. He sprang toward the falling stones, leaping and somersaulting between them while swiftly drawing his trusty bow.

"If you're that damn hungry…then eat this!!"

The child—or, to take him at his word, Bisco Akaboshi—exhaled deeply, and golden spores enwreathed his tiny body. They clung to his bow and arrow, and caused his cloak to gleam, until the boy himself resembled nothing less than a miniature sun.

"Take thiiiis!!!"

Ka-chew!

The force of Bisco's sunlight arrow catapulted him backward, and the projectile birthed a row of Rust-Eater mushrooms that sprouted up in front of the encroaching land like a great wall, daring it to approach.

"Yeah! See that? Huh? Huh?!"

However, Bisco's triumphant grin lasted only a moment, for with a gigantic *Crunch!*, the great land-beast gobbled up the Rust-Eaters.

"Dammit, why are the mushrooms so weak?!" Bisco cursed. "If only I was big again!"

He landed on his feet, and just as the giant mouth threatened to close around him…

"Bisco! Get out of there!!"

Gaboom! Gaboom! Gaboom!!

A bundle of King Trumpet arrows hit their marks, and a wall of ivory stalks sprouted out of the ground, holding back the jaws for an instant. In that moment, a second Mushroom Keeper landed beside Bisco, heroically this time, and leaped away with the boy in his arms.

"I told you not to go wandering off on your own!" the second boy reprimanded, his soft, sky-blue hair gleaming in the sunlight. This was none other than Milo Nekoyanagi, Bisco's attractive partner and doctor-slash-Mushroom Keeper.

"This is nothin', I said!" protested Bisco. "Let go of me! I can handle myself!"

"Listen to me, Bisco! If I've told you once, I've told you a thousand times!"

Milo landed on one of the rooftops and placed Bisco down, clasping his shoulders and looking him straight in the eye.

"You're a child now, Bisco. You don't have access to your usual strength!"

"I told you, I ain't a kid!"

"It's good to have confidence in yourself, Bisco, but you need to know your limits! It was you who told me that misjudging your own abilities is a fatal mistake!"

Milo looked to the last of the support choppers as it took off, and he heaved a sigh of relief. With its departure, the evacuation of the city was complete. He turned back to the scowling Bisco and ruffled his spiky hair.

"But don't worry!" he said. "I'll find a way to turn you back to normal! Just promise you'll stay by my side until then."

"I already promised to stay until death. How much more do I gotta say?"

"Gosh, you're so unaccommodating, Bisco! What do you want me to do?!"

"I made my promise, so now it's your turn. *You* promise to stay with *me* until you find a way to change me back!"

"But that's just the same thing…! Ahh, Bisco, come back!!"

Just as Bisco was about to go off alone once more, Milo hoisted the child-sized Mushroom Keeper onto his shoulders and took off across the rooftops, dodging the rocks that seemed to fall with malicious intent.

"We can't just keep on runnin'!" said Bisco. "Put me down, and I'll tear him a new one!"

"You can't just 'tear him a new one,' Bisco! That thing's as big as an island! It's larger than anything we've faced before! It'll squash you flat before you can even draw your bow!"

"Then what're we supposed to do, dumbass?! That thing'll eat all of Kyushu like a rice cracker if we don't stop it!"

"…Trying to get through its hide is like firing at a mountain," Milo explained. "But what if we aim for its beak?"

Milo suddenly pulled the cat-eye goggles from Bisco's brow and, ignoring his cries of "Give them back!", zoomed in on the approaching landmass.

"Just as I thought," he said. "Look at the top of the 'beak' curving over us. The land is clearly thinnest there, can you see?"

"How can I when you took my goggles?! Give 'em back!"

Indeed, the wave of land that towered over the city did look like a curved beak, and the earth's crust seemed to grow thinner toward the tip.

"When that comes down, let's pin it to the ground," he said, fitting the goggles neatly back on Bisco's head. "Just like a massive stapler!"

"Eurgh. Gross. Talk about an intervention. But this guy's eating habits are outta control!"

Milo raised his right arm, and a green cube appeared in his palm, spinning rapidly while emitting a bright light.

"The Mantra Bow with spearshroom arrows ought to do the trick," he said. "We'll skewer that monster's mouth shut!"

"You've been gettin' pretty bold lately! You know how crazy that sounds?"

"What's the matter, Bisco? Too difficult for you?"

"Ha! Just you watch. Ask and you shall receive!"

Milo chanted his spell, and the Mantra Bow appeared in the young Bisco's hands. He gave it a pull and grinned a canine-flashing smile, satisfied.

"Nice. This bow's just my size. Couldn't have asked for one better!" said Bisco.

"*Well, that's because I made it child-sized for you,*" muttered Milo so he wouldn't hear.

Still riding on Milo's shoulders, Bisco reached down and pulled a sheaf of arrows from his partner's quiver, aiming them at the attacking landmass.

"Now, Bisco!"

Milo's King Trumpet arrow threw them high up into the air, and Bisco watched as the force of the launch tore the mushroom apart.

His eyes sparkled. "Take thiiiis!!" he yelled.

Twang! Gaboom! Gaboom!

His arrows flew like emerald meteors, driving into the soil of Kaso Prefecture one after the other. Though the power of the bow was scaled to Bisco's reduced strength, his aim was no less precise, and the spear-like mushrooms shot up from the ground, impaling the jaw of the Hokkaido land-beast.

"GRGRGRGRGRGRGR"

The island's jaw ceased moving, skewered by the fungi, and the wave of land engulfing Kaso slowed significantly. A noise like grating stones, the cry of the great beast, rang out over the land.

"It's working, Bisco! Keep it up!"

"You got it!"

"Won/ul/eroad/snew!"

Milo chanted another mantra and tossed his spinning cube. It swept through the sky, tracing a smooth path of emerald light.

"Since when could you make roads outta nothin'?!" Bisco shouted. "You been practicin' while I wasn't lookin'?!"

"It doesn't last very long!" Milo yelled back. "Stay focused!"

Milo hit the road and immediately started running, while Bisco reached down and took another bundle of arrows.

Twang! Gaboom! Gaboom! Gaboom!

Another row of spearshroom arrows erupted through a line of buildings, piercing the tsunami of land overhead. From where the spears hit, hundreds of rocks and boulders came raining down upon the duo.

"Milo, take care of those for me!"

"Okay!"

Milo's mantra generated a protective barrier that deflected the falling stones, while Bisco fired yet another handful of arrows with unmatched accuracy. At last, the wave of earth was completely pinned to the ground.

"GRGRGRGRGRGRGRGR"

"Bisco! One more! Let's end this while we have the chance!"

"Time to finish it off with a bang, then!"

Brow dripping with sweat, Bisco wrung out the last of his strength to fire the finishing shot.

Gaboom!

As if proving Bisco's inability to keep his power under wraps, the final arrow produced not a spearshroom as was intended, but a golden Rust-Eater cap that tore its way through the center of the island's upper jaw.

"GR GR GR

"GR GR

"GR…"

"…We did it, Bisco! It's stopped!"

"*Wheeze.* See that, sucker? Lunchtime's over!"

Before their eyes was a spectacle too fantastic to be believed. Multiple mushroom spears extended up from the earth of Kaso Prefecture, pinning the island's upper lip in place.

"…So?" Bisco asked after wiping his sweat. "What was that thing in the end?"

Milo looked a little troubled. "An island… At least, that's what I think it was."

"An island?! What kind of island just swims over to Kyushu for a bite to eat?!"

"An Assault Island. It's a kind of weapon I read about in accounts of past wars. They would install a ginormous engine onto an island and use it to ram into enemy lands. I think this must be the Benibishi's secret weapon in their war against humanity… H-hey, Bisco?!"

Bisco suddenly placed both feet on Milo's shoulders and stood up, training his cat-eye goggles on the island for a better look. Atop the cliffs, on the island's surface, a raging blizzard covered the whole region, making it hard to see what was up there.

"You're right—there's land! That means this *is* an island! Crazy as it sounds…"

"What can you see?"

"Not much through all this snow. If only I had somethin' to go on… Hmm?!"

"Bisco, over there!"

Bisco turned his gaze upward and spotted a small figure in a luxurious gown looking down from a high cliff. With pale skin, crimson eyes, and a camellia flower nestled behind her ear, it was clearly none other than the Benibishi girl whom both boys knew very well.

""Shishi!""

It was unlikely their words would reach her, given the distance, but Shishi had very clearly noticed them. She examined the pair for a moment, her expression glacial and unchanging, before turning and disappearing into the snow as her gown fluttered in the wind.

"Shishi!!" Bisco yelled, his cherubic features rosy-cheeked with anger. "Get down here and fight me like a man!"

"Bisco!" cried Milo from atop the crumbling walkway. "Settle down! You'll make us fall!"

"Milo, get it together! That was Shishi! That means she's the one who sent this island after us! We need to get up there and teach her a lesson!"

"I know, I know!" protested Milo, barely managing to set Bisco down on the ground without dropping him. "But our King Trumpets can't get us up there, even combined! It's just too high! Besides, you're still in kid form—"

"I told you, I ain't a damn kid!"

"Don't interrupt me while I'm speaking."

"Sorry."

"If our King Trumpets won't get us up there, there's only one thing to do."

Milo looked up at the walls of earth supporting the encroaching land and smiled.

"Whaddaya mean?" asked Bisco. "You got an idea? Out with it!"

"As a wise man once said," said Milo enigmatically, "'because it's there.'" He turned to face Bisco and, in lieu of an answer, asked a question.

"Have you ever been rock climbing before, Bisco?"

Illustration by **K Akagishi**

World Concept Art by **mocha** (@mocha708)

Map Art by **hatena to kinoko**

"I told you, there's no freakin' way we're gonna be able to climb up this!" shouted Bisco, at the approximate halfway point up the precipitous overhang. The two boys had used their King Trumpets to make the initial climb, but now they were clinging to the bare rock as wind ruffled their cloaks, with no ropes or tethers to save them should they fall.

"I thought you said you'd been rock climbing before, Bisco. Getting cold feet?"

"Shut it. I ain't gonna let no wall get the better of— *Shit!*"

"Whoopsie-daisy! Stay focused, Bisco. The rock is awfully fragile around here."

Bisco had been up many walls on Actagawa, but doing it unaided was a different matter entirely, and much harder than it looked, even for a seasoned Mushroom Keeper like him. He was jamming his mushroom arrows into the walls barehanded, creating platforms of oyster mushroom clusters for his hands and feet, but this was not easy, for too much force and the explosion would blow the wall apart. It was a task that demanded Bisco's full and complete attention.

"Hey, Milo!"

"Yes, Bisco?"

"Just makin' sure, but the plan *is* to beat the crap outta Shishi, right?"

"Of course! We can't let her conquer humanity! Why do you ask?"

"…Well, how the hell did we end up climbin' this freaky-ass cliff?!"

Milo answered Bisco as diplomatically as he could, but even he was a little put off by the situation. After all, the cliff in question had just attacked the entire island of Kyushu out of nowhere.

I never knew the Benibishi had something like this up their sleeve. Honshu might be next, for all we know. I wonder what's happening in Imihama right now...

An image of his sister, her long black hair, her cunning smile, flashed in his mind.

I hope Pawoo's all right...

He worried for her safety. He hadn't seen her since Satahabaki had sent her packing back to Imihama.

Just then, a pebble fell from above and struck the daydreaming Milo on the forehead. He looked up to see Bisco, struggling with the cliff a short distance above.

"Grrr... You goddamn wall... I'm gonna give you a piece of my mind..."

"Bisco. I'm sorry, I don't think this is going to work. I'll carry you the rest of the way. Just stay there!"

"Shaddup! I ain't so weak I need some string bean to carry me!"

"String bean...?!"

Clearly irritated by Milo's offer, Bisco scrambled up the cliff with renewed vigor. After clambering onto a ledge, he turned back and stuck out his tongue at his partner below.

H-he's such a little brat! thought Milo, and he began climbing up after him. As he did, though, he started to notice something strange about the land in general.

First, the rock was rather warm, and Bisco and Milo were both sweating from the heat radiating off it.

Second, the earth seemed to be *pulsating*. If Milo placed his ear to the wall, he could just about hear what sounded like a person's heartbeat.

...Something's not right with this cliff. It's almost like it's alive...

"Come on, Milo! Get up here already! I could have a cup of tea in the time you're takin'!"

"Y-you little brat!"

Stirred from his thoughts by Bisco's taunts, Milo looked up at his childlike partner, when suddenly he witnessed something very strange. A large hole slowly appeared in the wall behind Bisco, stretching open like the mouth of a dark cave. Milo was too surprised by the incredible sight to do anything at first.

...Wh-what's that?!

Since Bisco seemed ignorant to the weirdness unfolding behind him, Milo shouted, "Look out! Get away from there!"

But Bisco seemed not to notice. "You're the one in danger, not me," he calmly shot back. "You ain't gonna get anywhere swinging your arrows like that. Put your back into it!"

"Behind you!! Look at the wall!"

Bisco turned around just in time to see the cave as it fired a blast of hot air at him. Lacking the body mass to stay upright, he was blown clean off the ledge by the gust.

"Whoa?! What the hell? Dammit!"

Bisco drew and fired an anchor arrow, but his juvenile strength wasn't enough to pierce the rock, and the arrow merely bounced off the cliff.

"Bisco!"

Milo drew his bow, but just as he was about to fire an arrow toward his falling partner...

"Hold on one nail-bitin' second!"

...an aerial drone roughly sixty centimeters across appeared out of nowhere and bolted toward Bisco with incredible speed.

"This rescue service don't come cheap, ya know!" came a familiar voice from an onboard speaker. *"Get yer wallets ready!"*

"What?!"

The drone extended four long arms like the tentacles of a jellyfish and caught Bisco mid-flight.

"Whoa?!"

"Batter out! That's how we play ball, ladies and gentlemen!"

The drone lifted Bisco back up and spun on the spot, triumphant.

"Ah-ha-ha-ha! Oh, boys, what would y'all do without me?"

"That voice...!"

"Tirol?!"

The ill-omened laughter that emanated from the miniature craft could belong to none other than the pair's longtime confidante and all-around bad influence, Tirol Ochagama.

"Wh-what are you doin' here?" yelled Bisco. "Wh-whoa, hold it! I'm gonna fall!"

"Pawoo asked me, ya see. To check out Kaso Prefecture, and also to get a bead on you two... Hey, whoever's climbin' around on top, get off! You're gonna waste my fuel!"

"Goddamn... The one person I didn't want to owe a favor..."

Bisco wiped the cold sweat from his face and dropped back onto the rocky ledge, just as Milo managed to climb up as well. As the two panted and tried to regain their breath, the pink, jellyfish-looking drone spun gleefully, displaying Tirol's face on a monitor attached to the front.

"You saved us, Tirol! What is this, some kind of remote-controlled robot?"

"Yep. Based it off the Mokujin designs. Ain't she a beaut? Best part is, I get to sit back in the VIP lounge of the Imihama Prefectural Bureau an' put my feet up!"

"Hey, wait!" roared Bisco. "How come you didn't help us earlier?! How long have you been watchin'?!"

"Oh, from around the time you two kicked Satahabaki's butt and Bisco turned into an adorable little kid!"

"Grh..."

Bisco choked back his words as the drone circled his little head.

"So tell me, what's it like bein' a kid again? Let me have a little look-see."

"Get off me!! This is serious, you know! It ain't funny!"

"How could you say that, Bisco? I'm your friend! Haven't we always been there for each other, through thick and thin? I just want to know if there's anything I can do to help you!"

"But...!"

"Come on, just let me see! I promise I won't laugh."

The drone stopped in front of Bisco's face, and a lens on the front slowly zoomed in. Bisco scowled for the camera, but he could do little to hide his innate childlike cuteness.

There was a short silence. And then...

"*Gyah-ha-ha-ha-ha-ha!!!*"

"I'll rip you apart!!"

"Bisco, stop! You'll fall off!"

Milo held Bisco back, desperately fighting to keep him from leaping from the cliff toward the drone and surely meeting his own demise.

Meanwhile, a large *Slam!* was heard over the microphone, as on Tirol's end, a door was kicked open and someone walked in.

"*Tirol! What are you doing with my husband behind my back?!*"

"*Shit, it's the Iron Lady! I swear I locked that door!*"

"*Is this your camera?! Out of the way! I'll take over... Milo, Bisco! Oh, how wonderful it is to see you both!*"

""*Pawoo!!*""

The face that replaced Tirol's on the drone's monitor was that of Governor of Imihama, Pawoo Nekoyanagi. She was wrapped in bandages as a result of her tussle with Satahabaki, but the look in her eyes was as formidable as ever.

"*Bisco,*" she said. "*Don't worry. I'll always love you, no matter what you look like. There is no age gap that can stand in the way of our marriage! No taboo too great for our bond!*"

"Pawoo, can we do this later?" said Milo. "We're in the middle of a pretty dangerous climb! We want to know what exactly is up there. Can you use your satellites to figure something out?"

"*Ah, yes. That's actually what I came to talk about. You two may want to sit down for this.*"

"Sit down on what, the freakin' air?!"

"I'll set up the bivouac. One second, Pawoo."

Milo placed his ear to the cliff and heard once more the steady beating coming from within. Then he reached down to his vial case and pulled out a syringe filled with a milky white liquid, which he stabbed into the wall with all his might.

…This should settle you down for a while…!

Milo listened to the wall again as the beating grew fainter and the pulsing stopped.

Good, that seemed to work.

"Whatcha doin', Milo? Givin' the wall its shots?"

"It's a sedative. Just in case."

"Huh?!"

Milo declined to explain further, instead fastening Bisco to a wire arrow, which he sank into the cliff wall. It was as stable as they could make it, given the circumstances.

"First, I have something to tell you about the cliff you two are currently climbing."

"We already know. Milo told me. This is some kind of secret weapon the Benibishi created, a desert island on booster rockets, right?"

"Not exactly. You're right it's an island, but… Look at this."

The drone's monitor suddenly changed to display a satellite photograph of the whole Kyushu region. The two boys were baffled by what they saw.

"The hell? It's eatin' the whole damn island!"

"What on earth?"

There were no other words to describe it. The invading land had come in from the northern coast, engulfing a whole chunk of the island of Kyushu. From the satellite imagery, it was clear that the prefectures of Fukuoka and Saga had already been swallowed, with what seemed to be the beak poised to take Kaso as well.

"This is the full scale of the entity you two have been fighting."

"We've been calling it Hokkaido, the Island Whale," added Tirol.

""Ho-Hokkaido?!""

The two boys gave a second cry of surprise.

"You mean that giant island off the coast of Aomori? The one that's so infested with mutated creatures, nobody's ever come back alive?!"

"But that doesn't make any sense! That's Japan's northernmost isle! Why isn't it up north where it belongs?!"

"*Enough! Stop talking over each other! Tirol, hurry up and show them the next slide!*"

"*I know, I know, keep yer tits on! Here.*"

The next image appeared to be the same as the previous one, but taken under a thermal camera.

"The hell is this supposed to be?" asked Bisco, turning to his partner. But Milo's face was one of sheer dismay. "What's up, Milo?" he asked. "You make anythin' of this?"

"Bisco... Hokkaido, it's...it's..."

Milo shook his head repeatedly, as though he didn't believe his eyes. Finally, he managed to spit out his words.

"It's alive!!"

"The fuck do you mean it's alive?!"

"*He's right, Bisco,*" came Pawoo's voice through the speaker. "*Look, the island of Hokkaido is emitting heat. There's no engine at all; it's a living, breathing creature! It's hard to believe...but we theorize that what was long thought to be land has actually been an animal weapon, sleeping below the sea this entire time!*"

"Wh-wh...?"

"*Just before it awoke, we observed the dispersal of some sort of attractor for animal weapons, centered on Six Realms Penitentiary, right where you were at the time. It was a kind of pollen, so you know what that means. The Benibishi really are behind this!*"

"I thought something seemed odd," said Milo. "I could hear a heartbeat, feel a temperature, and just now, when Bisco got blown away, that must have been some sort of breathing hole!"

"Listen to yourselves—this is freakin' insane!" yelled Bisco, unable to take the ridiculous conversation any longer. Looking into the camera, he pointed a pudgy finger behind him at the cliff overhead. "Look at all that rock and earth. You tryin' to tell me that's alive?!"

"Bisco!! A-above you!"

"Huh?!"

Bisco looked where he was pointing, to see a crack appearing in the cliff wall hanging over him. The fissure worked its way across the rock face before suddenly and very deliberately opening wide.

"Wh-what the hell is that?!"

"It's the creature's eye, Bisco! Hide!"

Milo grabbed the dumbstruck Bisco and pulled him close to the cliff wall, while Tirol's drone zipped underneath the ledge and hid out of sight. The pair held their breath as the eye swiveled, looking around, before giving up and reverting to sheer rock once more.

"...Pawoo's right, Bisco," said Milo when the coast was clear. "This wall's alive. We need to get up high quick, or we're in trouble."

"...It's alive. It really is alive," Bisco muttered, ghastly pale. "A livin' island... That's gotta be, like, a god or somethin', right?"

"Bisco, snap out of it! We're going!"

"O-okay!"

"There's no telling what this thing'll do after it devours Kyushu. It might decide it's still hungry and move on to Honshu next! It's up to you two boys to put a stop to this Benibishi weapon and save Japan!"

"You don't gotta tell me twice. Shishi's the only one who can turn me back to normal," said Bisco. "Beatin' the crap outta her was my plan all along!"

"That's the spirit, Bisco! And don't worry about the journey. Tirol will be scouting ahead with the drone. She'll be able to update you on the lay of the land, and—"

But Pawoo was unable to say anything more before a large stone fell from the overhang above, landing square on the drone.

""Ah.""

"Waaaaagh?!?!?!"

The pink drone spiraled out of control, plummeting toward the base of the cliff. Pawoo's and Tirol's screams became more and more distant, eventually disappearing completely.

"Oh, poo," said Milo.

"...Well, could be worse. At least they weren't here for real."

"You're awfully pragmatic for a child, Bisco."

"Oh, shut it. Keep climbing! This cliff's alive, you know. There's no telling what it'll do!"

"That's what *I've* been trying to tell *you!*"

Sparing little concern for the fate of Tirol's drone, the two boys pressed onward, the cliff only growing more rugged and precipitous the farther they climbed.

"Come on, Bisco, just a little farther... Grab on!"

"Get your hand away from me! I don't need your help!"

Along the way, the boys had nearly been sucked into a set of gigantic gills, been scalded by hot air from the breathing holes, and generally risked life and limb to reach the top. Drenched in sweat, the two scrambled over the final ledge and stopped to catch their breath.

"W-we finally made it..."

"B-but why's it so damn cold?!"

Bisco and Milo expected at least a moment of solace after their arduous climb, but the landscape that greeted them was cold comfort, so to speak. It was almost impossible to see through the dense blizzard that swept the land, and Milo's legs were buried to the knees in packed snow.

"It was sunny down in Kaso," said Bisco. "How come it's snowin' up here?!"

"Maybe the altitude?" suggested Milo. "What do you think, Bisco? Can you handle it?"

"I ain't an old man! Whoa... *Pff.*"

"I guess that means no. Come on, I'll carry you again. The snow's almost up to your ears."

"I told you—*ptoo*—I can do it myself!"

"Don't be silly. You'll freeze to death down there!"

Milo pulled Bisco up onto his back, where he sat and sulked, pulling down his cat-eye goggles to peer through the snow.

"We really could have done with Tirol's drone," lamented Milo. "We're never going to find Shishi in all this."

"…I wouldn't be so sure," said Bisco.

"Huh?"

"It looks like she's already waiting for us."

Bisco lifted his goggles and glared off into the snow. From that direction, Milo heard the sound of footfalls crunching the ice underfoot, and several figures appeared before them. Leading the group was a purple-haired girl, gown fluttering in the blizzard, who eyed Bisco and Milo carefully.

""Shishi!!""

The pale and enchanting face of the Benibishi's new king betrayed none of her former cheer. Now she wore a cold mask of ice that made it impossible to tell what she was thinking. With her dignified and frigid expression, Milo wondered if she was still the same girl at all.

What happened to the Shishi we knew?

"Thanks for the warm welcome, Shishi!" shouted Bisco in order to be heard over the roaring blizzard. "Guess you shoulda finished me off when you had the chance, huh?" He leaped off Milo's back, landing on the snow and drawing his bow. "It's time for our rematch! If I win, you gotta turn me back to normal! Now draw your sword!"

The flames of anger flickered in his jade-green eyes. Shishi's expression changed almost imperceptibly in response to his words, and her crimson eyes glimmered. She parted her lips ever so slightly and expelled a white breath of mist, and the ivy gathered in her hand, taking the form of a shining golden longsword.

H-he can't fight her here! He'll lose for sure! I have to do something!

Milo stepped in front of Bisco, and just as he did, a member of Shishi's party did the same for her. The two ran their eyes up his massive frame, barely managing to stammer out a cry of shock.

"It…it's you!"

"Satahabaki?!"

It was impossible to mistake the trademark blue helmet and bare teeth, like white pillars, that identified the former warden of Six Realms Penitentiary, Someyoshi Satahabaki. Only now, instead of the Sakura Storm tattoo, it was the camellia plant that enwreathed his exposed skin, a sign that Shishi had overwritten Satahabaki's Bountiful Art with her own and brought the monstrous man under her control.

"Hey, judge guy!" Bisco shouted. "That's a criminal you're helpin'! Have you lost your mind?!"

"It's no use, Bisco! He can't hear you! Shishi's controlling him!"

Satahabaki kneeled over and whispered something in Shishi's ear. She listened quietly, before giving a single nod and dispersing her ivy sword. As if no longer interested in Bisco, she turned and walked away.

"Shishi! Get back here!" cried Bisco, running after her.

"Mmrh!!"

Satahabaki interposed his enormous frame. He lifted his huge arms, as thick as tree trunks, above his head and slammed his fists down on the ground.

"Grrh! Who invited this guy?!"

"Bisco, get back!"

"Mmmmrhhh!"

Ka-booom!!

The ground split open, and a fissure appeared where Satahabaki struck. The cracks in the ground grew larger and larger, and chunks of snow and ice started cascading inward, like a waterfall.

"He's tryin' to block us off!"

"Bisco, watch out! Grab my hand!"

Milo swiftly fired an anchor arrow at a nearby tree and held on to Bisco, who glared across the newly crafted ravine. There he saw Satahabaki calmly turn around and make as if to leave.

"What're you tryin' to say? Had enough of me? Goddammit, don't you dare look down on me!!"

"Bisco! We can't possibly take both of them on at once, especially not with you at that size! We need to come up with a plan and—"

"What's size gotta do with it?! There ain't no war that can't be won by kickin' enough ass!"

Milo wanted to say something, but Bisco's irrepressible confidence awed him into silence.

"We can jump a rift like this no problem," Bisco said. "Come on, follow me!"

"Whaaat?!"

"We ain't got time to grumble! Get your ass in gear, or I'll leave you behind!"

After seeing that the snow had settled, Bisco slipped free of Milo's grip and, with characteristically striking form, launched himself across the pit on a King Trumpet mushroom.

That's right... Bisco's like a mushroom. He keeps pushing on no matter the circumstances... Bisco will clear this obstacle, just like every other!

Milo attempted to put his fearful thoughts behind him and turned to follow his partner. He watched as the child vaulted the ravine, cloak flapping magnificently behind him.

"...Milooo..."

"Bisco?!"

"I ain't gonna make iiit..."

He watched as Bisco fell spectacularly short of the far cliff and plummeted into the bowels of the earth below. Without his usual strength, the power of his mushroom had been woefully insufficient.

For a moment, Milo gazed, open-mouthed, before...

"...H-hey!! What are you doing?! Just when I thought I could trust you!!"

...he immediately leaped into the chasm after his partner, firing a King Trumpet to launch himself downward and catching the falling Bisco in his arms.

"Hmm, yeah, I messed up that one," Bisco admitted. "Don't worry, Milo. I'll get it next time."

"There isn't a next time!!"

As the pair fell, Milo wrapped them both in a mantra barrier, and they went bouncing off the walls into the darkness beneath the earth.

Kaso Prefecture, Six Realms Penitentiary.

The weighty iron doors hung battered and open, a dark symbol of the prison's downfall. In the main entrance yard, thick with ivy and flowers, red camellias coated the walls and floor and cried out in praise of the victorious Benibishi. At the center of it all stood one Mushroom Keeper and one crazed young girl, doing battle as if on the gladiatorial sands, two finely honed souls clashing against each other.

"Bisco Akaboshi!" Shishi screamed. "The flowers spell your doom!"

She thrust her ivy sword, landing it in Bisco's shoulder. But his eyes sparkled.

"No flower's gonna stop a Mushroom Keeper!!"

With superhuman strength, Bisco leaped into the air, pulling the sword free, and whirled like a gale, delivering his signature spinning kick into Shishi's slender neck.

"...Ghh!!"

"Take this!!"

Crack!!

Bisco heard her bones break as his lightning-bolt kick connected.

"Ghh...ah!"

However, though Bisco's blow could fell trees, it did nothing to abate the fire in Shishi's eyes. In fact, the more blood she spilled, the fiercer she seemed to become, and the deeper her crimson eyes shone.

"You are strong… Brother…"

"Dammit! How are you still alive?"

"…But I am strong, too! Strong enough to block your kick!"

The instant Bisco's attack struck, Shishi had dispersed her ivy sword and redirected the vines to reinforce her neck, quelling the impact at the very last second.

This ain't good!

His ultimate attack blocked, Bisco was knocked off-balance.

"Let this be the sign…," said Shishi, retracting the vines from her neck and re-forming them into her sword. Before Bisco could react, she swung. "You are Japan's champion, Brother. May your blood mark the beginning of our reign!"

"Shishiiii!"

"Flourish! Lion's Crimson Sword!!"

Splat!!

"Graahhh!!"

Shishi sliced into Bisco's flesh with enough force to send him spinning through the air.

"The flowers have taken root," she said. "This is the end for you, Brother."

She swiveled, pointing a hand toward the flying Bisco, and unleashed the full extent of her Bountiful Art upon him.

"Flourish! Lion's Camellia!!"

Bwoom! Bwoom! Bwoom!

Embedded into Bisco's flesh by Shishi's slash were camellia seeds, which bloomed one after the other into bright-red flowers that launched him faster and faster. Eventually, he collided hard with a stone wall, which then collapsed into a cloud of dust and rubble.

"The power of the camellia is that of servitude, Brother. It weakens the spirit, making the victim a slave."

Shishi gasped for breath, but her victory was already assured.

"This is checkmate, Brother. You will defy me no longer."

She watched the rising dust for a few seconds, then dispersed her ivy blade…when suddenly a silver gleam caused her eyes to go wide.

"Let's see if you still say that after this!!"

From out of the dust came a streaking arrow, hurtling toward Shishi with deadly precision. She brandished her sword once more, parrying the projectile out of the air and into the ground behind her, where it exploded into a somewhat smaller-than-usual oyster mushroom.

"This fight ain't over yet. If you think this flower of servitude or whatever can suppress *my* soul, then you better guess again, 'cause I ain't going nowhere!"

"…Well. You are just full of surprises."

Shishi seemed vexed at Bisco's miraculous survival, but it did little to topple her composure.

"Your heart is mighty indeed. Mightier still than my flowers. I should have expected as much from the man I chose to follow."

"You'll pay for underestimatin' me, Shishi. I ain't your regular foe! Come on, it's time for round two! Get ready!"

The dust cloud burst, and the earth's strongest Mushroom Keeper flew out and landed before Shishi, cloak flapping, standing strong and tall…

Well, standing strong anyway.

His Mushroom Keeper garb, his bright-red hair, his glimmering jade-green eyes; these were all the same, but there was one very important difference that marked this Bisco apart from the one of only a few moments before.

He was a child.

His stature had been reduced to that of a boy of only ten years or so, and so his clothes were baggy and loose. The bow in his hands seemed so large and ungainly by comparison, it was a wonder he could wield it at all.

"…Hmm?!"

Training his bow on Shishi, Bisco finally seemed to notice something strange.

"You've gotten a lot bigger all of a sudden! This another one'a your powers?"

Shishi released the ivy sword again, revealing the pure-white skin of her hand.

"My Bountiful Art is persistent. It is supposed to regress the mind, but if it cannot do that, it will regress the flesh instead…just like it has done to you."

"…Hmm??"

Bisco was baffled by Shishi's behavior. She was acting like the battle was over, already patting out the creases in her clothes.

"You are nothing now but a powerless infant," she said. "There is no point in killing you."

"Regress…the flesh…?!"

Bisco didn't like the sound of that, whatever it meant. And he was starting to feel strange, to boot. "Explain yourself, Shishi!" he squeaked. "What have you done to me?!"

Shishi turned and picked up a large shard of glass that had fallen in the battle, tossing it to Bisco.

Bisco caught it and peered at the reflection, wondering who exactly the childlike face staring back at him belonged to.

Then, at last, it dawned on him.

"…Wh…? Wha…? What…? What the hell is this?!!"

* * *

"Damn you, Shishi, turn me baaaaack!!"

Bisco sat bolt upright, panting and wheezing and drenched in a cold sweat. It was the same dream again. When at last he recovered from the painful memories therein, Bisco shook his head and looked around.

"Wait…where am I?"

It was dark, but unnaturally warm. Bisco blinked his eyes in surprise. "…Milo!"

Suddenly remembering his partner, Bisco drew some glowshroom spores from his pouch, placed them in his mouth, and blew them onto the floor. There they sprouted with a *Pop, pop, pop!* illuminating Milo's unconscious form a short distance away.

Bisco leaped to his feet and dashed over to his partner's side.

"Milo! Milo, wake up!"

"Mph…"

The dashing young doctor slowly lifted his eyelids and looked up sleepily at Bisco, whereupon he gave a faint smile.

"Bisco! …Oh, thank goodness, I was hoping we'd both end up in Hell together! …Ow!!"

Bisco pinched Milo's nose, squeezing it with incredible strength for such a small child. His roughness swiftly brought the daydreaming doctor out of his reverie.

"Ow, ow, ow, ow, ow! Wh-what are you doing?! It's me, your partner!"

"Tryin' to wake you up, dumbass! Look around you. We ain't dead yet!"

"Huh? Oh yeah! Where are we, Bisco?"

Sitting upright, Milo took a look around at the dark, liver-red walls. They glowed with a faint heat and light and pulsated rhythmically like the cliffs from before, only now it was loud enough for both boys to feel it in their bones.

"We fell down a hole, I thought," said Bisco. "But I can't see the sun…and this place smells real bad."

"It's best not to act in haste," Milo suggested. "Let's make sure everything's ready… Huh? I can't find my medical bag. I must have dropped it somewhere!"

"Stay where you are. I'll give us some more light."

The child Bisco sprang into the air and unleashed two cheekfuls of glowshroom spores. Milo found the sight simply adorable, but feared that if he said anything, he'd get another nose-pinching, and so opted to stay quiet.

"Hey, Milo. Isn't that your bag over there?"

"Oh, yes! How did it get so high up…?"

The strap of Milo's bag had gotten caught on the end of some sort of stiff white pillar poking out of the wall, and it hung about ten meters off the ground.

What is that? Milo thought. *It looks familiar, somehow…*

"Stay there," said Bisco. "I'll go get it for you."

He seemed a little apologetic, almost as though he felt guilty for the two of them ending up down here, and hopped up a few more of the white pillars to get to Milo's bag. Milo watched with a sense of vague apprehension, until finally he realized what had been bugging him. He looked up to the ceiling, and what he saw gave him goose bumps.

"Milo! I got it! This one, right?"

"Bisco! Get down! Hurry up and get down from there!"

"Geez, all right! A little thanks would be nice!"

"No! Look up!"

Sensing something amiss, Bisco craned his neck upward, and his eyes went wide with shock. High up in the gloomy cave roof were more of the huge white pillars, and these swiftly plunged toward Bisco.

"Whoaaaaa!!"

Bisco jumped away as quickly as possible, moments before the pillars came crashing down behind him. They crashed together from above and below, trapping Bisco's cloak between them. Bisco dangled as it tightened around his neck, causing his face to turn bright-red.

"Bisco!"

After a moment, the pillars shuddered apart again, releasing Bisco's cloak and dropping him down below. Milo caught him in the nick of time and heaved a sigh of relief.

"Th-that was close, Bisco. You almost became fish food!"

"*Cough! Cough!* What the hell *was* that?!"

"That was its teeth, Bisco."

"Its…teeth?!"

"I just figured it out. Look around; we're inside Hokkaido's mouth!"

At Milo's words, Bisco took a second look around. While the pillars were all different sizes, now that it was pointed out, there did seem to be some order in their arrangement. While he gazed in wonder, the teeth came together a second time, shaking the ground and knocking Bisco and Milo off their feet.

"Th-this guy means business! Let's get outta here before we become his next meal!"

"Right! But…hold on. If there are teeth here, then that means…"

The two boys felt a sudden chill and slowly peered over their shoulders into the depths of the cavern. Then, from out of the darkness appeared an enormous, slimy hunk of flesh. Before either one of them could move a muscle, it wrapped around the pair, immobilizing them both.

"I knew it!! There's a tongue as well!" screamed Milo, holding on tight to Bisco like a mother protecting her child. The tongue, however, pushed them both indiscriminately toward the back of the mouth, trapping them between the back teeth.

"Waaah! We're stuck!"

"Stay calm, Milo! King Trumpets on my mark!"

"O-okay!"

With split-second decision-making, the pair fired their mushroom arrows at one of the back teeth. The King Trumpets sprang upward out of the enamel and held up the upper teeth just before the creature's jaws closed, thus sparing the boys.

"The mushrooms ain't gonna hold it for long. This thing packs a punch!"

"Bisco, I can't get through the tongue!" cried Milo, firing his oyster mushroom arrows at the appendage. The tongue appeared utterly undamaged, trapping the boys in their enamel prison with no choice but to await their inevitable demise.

"What'll we do, Bisco? The next time those teeth come down, they'll turn us into mushroom sauce!"

"All your book learnin' ain't worth squat if you freak out at the first sign of trouble. Why don't you start usin' your head for a change?"

"You're the last person I want to hear that from, Bisco!"

"Think: If this thing's a tongue, then how about we let it taste one of these?"

Bisco produced a bundle of curious arrows fletched with emerald feathers and affixed them to his bow. He aimed them at the wall of flesh mere centimeters in front of him and fired.

Goom! Goom!

Bisco's arrows stuck into the slimy mass and exploded into a cluster of green mushrooms not unlike an oyster mushroom. In the blink of an eye, they spread across the surface of the tonguelike mass, but even Milo could see that there was not enough force there to extricate them from this perilous situation.

"It's no use, Bisco! We'll have to try the Mantra Bow!"

"Keep yer pants on! There's times you can't rely on brute force, y'know! Quick wits are the essence of any Mushroom Keeper!"

"What are you talking about?!"

"Sit still and watch… It's startin'."

Once Bisco's mushrooms covered enough of the tongue, it suddenly retracted into the mouth cavity and began turning and wriggling wildly. Milo watched in amazement, wondering what on earth was happening, and was only broken out of his trance when Bisco grabbed his sleeve, yelling, "Get outta there, dumbass! You're gonna die!" Not a moment later, the teeth came crashing together, pulverizing the spot where he had just been standing.

"Th-the tongue, it's gone berserk! Bisco, what kind of mushrooms were those?!"

"Devil's head mushrooms. They spread like the plague."

"Devil's…head?"

"And they got a real diabolical kick to them, too. Spicy as hell, just like the name! Pop one in your mouth, and you lose your sense of taste for a whole year!"

Bisco grinned like a mischievous child and tossed a few of the mushroom arrows to Milo, who swiftly got the message. The two of them leaped in opposite directions, firing the unbelievably hot mushrooms at the tongue from both sides.

The tongue, meanwhile, scraped against the walls of the mouth-cave in an attempt to rid itself of the infernal fungi, but the mushrooms spread too fast, and soon it collapsed in the center of the mouth, exhausted.

"W-we did it! We beat it! I can't believe it!"

"Guess even a whale the size of an island can't handle the spice," Bisco added, leaping atop the motionless tongue and jumping up and down to make sure it really was out for the count.

"That was amazing, Bisco!" cried Milo, unable to contain his admiration any longer. "I can't believe you beat that thing while just a child!"

"Age don't matter to a Mushroom Keeper! I've always been Bisco Akaboshi, from the moment I was born!"

Milo couldn't be happier to hear his friend and partner in high spirits again. It was a while before he noticed the thick fluid oozing toward his boots below. When it reached them, it sizzled and gave off a thick white smoke.

"Wah!"

"What's wrong, Milo?!"

"What on earth?!"

Milo jumped up onto the tongue alongside Bisco and looked at the yellow fluid eating away at his boots.

"It's the saliva from the tongue, Bisco. It must be because of those mushrooms; it's trying to wash away the spice. Such a powerful acid… I've never seen anything like it. If this gets on your hands, it'll strip the flesh clean off!"

"This ain't good," muttered Bisco, peering off the tongue at the cave floor below. "The level's risin'. I don't much fancy stayin' here and seein' what my bones look like."

Milo pondered for a while, casting a glance over his shoulder at the back of the cave, toward the dark tunnel that led farther into the beast. Making up his mind, he nodded and turned to Bisco.

"Okay, Bisco, then let's go!"

"Go? Go where?!"

"Down the hatch, so to speak. That cave back there."

Milo took Bisco's hand without further argument and led him down toward the base of the tongue. Bisco's eyes went wide with fear when he realized what his partner was saying.

"Down there? Have you lost your freakin' mind? Why are we goin' farther in when we can get back out? We came down from above, so all we have to do is find a way back up!"

"We'll be one step behind Shishi if we do that. To topple the king, you have to take out his horse. Isn't that what they say?"

"No? Mushroom Keepers always go straight for the king."

"Well, whatever! The point is, we have to take down Hokkaido to have a chance at beating Shishi. If we disable her secret weapon, it'll throw a wrench in her plans that we might be able to take advantage of."

"Easier said than done! We don't even know our way around this thing!"

"Not yet," Milo said, stopping and turning to Bisco with a satisfied grin. "But remember who your partner is. I'm no ordinary Mushroom Keeper; I'm Dr. Panda of Imihama! If biology's the game, then I'm your man!"

"R-right," said Bisco, momentarily stunned, as the matter of his partner's medical know-how had not come up for such a long time that he had almost forgotten it. "That's amazing, Milo! You mean you've seen something like this in your clinic before?"

"Well, no, but how different could it be? You've seen one living thing, you've seen them all."

"They should take away your medical license, you quack!"

With that, Milo pulled on Bisco's arm, and the two disappeared down the gullet, with courage and quick-wittedness as their sword and shield.

☈⚡☉♒ **3**

This far into the cavern, the glowshrooms were no longer necessary, for the enormous blood vessels visible within the liver-red walls illuminated the surroundings with each rhythmic pulse. From time to time, Milo noticed white flowers and some sort of mosslike plant growing on the walls and floor, and the curious sight tantalized his academic sensibilities. It was difficult to say either way whether the titanic organism was fully beast or landmass.

And the most curious thing of all was a cloud of strange white spheres of various sizes that floated in the air ahead.

"Look, Bisco! Those must be blood cells!"

Milo snatched one of the floating balls and examined it with excitement. He squeezed it, rubbed it, and shook it, just like a hamster playing with a new toy.

"So its blood is white! Look at this, Bisco! It's all squishy like putty! I must be the first doctor in all of Japan to find out what Hokkaido's blood feels like!"

Bisco heaved a deep sigh. "It's nice to see the great Dr. Panda in his element, but do you think we could get a move on?! I've seen all I wanna see, and I'm about ready to get outta this place before anything else jumps out at us! Do you even have a plan for how we're gonna take this thing down?"

"Bisco! Think what this could teach us about the mysteries of life! Don't you have any sense of adventure?"

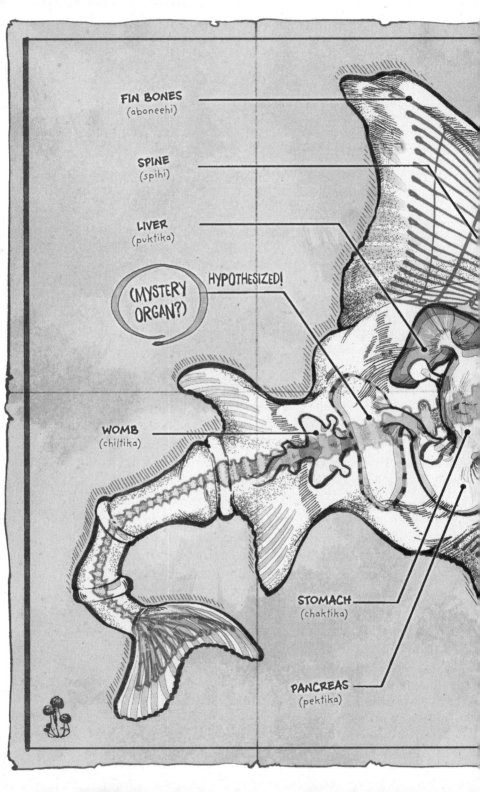

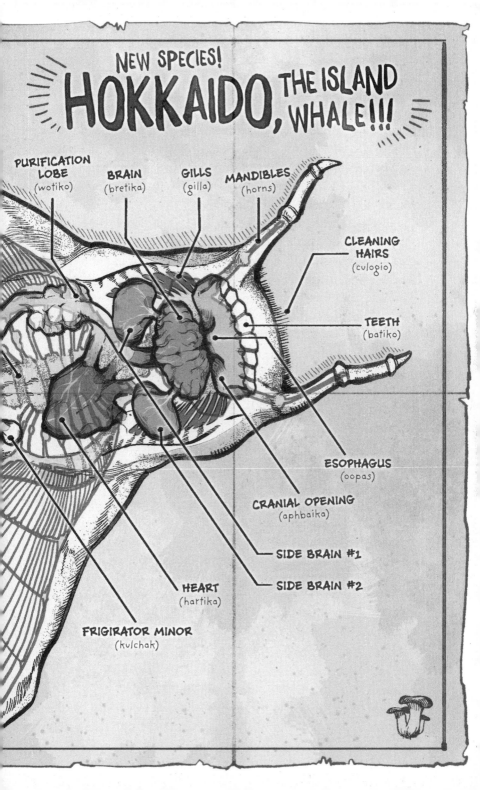

Sounding a little fed up, Milo produced from his breast pocket a sheet of paper and handed it over. Bisco snatched it away and peered at the page, which featured "*Hokkaido Island Whale Anatomical Sketch!*" written at the top in Milo's frenetic handwriting, and beneath that, an oddly detailed drawing of what was presumably the creature the pair presently inhabited.

"...Hee-art...heart," he read. "Lungs, spine...kid...kid...nay? Kidnay."

"Kidney. From what I can tell of Hokkaido's internal structure, it seems similar to the species of the genus *Mollusca evolutus*, such as the Platinum Snail or the northern sea slug."

Milo leaned in over Bisco's shoulder as he struggled with the diagram and pointed out some of the features.

"This is the esophagus. That's where we are. There should be a fork somewhere where it connects to the respiratory system, and from there we can reach the brain stem. Most animal weapons have a control pin in the brain. We remove that, we shut down Hokkaido for good."

"You sure?! I mean, you basically just sketched this from your imagination!"

"Just trust in Dr. Panda. Oh, look, there's another one of those blood cells!!"

Spotting one floating close to the ground, Milo bounded off after it, leaving Bisco to sigh in despair at his partner's airheadedness.

Just then, Bisco spotted something far off in the distance, sprinting toward them. Squinting his eyes, he managed to make out the outline of a person, followed by a horde of white things. Whatever they were, they were clearly hostile, and the person seemed to be fleeing for dear life.

"Milo... Hey, Milo!"

"Yeah?"

"There's someone out there! Look, it's a kid! They're in trouble!"

"What?! What's someone else doing in a place like this?!"

"How would I know?! We gotta do something, fast!"

The two boys looked to each other and nodded, before dashing toward the distressed individual, kicking off the springy cells to gain speed.

"Eep!"

The poor figure tripped on a clump of moss, falling flat on their face. The closest of the white things opened its jaws wide, revealing rows of teeth with which it pounced upon the fallen victim.

"Noooo!!"

Fwp!!

At the last moment, Bisco's arrow swooped in and stuck in the head of the white organism, blasting it away. It landed with a thud and a *Bagoom!* in the far wall of the tunnel, and a bright-red oyster mushroom sprouted into being. The white creature itself was covered in fur and looked an awful lot like a polar bear, except instead of eyes, it possessed a huge pair of jaws that covered its entire face.

The victim, a girl, looked around in confusion.

"H-huh?!"

"Don't just stand there! Move!"

The girl stood up, not knowing what was going on, and continued running as fast as her little legs could carry her. Milo and Bisco unleashed a hailstorm of arrows at the white creatures, narrowly whisking past the girl's hair and neck as she squealed in terror.

"Bisco, there's too many of them!"

"They're comin' up behind us, too. We're trapped!"

Perhaps alerted by the mushroom arrows, more of the eyeless polar bears began squeezing their way through cracks in the walls, coming after the new prey in the form of the two boys.

"We need to hide, Bisco! What about the smokeshroom arrows?!"

"That ain't gonna work! They don't have eyes! But they got mouths, so…"

Bisco reached for his quiver and pulled out a stack of pink-fletched arrows, firing two behind him and one in front at the girl's feet.

Gaboom!!

"Eeeeek?!"

The force of the mushroom's growth launched the girl through the air and into Bisco's arms.

"It's okay. You're safe now— Whooaaa?!"

Bisco meant to land heroically on the floor, but as the girl was larger than he was, he instead lost his balance and went rolling across it, crashing in a heap some short distance away.

"Nooo!" the girl screamed. "Please don't kill me! Pleeease! Let me go!"

"Calm down! I used a very strong drunkshroom arrow. Hold your breath, or you'll be sick for two days straight!"

"Wh-what? Eek!"

Just as the girl opened her mouth to object, three polar bears reared up before them, casting a shadow over the pair. With no way out, the girl squeezed her eyes shut and awaited the inevitable, when all of a sudden one of the polar bears collapsed to the floor.

"Hwa?!"

"Shhh. Look closely."

The girl did as Bisco whispered and saw that the polar bear was sound asleep, its face flushed and jaws open wide. The other bears began tottering and flopped to the ground one by one.

"The spores have gotten to work. Let's get outta here while they're snorin'."

"...Ah...ah..."

"Snap out of it. Your legs ain't hurt, right? Then let's go!"

"...!!"

The girl nodded repeatedly and followed Bisco, tiptoeing away from the horde. The bears could no longer distinguish friend from foe, play-fighting merrily with one another before collapsing to the floor in a daze.

"Bisco. Those are white hair antibodies."

"White hair whatsits?"

"Their purpose is to eradicate any foreign material in the body. It was good you left them alive; they're good guys, and they would have just kept coming anyway."

Milo rushed over to Bisco's side and put on a medical mask from his bag. But just as he went to put a mask on the girl, she suddenly fainted onto the esophagus floor.

"Huh?! What's wrong? Hey, get up!"

"Her face is all red. She must have inhaled some of the drunkshroom spores..."

"What a lightweight. All right, I'll carry her."

"You can't, Bisco! She's bigger than you are! I'll do it."

"Krh!"

A few of the white bears turned around at the sound of the disturbance. Milo quickly lifted the girl onto his back and exchanged glances with his partner, before the two of them set off down the tunnel with nary a sound.

Water fell from high above into a clear pool, filling the room with a calming trickle sound.

"This girl's even more surprising than the damn bears," said Bisco. "How the hell did she end up in the belly of the beast all by herself?"

"Your guess is as good as mine," replied Milo. "Perhaps she was eaten just like we were?"

"Does she look like she's from around here?! The only people I've seen with skin this pale come from all the way up north!"

The two boys' whispering voices brought the mysterious girl out of her slumber. She felt a cool breeze, and every now and then she groaned as cold droplets of water struck her bare skin. Soon, her large eyes fluttered open.

"Oh, I got it. She's a fairy, Milo. I remember reading about it in a picture book once. The Organ-Pinchin' Child. She takes the form of a kid, and if you carry her on your back, then she steals your—"

"Shh! Bisco, I think she's listening!"

"..."

"Hey!" shouted Bisco at the girl. "You okay? Got a hangover? Want some water?"

"Eeek! *Devika!!*"

The girl's mighty scream sent Bisco tumbling head over heels. His eyes spun as he sat up, dumbfounded.

"D-devika?"

"That's a word you don't hear every day," said Milo "It's old Sakhalinese. I think it means…'little devil.'"

"Little devil?" Upon hearing Milo's translation, Bisco went bright-red in the face with anger. "Hey, you pint-sized brat! Is that any way to treat someone who just saved your life?! At least call me a big devil!"

"Please don't kill me! I want to go home! Please take me back to the *pektika*!"

"It's okay. We're not going to hurt you. Calm down," said Milo. "Here, have some water."

Milo kneeled next to the girl and offered her a drink. For some reason, as soon as she looked into his starlike eyes, the girl seemed to calm down, and she took the water.

"We're inside a part of the body unique to mollusks called the purification tract," explained Milo. "It takes the water the creature inhales and makes it safe to drink. That means it's cool, tasty, and good for you as well."

The girl looked up at Milo warily, but Dr. Panda's beaming smile broke through all her mental defenses, and she took a tentative sip… followed by another, followed by gulping down the whole lot in an effort to quench her parched throat.

"Wow, you finished that off quick! Fetch some more water, Bisco."

"Who am I, your waiter? Goddammit…"

Despite his grumbles, Bisco did as he was asked and dipped the canteen into the nearby pool. The girl darted her eyes between him and the smiling Milo with a confused look on her face.

"Um…who are you? You don't look like Benibishi…but you aren't *sporko* from the village, either. A-are you, perhaps, *saushaka*?"

"S-saushaka?"

"I mean, did you come from outside Hokkaido?!" yelled the girl, clearly frustrated.

Oh, I wish I'd paid more attention in Sakhalinese class!

Milo struggled to keep up with the girl's incessant use of her native tongue and chose his words carefully so as to put her fears to rest.

"Y-yes! That's right, we're *saushaka*—southerners. I'm from Imihama, and my name's Milo Nekoyanagi. I'm a doctor. Dr. Panda, they call me!"

"Milo...Nekoyanagi? And that *devika* over there?"

"He's Bisco Akaboshi. He got turned into a child by the Benibishi, but he's supposed to be—"

"Bisco...Akaboshi?!"

The girl suddenly grew fierce and began railing at Milo.

"You're lying! Bisco Akaboshi and Milo Nekoyanagi are the strongest *sporko* of all the *saushaka*, not little boys like that! You must be servants of the Benibishi here to take me away!"

"Awawa... N-no, we're not, I swear...!"

"For cryin' out loud, are you scared of us or not? Make up your damn mind!" Bisco yelled, leaping across the moist meat floor to interpose himself between Milo and the girl. He offered the newly filled canteen to the girl with a "Hmph" that translated to *"Here, take it,"* but the girl simply turned her head away like a disgruntled infant refusing their food. Bisco shrugged and brought the water flask to his lips, whereupon the girl finally cracked, swiping the canteen from his hand and gulping it down in an instant.

"What a selfish brat! I wish we'd left you for the bears now. C'mon, Milo, let's get the hell out of here and leave her behind!"

"Um, excuse me," said Milo to the girl, pushing Bisco's angry face aside. "What's your name?"

The girl eyed the pair of them suspiciously, but it soon seemed to dawn on her that these two idiots meant her no harm, so she reluctantly answered.

"...I am Chaika, daughter of Cavillacan, Hand of the Ghost Hail," she replied, turning away defensively. "Everybody simply calls me 'Chaika.'"

Here Bisco took another close look at the girl. She reminded him of Nuts and Plum in terms of her age, but Chaika was surprisingly curvaceous for her years and not like the skinny Honshu folk at all. Her bright-blond hair came down to her shoulders and contrasted brilliantly with her pale white skin. She was dressed in a thick, fur-lined coat and boots, decorated with intricate patterns that made Bisco think she must be from a pretty well-off family.

"...Hey!" she said at last. "Where do you think you're looking?! *Kyabi! Bedelero!*"

"Kyabi...? Bedelero...?"

"Err...I think she's calling you a coward and a pervert, Bisco."

"What?! I ain't into kids! Where'd you get that idea?!"

"You're a kid, too!! A stinky, pervert kid!!"

"Whoa! Calm down, you two! Don't start another fight!!"

Milo threw himself between Bisco and Chaika and looked into her eyes once more.

"Chaika," he said. "I need to know if you've been hurt. I'm a doctor; you can show me. Do you have any injuries?"

"Hurt... Ah!"

Milo's words seemed to suddenly remind Chaika of something, and she tore open her coat to reveal a small part of her shoulder where her soft, clear skin was marred with ivy, with a bright-red camellia flower blossoming from it.

"What the hell...?"

"A flower. It's Shishi's camellia!"

The two boys gulped, while Chaika herself burst into tears as she explained.

"I was trying to run away when one of the Benibishi got me with their sword! Now it's gonna turn me into a *slevi*! Waaah! I don't want to be a *slevi*!"

"Calm down, Chaika! There's got to be some way to cure it!"

"Please take me back to my village!!" she cried, throwing her arms around Milo, shaking in fear and dismay, and showing none of her guarded attitude from earlier. "My father can erase the Florescence with the Hand of the Ghost Hail! I don't care if you're *saushaka sporko* right now. Take me back to the village so he can cure me!"

"Chaika…"

Milo gently embraced the poor girl while Bisco looked on in displeasure.

"There you go again, helpin' people like usual. You sure we got time for a detour? We need to head to the brain and take this thing down, remember?"

"No!!" cried Chaika. "You mustn't go to the *bretika*! The whole area has been overrun by Benibishi plants! There's another way to stop Hokkaido, but only my father knows the secret… I haven't ever been this far from the village before, and I am lost. Take me back to the *pektika*! I need to see my father!"

"Pektika…," said Milo. "I think that means 'pancreas.' Is that where you live, Chaika? Hey, Chaika, listen to me!"

The girl seemed unable to do anything but cling to Milo, sobbing into his chest. The two boys gave each other a troubled look.

"I can barely make out a word she's sayin'," said Bisco. "Besides, could there really be a tribe livin' down here, like she says?" He scowled and cracked his neck. "It's a little hard to believe, don't you think? Not that leavin' her here is a good idea, neither. I just…"

"It might not end up being that much of a detour," said Milo, rubbing Chaika's back. He pondered for a moment, then continued. "She said her father has the power to remove the Florescence. Maybe he knows a way to turn you back to normal as well!"

"Hmm. But who knows if we can trust her?" replied Bisco, scratching his chin. After a moment's thought, however, he could come up with no reasonable objection, so he looked at Milo and nodded. "I guess you're right. We'll help her. But she said she's from the pancreas, right? Ain't that quite a way from here according to your map?"

Bisco pointed to the diagram, which indicated that the purification tract the pair currently occupied was located near the head of the creature, as opposed to the pancreas, which was far deeper within the abdomen. Considering that the beast was the size of an island, it was not a small distance to traverse.

"Oh, it'll be okay! I'm a doctor, remember? As long as it's a living creature, and not a man-made maze, I'm sure I'll figure something out!"

"How do you figure?"

"Well, I did go to school."

"Ech. That's what you always say."

Bisco looked as though he was going to throw up at Milo's signature catchphrase. Meanwhile, Milo helped Chaika dust off her coat and get back on her feet.

"Don't worry. Bisco and I will make sure you get back to your village safely."

"Y-you mean it…?"

"Yep. But you have to trust us, too. Now, let's get going. Bisco, watch my back!"

"You got it!"

"Huh? Wha…? Eeek!"

Milo hoisted Chaika up onto his back, then leaped to the top of the waterfall, heading farther into the body. At first, Chaika was too scared to open her eyes, but after a moment she turned and looked around her.

"…*Ouya*! Wow! It's like we're flying!"

Chaika turned to look over her shoulder and made eye contact with Bisco, who was watching the rear. The beating walls illuminated his canines as he grinned back at her.

"Kids better keep their eyes shut. I don't want you cryin' all over *me* this time."

"…But you're a kid, too!"

Just as Chaika had been starting to relax, she was filled with anger once more, and she glared at Bisco, rosy-cheeked, before going "Hmph!" and facing forward again.

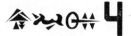

"Are you keeping up?!" Milo called back at his partner, who had stopped to look around.

"'Course I am! Quit worryin' about me!" Bisco shot back, following after Milo again. "So where are we, anyway? The ground's all spongy, and it's givin' me the creeps!"

"We've just entered a dead vein. On occasion, a *Mollusca evolutus* will abandon a damaged blood vessel and create a new one to replace it."

"I wish you'd abandon that smart-ass grin of yours!"

"I thought you'd be interested! Anyway, the point is, if we follow this dead vein, we should end up at the heart."

"The *hartika*? Is that where we're going?" asked Chaika, a worried tone in her voice. Just then, Bisco caught up and asked the question she had been thinking.

"So we're on the way to the heart, then. What are you plannin' to do once we get there?"

"It's probably easier to explain if you look at the diagram. The main artery travels from the heart to the pancreas. If we hop into the bloodstream, it'll take us straight there."

"Th-the bloodstream?" exclaimed Chaika, so surprised she nearly fell off Milo's back. Bisco quickly propped her up.

"Hey! Didn't Milo tell you to hold on tight?!" he yelled.

"B-but swimming through the *blodika* is simply unthinkable! Are all *saushaka* this damaged upstairs, or is it just you?"

"Chaika, the camellia progresses fast. We can't afford to waste time. But don't worry; in a beast of this size, the blood will have to be moving incredibly fast!"

"That's exactly what I'm worried about, you fool! In the village, we only use the *blodika* to move heavy objects around. If an ordinary person went inside, they'd drown!"

"Milo!" shouted Bisco all of a sudden. "There's something ahead of us."

Looking where Bisco was pointing, Milo noticed that the vein they were traversing ended in some sort of fleshy door that blocked the way.

"That's it!" Milo cried. "The main valve! We've reached the heart!"

"But it's closed. How do we get in?"

"We just have to force it open. Bisco, do you have any mushroom arrows that'll do the job?"

"Sure. One boomshroom should blow it wide open."

"N-n-n-n-no, wait!!"

Her face now bright-red, Chaika grabbed Milo's head and shook it.

"Don't destroy the valve to the *hartika*! If you do that, the blood will all come rushing out and wash us away!!"

"Is that right, Milo?"

"I suppose so, but it's nothing we can't handle."

"Fair enough."

"It's not fair enough at all!! Where do you two get your confidence from?!"

""Each other,"" they both replied at once.

"H-how did you do that?!" Chaika cried.

By now, she expected such ridiculous claims from the mouth of the intrepid Bisco, but Milo had represented her last island of sanity, now utterly sunk beneath the waves. The boy doctor fired a spearshroom into the ground, which sprouted straight up like a bamboo shoot all the way into the cavern roof overhead.

"Hold on to this, Chaika. I'll be right behind you to catch you if you fall."

"W-w-w-wait! Surely you can't be serious!!"

"All yours, Bisco! Make a nice hole for us!"

"Yep. Leave it to me."

"Wh-what do you mean a 'nice hole'?!"

Bisco cleanly nocked his arrow and pulled the bowstring tight, firing it toward the door.

Gaboom!

The explosion tore a hole in the valve of Hokkaido's heart, and the entire room began to tremble in anticipation of the impending torrent.

"Hold on tight, Bisco! Remember, you're not as strong as you think you are!"

"I learned that last time! I'm not gonna let it happen again!"

"Eeeek!!"

Chaika's scream was almost erased by the gushing river of milky blood as it swept into the disused vein. The three clung to Milo's spear-shroom for dear life, lest the current wash them away.

"Oh, the blood *is* white, just as I hypothesized! I wonder what makes it that color."

"Stop acting so casual!" yelled Chaika. "Glph…! Phah!"

"And you quit flounderin' around like a dyin' fish!" said Bisco. "You're gonna be okay!"

Just as Milo predicted, the flow of blood did not last long (although the heart still released a few hundred humans' worth), and after about a minute, the stream died down.

"Haah…haah… I feared I was about to perish… And my clothes are sopping wet…!"

"Now, was that a nice hole or was that a nice hole? Are you gonna trust us *now*? Or are you gonna let your worries burn a hole in your stomach?"

Chaika was gobsmacked by Bisco's sheer unwarranted pride. "Th-that could have just been a coincidence! Besides, I'm just a child! What would my father say if he knew about you two forcing me to undergo such perilous activities?!"

"I thought you were sayin' we were both kids before, weren't you?"

Unable to come up with a satisfactory comeback, Chaika fumed, before turning away from Bisco with pouted lips and another "Hmph!"

"Bisco! Chaika! Come look at this! It's just as wonderful as I imagined!"

The two joined Milo at the ruptured valve, peering through it into the heart, where they were met with the sight of a swirling pool of white liquid.

"Isn't it amazing?" said Milo. "It looks like a sea of milk!"

"It's nothin' like a human's at all," said Bisco. "Guess I shoulda expected that."

The two boys couldn't take their eyes off the magnificent sight. Chaika, on the other hand, gazed solemnly at the pool, then opened her mouth to speak.

"Milo, Bisco. I'm sorry, but I don't think your plan is going to work."

"Huh? What do you mean, Chaika?"

"The *hartika* is weakened," she explained, watching it pump the white fluid to other parts of the body. "When Father brought me here before, it was much stronger. The Benibishi flowers must have robbed Hokkaido of its former strength."

"The 'hartika'?"

"I believe that means 'heart,'" said Milo.

"The heart's been weakened? How can you tell?!"

"The heartbeat feels softer than I remember," she said, looking forlorn. "I do not believe this will be strong enough to ferry us through the *blodika*."

The two boys shared an uncertain glance and thought for a moment.

"Hey, Dr. Panda! What's your usual plan for somethin' like this?!"

"What's the cure for low blood pressure? Let's see..."

Milo took a look around, voicing his thoughts as he did so.

"The best treatment is cardiac massage... In other words, we need to give the heart a shock to resuscitate it. But how do we do that on something so big...?"

"Sounds like my specialty," said Bisco. "Get over here. I'll take care of it!"

"Wha—?! Wait! Bisco? What?!"

Without letting Milo speak, Bisco grabbed him and leaped into the milky white pool. Chaika screamed after them, "What are you doing?!" but Bisco ignored her and climbed up onto Milo's shoulders.

"Milo, give us the Mantra Bow!" he shouted. "Can you do it?"

"I—I can, but what are you going to do with it?"

"The only thing you *can* do with a bow! I'm gonna fire a Rust-Eater into this thing and see if that wakes it up!"

"Whaaat?!" cried Milo, treading water in the white blood. "Don't you think that's a little drastic?! The power of your Rust-Eater is out of this world! That's not a massage; it's an onslaught!"

Just then, Milo realized what Bisco was getting at. "Ah, but as a child, your arrows are much weaker than before! They might not tear through the walls of the heart after all! In fact, it might be just the shock this creature needs!"

"Then hurry up and give it to me, Milo, before the heart shuts down for good!"

"…Okay! *Won/shad/viviki/snew!*"

The moment Milo finished speaking his mantra, glowing motes scattered from his palm, coalescing in Bisco's ready hand and taking the form of a small glittering emerald bow.

"…What?!" came Chaika's cry of surprise. "He just created a bow out of thin air!"

She watched from above, by the valve, as Bisco took a deep breath, expelling the Rust-Eater spores. They gathered into the shape of a golden arrow, which Bisco nocked against the bowstring of the Mantra Bow, filling the cavern of the heart with green and orange light. For a moment, Chaika stood in wonder, entranced by the sight.

It's so pretty…

Then, all of a sudden, she realized the ludicrous nature of the boys' plan.

"W-w-w-wait! You're firing an arrow into the *hartika*?! I knew it, you really *are* crazy! What on earth are you thinking?!"

"Now, Bisco!"

"Wait!!"

"All right, here we go!"

Pchew! Gaboom!

Bisco launched his arrow at blazing speed into the floor of the pool, and an enormous Rust-Eater mushroom sprouted from the lining of Hokkaido's heart.

Gaboom! Gaboom! Gaboom!

When Chaika noticed the sunlight-colored dust in the air, she gasped.

Impossible! Those are Heaven's Light spores! How could this child possibly command them?!

Bisco, on the other hand, went white as the pool itself when he saw the cluster of proud mushroom stalks lining it.

"Crap, I got a little excited," he said. "Think I overdid it?"

"I don't think so!" said Milo. "The pulsing is back to normal!"

Indeed, soon the whole heart twitched with a steady beat, which grew faster and faster, pumping the white blood out of the cavity.

"It's back to life again!" said Milo. "The blood pressure should be strong enough soon!"

"What're you standing around for, Chaika?! Get in, or we're gonna leave you behind!"

Chaika couldn't move for a second, still awed by the sight of Bisco and the Rust-Eater spores. Then she hopped back to her senses, shaking her head vigorously.

"I—I can't! It's too scary! You *saushaka* are out of your minds! Now that the *hartika* is restored, the *blodika* will surely drown us all!"

"Don't worry—we'll protect you!" said Milo. "Hurry up and get in, before it's too late!"

"No... No! Somebody help... Please...somebody take me back to my father!"

Unable to handle the pressure any longer, Chaika fell to the floor and began bawling her eyes out. Just then, an arrow sailed cleanly overhead and landed in the floor behind her.

Gaboom!

"Whaaaah?!"

The humble oyster mushroom launched Chaika into the air, where she flapped and kicked helplessly before landing in Bisco's arms.

"Geez, you sure are a handful," he grumbled. "Have a little faith. We hafta do crap like this every day!"

"Stop talking like you know it all; you're just a kid, like me! You *evie*! You *murderer*!"

"'Murderer' means 'bully.'"

"I understood that last one!" Bisco yelled. "I don't need you to translate everything!!"

"The bloodflow is speeding up! Bisco, Chaika, are you ready?"

"No! I'm scared! Hold on to me! Don't you dare let go!"

Chaika wrapped both arms around Bisco's neck and squeezed him tight, his choked groans eliciting a chuckle from Milo. The two of them wrapped their arms around her in turn, swaddling the child between them.

Then there was a huge *Ba-bump!* from the heart, and a wave of white carried the three through an exit and into Hokkaido's main artery.

"*Pwah!* It's just as I suspected, Bisco! Hokkaido's blood is dense enough for humans to float on! We're moving quite fast, but so long as we stay still, we should be able to avoid drowning!"

"Gblblblblbl! Ghah! Gablblblblbl!!"

"Tell that to the kid!" cried Bisco. "At this rate, she's gonna drag me down with her!"

The blood ferried Bisco, Milo, and Chaika through the veins of Hokkaido at breakneck speed. It was good for their travel time, as Milo predicted, but the journey was quickly proving unbearable for the poor girl dragged along for the ride.

"Chaika's gonna run out of energy before we get there," said Bisco. "I guess I'd feel a *little* bad if she drowned."

"What should we do? Oh, I know! I'll make her a snorkel…! What's the mantra for a snorkel, I wonder?" Milo began scratching his chin, pondering. "Won, shad, kel…hmm."

Bisco turned his attention forward, down the artery. From there, he could hear a low, rumbling sound that seemed to be very quickly drawing nearer.

"…Milo! Look out ahead! There's somethin' there!"

"Huh?! What is it?"

"It's like some sort of geyser; the blood is bein' shot upward. What is that?"

Milo turned and looked. Just ahead, the raging stream of blood

suddenly pointed upward and went gushing out of the vein like a fountain high into the air.

"Oh no! Something must have damaged the artery!"

"Damaged the artery?!"

"The blood is escaping to the surface! We'll be thrown out with it at
this rate!"

"I see. Then what's the plan? The great Dr. Panda musta thought of
somethin', right?"

Bisco looked hopefully to his partner as Chaika floundered for
breath. Milo pondered for a moment, before giving a trustworthy nod.

"...I'm sure it'll work out somehow. Let's just cross that bridge when
we come to it!"

"You ad-libbing madman!!"

"Well, I learned from the best."

The two boys held on to Chaika as all three of them were swept up
through the geyser of blood.

""Whoooooaaaa!!""

"*Phah!* Wh-what? What's going on?"

The current was much stronger than expected, and the three sailed
high into the air above Hokkaido's surface, looking down upon the
creature's vast back. However, what they saw there sent a shiver down
their spines, for it was far from the snow-covered wonderland they had
expected to see.

"Wh-what? What the hell happened here?!"

"Bisco, it looks like Hokkaido's already been conquered...!"

The two boys looked at each other and gulped.

"This is Shishi's domain now. Everything's been turned into..."

""Flowers!""

Seeing the field of flowers that coated the entire land, Bisco and Milo
stifled a shudder and fell helplessly through the air toward the snow
waiting below.

* * *

The landscape of Hokkaido's back was a true spectacle of natural beauty. The snow fell constantly all year round, even when the sky was absolutely cloudless, each and every snowflake akin to a jewel gliding softly in the air.

And after a thick layer of snow covered the land, the very heartbeat of the great megabeast would rouse it, causing swiftly flowing rivers of snow that could ensnare the foot of the unwary traveler like quicksand. Though dangerous, these marvelous snow-rivers were incomparable in the way they shone and glittered in the light; a true miracle of nature known only to this strange and untrodden land.

However, that all changed when the Benibishi invaded, threatening to warp this land's terrible beauty beyond all recognition.

"How is the garden faring?"

"My, Lord Satahabaki!"

The Benibishi soldier bowed his head at the giant man towering over him.

"I have excellent news, My Lord. We have struck one of Hokkaido's main arteries, and the beast's white blood proves a most splendid fertilizer. I pray this garden will soon meet your honored esteem."

"Hmm."

Satahabaki nodded in response to the man's joyous report. Before him, a garden of ivy and bright-red camellia flowers stretched across the snow as far as the eye could see. The roots extended deep beneath the thick snow and into Hokkaido's back, from where they drew their nourishment. Plus, at the center of the garden, the beast's white blood spouted like a macabre lawn sprinkler.

"All is going well, I see," he boomed. "But keep your spirit firm. Our victory is far from assured."

With that, Satahabaki turned his back on the soldier.

"Let them flourish. Drain the life out of Hokkaido. And never neglect your duties, even for a moment."

"Yes, sir!"

The soldier watched Satahabaki leave, then turned and surveyed the fountain once more.

"It should be safe to widen the hole in the artery a little," he pondered aloud. "That should spread the nutrients over a far larger area..."

Just then, he heard a strange noise.

""Whoooooaaa!!""

"Eeeeeek!!"

He looked to the screams coming from overhead to see a young man, a boy, and a small girl falling toward him. One of them, the red-haired little boy, wrapped the girl in his cloak and protected her as the pair hit the ground. The soldier watched, open-mouthed in shock, before...

"Y-you are not Benibishi! Brothers! Come to me! Humans have—"

Fwip!

Before the soldier could raise the alarm, the young man tossed a syringe, which landed point-first in the Benibishi's neck and caused him to pass out immediately. The assailant ran a hand through his sky-blue hair and breathed a sigh of relief.

"Damn, did you just kill him? Ice-cold, dude. Guess that's why they call you the Man-Eatin' Panda."

"Of course not! He's just sleeping... In any case, it looks like they're the ones responsible for damaging the artery."

"Geez, and their flowers are all over the place. Can't move for the damn things. You think they've been growin' them?"

The two gazed across the field of flowers, stretching all the way to the horizon. Meanwhile...

"Ahh... How awful..."

Chaika took a few careful steps before dropping to her knees and weeping.

"Whoa, Chaika?! What's the matter? Does it hurt?"

"Of course it does... Not me, but Hokkaido... His beautiful white back, sucked dry of life by the flowers..."

Bisco took one look at Chaika's tearstained face and shot Milo a questioning glance. Milo nodded gravely and looked out over the field, stroking his chin.

"I thought they wanted to use Hokkaido as an animal weapon," he said, "but this is only going to make it grow weaker. Why would they...? Wait!" he exclaimed all of a sudden. "Of course! Using Hokkaido to crash into Kyushu was only the first step of their plan! Shishi's true aim is to suck up his life force into the flowers!"

"Suckin' up his life force? Can they do that?"

"...They can," answered Chaika. "And by stealing Hokkaido's energy, they make their own Florescence more powerful. Hokkaido is gentle. He would never attack the lands of the *saushaka*. He's being forced to, by the Benibishi, against his will! He's suffering!"

Her voice strengthened into a scream, and the tears fell in large droplets from her face and mixed with the snow. Bisco and Milo looked at each other, and were just on the verge of offering Chaika some comforting words when...

"There they are! Humans spotted!"

"It's Akaboshi and Nekoyanagi! Kill them! Don't let them get away! We shall offer their heads to King Shishi!"

...a great number of Benibishi suddenly crested a hill far in the distance and began marching toward them.

"Crap, they've found us!"

"Oh no, it's the Benibishi! Please, don't let them hurt me!"

"Get on my back, Chaika. We're going!"

Milo helped the girl up, and he and Bisco began fleeing the garden. Thanks to the Mushroom Keepers' practiced running skills, the pair were not slowed by the snow and ice, but fairly soon more Benibishi appeared from the opposite direction, cutting them off.

"They've surrounded us! They must be super fast, thanks to Hokkaido's power boost!"

"Then we're just gonna have to fight our way through! Cover your ears, kid!"

"Wait...wait, you two! We're in luck!" shouted Chaika with a relieved smile. "Look down! We're right above the *nordika*!"

"...The nordika?"

"That's the blowhole."

"I've never met such a complete simpleton," Chaika said, sighing. "Does he have to explain everything for you?"

"How the hell am I supposed to know a language I've never even heard of before?!"

Still, Bisco had to agree she had a point. Not about his intelligence, but on the existence of a strange circular protuberance that encircled the land beneath their feet. Milo nodded and, keeping an eye on the approaching Benibishi soldiers, turned to Bisco.

"Let's trust her. Okay, Chaika, how do we open this *nordika*?"

"Hweh?"

Chaika suddenly stiffened, and a look of embarrassment spread across her face.

"...I don't know. It'll open when Hokkaido needs to breathe, I guess."

"Don't act so smug if you don't even know how to open it!" Bisco roared.

"Oh, shut up! That's your job! Use your mushrooms or whatever! You're *sporko*, aren't you? Show me what your *saushaka* mushroom arts can do!"

"This kid just won't shut up...!"

"Of course! Bisco, the tickleshrooms!" Milo swiftly pulled an arrow with vermilion fletchings from his quiver. "It's a bit cruel, but if we can make Hokkaido sneeze, we should be able to open that hole!!"

"Urk! Can't say it sounds like fun..."

Still, when compared to the advancing Benibishi armies, it was clear which was the more appealing option, so Bisco timed his arrows with Milo and fired the tickleshrooms into the ground around the blowhole. They exploded into small yellow mushrooms and immediately began scattering their spores, which were quickly absorbed into the breathing pore.

"Wow, they're so pretty."

"Don't touch 'em! Not unless you wanna know what it's like to be stung by a thousand mosquitoes at once!"

The two boys held Chaika back, and soon enough the blowhole began slowly opening, the snow cascading into the chasm beneath.

"All right, it's open! Nice one, Chaika! Now let's get going!"

"Err... Oh, are we really going down here? I don't know... It's scary, and we don't know what's down there! No! Stop! Let go of me!"

"What the hell? You're the one who suggested it in the first place!!"

"On the count of three," said Milo. "One, two, three!"

"NOOOOOOO!!"

Just as Hokkaido took a deep breath to sneeze, Milo and Bisco leaped into the hole and were sucked down a long, winding tunnel, deep into the airways of the beast. They heard the sounds of the Benibishi soldiers echoing from far behind them.

"They're gone! Where did they go?!"

"There's a hole! They must have escaped down here!"

"Into the hole, men! Charge!"

But just as they attempted to follow...

"*A C H O O O O !*"

...Hokkaido's gargantuan sneeze blasted dozens of soldiers high into the air, and the blowhole resealed, ensuring the two boys' successful escape.

☆⚯〜Ө⚟ **6**

"Cough! Cough!"

The milky white blood of Hokkaido spilled from Chaika's lips. It glistened in the light emitted by the creature's internal organs, then seeped into the surface and disappeared.

The long, winding tunnel had deposited the three in a large cavern of meat, where they waited for Chaika's ear canals to discern up from down again.

"M-my head is spinning... I've had to swim through seas of blood, been chased by the Benibishi... I've seen enough today to last me a lifetime..."

"But still kickin', ain't ya?" replied Bisco. "And not a scratch on you, to boot. I'm still waitin' for my thanks, by the way."

"It isn't coming!!" Chaika yelled. "After all you put me through, you want me to *thank* you? In fact, when we find my father, I'm going to make him beat you to a pulp!!"

"Listen here, you ungrateful little brat! That was all to help you!"

"Bisco, Chaika! Good news! I think we just took a shortcut!"

Just as the two children were about to start another fight, they heard Milo's voice. He came over and showed them his diagram, now drenched with white blood but still legible.

"This is where we are," he explained, pointing. "Inside the abdominal cavity."

"So?" asked Bisco. "Does that mean we're any closer to gettin' the little one back home?"

"We've made good distance, but the pancreas is still a ways to go yet, and the abdominal cavity is really big. It would be nice if there was a shortcut we could take…"

"…There is," said Chaika.

""…What?!""

The two hadn't expected to get anything out of Chaika the way she was acting, so when she suddenly chimed in, it came as quite a shock. Chaika was a little surprised in turn by their overblown reaction, but she carried on.

"…I'm not *completely* useless, you know. The others go via the *stomagre*— that is, this cavity—quite often. I've been here a couple times before."

"Then does that mean you know the way through this massive cave?"

"Mm-hmm!"

Chaika, still a little standoffish, pointed toward the roof of the cavern. The two boys looked up…and gasped at what they saw.

Along the top of that cave, so wide even the walls were too far to be seen, was a row of white bones, obviously standing out against the reddish flesh behind.

"That's Hokkaido's *spihi*—the spine," she said. Seeing the boys' astonished faces, Chaika quickly regained her pride and gave a triumphant snort as she went on. "The villagers all travel across that when they come to check on the organs. It's common knowledge around these parts."

"They travel across it?" asked Bisco, incredulous. "How? Can they walk upside down?"

"Look closer, silly. Don't you see the black rail running along it?"

Sure enough, there was an iron rail set into the white bone of Hokkaido's spine. Furthermore, hanging from that rail, and directly above the boys' heads, was what looked like a cable car. The car had spindly white legs extending from both sides, so it was apparently a modified creature of some sort, rather than an inanimate object.

"It looks like a stray car has just happened to stop here. Those are called *spanagoi kaparey*. I suppose in your tongue, that would be…'spinal bugs.'"

"Spinal bugs?!"

"Quite. They're a parasite that we've turned into vehicles. The *sporko* of the village use them to travel all throughout Hokkaido."

"W-wooow…!"

Once more, Bisco and Milo were struck by the sheer scale of Hokkaido, halfway between island and creature, and even more so by the ingenuity of its inhabitants.

"Anyway. That's how we'll get to my village. Now take me up there."

"And how are we supposed to get on it when it's danglin' from the ceilin' like that?!"

"…W-well, we need to first go uphill to the boarding area. There should be one nearby…"

"I ain't got time for this bullshit!"

Bisco nocked a wire arrow and fired it into the ceiling, reeling him up into the air.

"Milo! Grab her and get up here!"

"Ah, I see…that's clever…"

"H-hey! You're not gonna do that to me, are you?! I-I'll have you know my father is the greatest *warriat* in the village!"

"Chaika, close your eyes and hold on tight. It'll all be over soon."

"Noooooo!!"

Pchew! Milo's wire arrow latched into the ceiling, lifting him and Chaika upward. Milo landed perfectly on the spinal bug's legs and slid gracefully down them to reach the cabin.

"There we go—all over! You can open your eyes now!"

"I—I thought my *hartika* was going to stop!"

"This all looks a lot more complicated than I expected," said Bisco. "How do you work this thing?"

"You're useless! Let me do it!"

Chaika pushed Bisco aside and began tapping at the control panel. Soon the spinal bug let out a groan like a steam whistle and marched onward, following the rail in the ceiling.

"…Phew. That should do it. Next stop, the *pektika*."

"Hear that, Bisco? Oh, thank you, Chaika! You're a lifesaver!"

"…M-Milo. Um…"

Now that things were safely back on track, Chaika seemed to grow a little reserved, looking shyly up at Milo.

"Th-thank you," she said. "I'd have died back there if it weren't for you. When we reach the village, tell my father you saved my life. He'll grant you anything you ask for."

"…Hey, Chaika. I'm still wondering why we found you running back from the brain stem. What were you doing all by yourself in such a dangerous place?"

"…I was trying to commune with the *bretika*—the brain. The only one who can speak with Hokkaido…is me."

"Y-you can talk to the brain?!"

Chaika paused for a moment, wondering if she should so freely share this information with outsiders, but when she looked into Milo's starry eyes, she found she couldn't resist.

"I…am Hokkaido's oracle," she explained. "The village raised me as the only one who could understand the great beast. When the Benibishi's pollen made him go mad, the village sent me along with lots of guards to the *bretika* to try to stop it."

"…"

"But it was no use. Hokkaido's *bretika* was already controlled by the Benibishi's plants, and my words would not reach him. Then the Benibishi sprang an ambush on us, and the guards all… They all…"

"Chaika! I'm sorry. It's okay—you don't have to say any more."

Milo took the trembling girl in his arms.

So there's been a tribe living inside Hokkaido all this time that can talk to it and keep it under control…?

"Hey, Milo," came Bisco's voice. "Somethin's comin'."

It's impossible to believe. How could humans live alongside a beast as large as this…?

"Snap out of it, Milo! There's somethin' behind us!"

"Whaaat?!"

Milo turned to see something traveling after them at incredible speed. It was another of the spinal bug insects, going so fast that it sparked against the rail.

"What a tailgater," said Bisco. "Don't he know he can't overtake?"

"Shut up, Bisco! Look at that!"

Milo pointed near the front of the bug, at the first carriage of the train that pursued them. It was covered in ivy, sprouting large red camellia flowers that scattered their pollen everywhere.

"I-impossible... That *kaparey*... No one's driving it!" cried Chaika, poking her head between the two boys. "It's the Benibishi! They're controlling the bugs just like they did with Hokkaido!"

"They can control the stuff livin' inside it, too?!" yelled Bisco. "Just how far does Shishi's power go?!"

Clanggg!!

The three lost their footing and stumbled as the train behind collided with theirs, and the spinal bug let out a low cry. Milo swiftly fired his hen-of-the-woods arrow at the beast, and although it blossomed with a *Gaboom!* the ivy quickly wrapped around it and sucked out all the nutrients.

"It's no use. Our mushrooms don't work against Shishi's flowers," he said.

"Hey, Chaika!" yelled Bisco. "There any way to stop that thing?!"

"There's an emergency lever inside the *kaparey*! But there's no way we can get in through that narrow opening at this speed!"

Following Chaika's eyes, Bisco saw that indeed the vehicle's windows were quite small and covered in tough-looking vines.

"Yeah. I guess you'd have to be a kid to make it inside..."

"B-Bisco?! Don't tell me you're going to try?!" cried Chaika.

"I don't got any better ideas! Milo! Use your mantra to clear away the ivy!"

"You got it, Bisco!"

"Th-this can't be happening. You two are insane!!"

Bisco tied his partner's wire arrow to himself to help him back up should he fall, while Milo focused intently on his right hand.

"Won/ul/viviki/snew!"

Emerald-colored motes gathered in his palm, taking the form of a sparkling green hand ax. As Chaika watched it happen, she began trembling fearfully.

"Y-you can control the Rust?! That is surely blasphemy!"

"I guess that's a cultural difference," Milo replied. "Everyone does it where I'm from. Just watch!"

"...The Rust obeys his words... I-impossible...!"

With Milo's white lie to soothe things over, he threw the ax as hard as he could at the vine-wrapped cable car behind. It sliced clean through the solid wall of ivy and smashed the reinforced glass of the window beyond.

"Bisco!"

"You got it!"

Bisco leaped into the air, just as the spinal bug came back for another ramming attack. He sailed cleanly into the open window, tumbling onto the floor of the driving room.

"O-ouya! I can't believe it!" Chaika cheered. "Bisco's inside!"

Bisco poked his face through the window and yelled back. "Chaika! There's too many levers here! Which one do I pull?!"

"H-how am I supposed to know?" Chaika muttered. "I can't tell without seeing them..." But she couldn't very well leave Bisco's question unanswered, so she shouted back, "I don't know, but it has to be there somewhere! Just try pulling all of them!"

"What kind of suggestion is that?" Bisco grumbled, tearing off the ivy from the control panel. The shredded vines released a green liquid that got all over Bisco's clothes and skin.

Crash!

"Whoa!"

The force of the collision slammed Bisco into the rear of the car. He quickly got up and peered through the front window to see that the vehicle carrying Milo and Chaika had come loose from the insect's back and was now positioned at a wonky angle, swaying perilously.

"Bisco!" Milo shouted back across the distance. "We can't take much more of this! We'll fall off if the spinal bug doesn't die first!"

"Don't rush me!" Bisco yelled back. "I'm doin' everythin' I can!"

Bisco looked around the control room for the largest lever, and when he found it, covered in vines, he took out his knife and cut it loose.

"This better work!"

Bisco hopped onto it, using all the weight of his tiny body to push the lever down. The vines holding it back split and broke one by one, splattering him in their green fluid.

"Move, dammit, move!!"

Ker-lunk!

The lever fell into place, and the entire cabin lurched back. Chaika watched as the vehicle began to slow down.

"You fool, that's the release switch! It uncouples the whole *spanagoi* from the rail! Hurry up and get back here before you fall!"

"Why didn't you tell me to look out for that?!"

"I'll reel you in, Bisco! Hurry!"

The spinal bug let out a cry, as with a cloud of sparks, the rail released its load, and the entire creature went plummeting toward the ground. Bisco narrowly escaped through a window, and Milo managed to pull him back to safety just in time.

Bisco turned to watch the falling insect before landing in Milo's arms, whereupon all concerned breathed a collective sigh of relief.

"Wow," said Chaika. "I can't believe you actually pulled the release lever. That's crazy..."

"Shaddup! I wouldn't have done it if I knew what it did!"

"...It normally takes several grown-ups. I didn't think you'd be strong enough..." Chaika turned to Bisco timidly. "I...I apologize for disrespecting you, Bisco. You are very strong and brave for your age."

"I keep tellin' ya, I'm not a—!"

Bisco was about to yell at her again when he saw how sorry she looked. He paused and rubbed his temples for a moment as he tried to come up with something to say back.

"Listen, Chaika. It's got nothin' to do with bein' big enough or strong enough or any of that crap."

"..."

"All you need to get stuff done is the spirit. Believe in yourself, and you become a bolt of lightning that strikes down anything in your way."

"Believe...in yourself?"

"Does that make sense?"

"...Yes. I think it does."

Chaika looked across into Bisco's jade-green eyes, then puffed out her cheeks in frustration.

"...But it's a little annoying being lectured by a child even younger than me!"

"You haven't listened to a word I've been sayin', have you?!"

"B-Bisco! Chaika! Look out!"

"Oh, don't you start!" said Bisco, wiping the plant fluid off his face. "Can't I have a little peace and quiet for—? Whooooaaa?!"

When he turned to Milo, Bisco froze in shock, and his spiky hair stood on end.

"Waah! Look at that! Chaika! Look!"

"Oh, please settle down. We aren't due to arrive at the *pektika* for a while now."

"No! Look! It's another bug, and this one's comin' right for us!"

Chaika turned dubiously and looked ahead and was struck with the sight of another ivy-clad spinal bug, just like the last one, except it was approaching from the front. It let out a low moan, hurtling toward the cabin with terrifying force.

"What do we do about this one, Chaika?! Any ideas?!"

"...Ohh..."

"She fainted!! What a useless brat!"

"We'll have to jump, Bisco! Tie Chaika to me with your wire!"

Milo was quick to come up with a solution. While Bisco did as he asked, Milo blasted the side door off its hinges with an unbelievably strong kick, and peered down into the darkness awaiting him below.

"Milo! Where are we now? What's down there?"

Milo thought for a moment, his sky-blue hair flapping in the wind, before turning to Bisco with a peaceful smile.

"Hmm, I don't know! I guess we'll just have to find out, won't we?"

"I'm gonna shut down your clinic when we get back, you useless panda!"

"Let's go, Bisco! Hold on to me…! *Won/shared/shed/snew!*"

Milo's mantra covered the three of them in a protective emerald sphere, then he and Bisco leaped from the moving vehicle alongside each other, plummeting into the gaping chasm below.

Ker-slamm!! Kaboom!

The vehicles collided in a screaming rush of metal, scattering debris that bounced off the barrier as the three fell silently into the darkness.

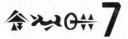

""Waaaaghhh!!""

Falling at terminal velocity, Bisco, Milo, and Chaika hit the ground to find it was surprisingly elastic as it flung them high into the air again. Even with Milo's mantra shield absorbing the impact, it took three or four bounces for the ball to settle.

"Haah…haah… We made it. I guess you won that bet."

"I don't believe it. I thought we were dead for sure! It's all thanks to our soft landing." Milo inspected the cube in his hand, which had now lost its glow, and sighed. "Though I think that's used up the last of my Rust power. I won't be using any mantras like that for a while…"

"But damn, is it hot around here! Milo, have you figured out where we are yet?"

"Let's see…"

Milo made sure Chaika was still safely on his back, then stood up and took a look around. It was a lot brighter than the gloomy caverns from earlier, and the walls now shone with an orange glow. Just like Bisco said, this glow appeared to warm the air, and the scorching heat made the two boys sweat.

"…Oh no," he muttered softly to himself. "I don't think we should stay here very long."

"What's wrong?" said Bisco "Out with it!"

"How did you hear that?! We're…we're in the stomach, Bisco. It's not a very safe place to be, and that's putting it mildly."

"Ech. The stomach?! Why the hell did you bring us here?!"

"I didn't! That's just the way it happened! But look on the bright side. The pancreas can't be far from here! Let's get out before something happens, Bisco!"

"Look on the bright side? Dumbass..."

Bisco cursed and took another look around. It almost seemed like the heart of a volcano, with glowing red pools and rivers of what looked like magma. The air was so hot it burned the lungs, and the ground seemed far too hot to cross barefoot.

"Those pools must be stomach acid," Milo explained. "It's so unlike human biology...though I suppose that's not surprising. It's more like walking through a volcano. Isn't it amazing?!"

"Take this seriously for once...! Hey, look at Chaika. She's bright-red. You think she needs water or somethin'?"

"Huh?!"

Milo quickly untied the wire strapping her to his back and laid the exhausted Chaika on the ground. She looked dangerously flushed, and she kept panting.

"Oh no, it looks like heatstroke," he said. "The camellia must have affected her resistance!"

Milo began stripping off her constricting clothing, to see that the ivy had grown significantly since they'd first met. Now it covered her whole shoulder, and it was still growing, fast enough that Milo could see it slowly stretching across her.

"It's speeding up because she's weakened!" Milo said. "We need to get somewhere cooler, fast, before the plants take over her mind!"

"All right," said Bisco, leaping into action. "You stay here and watch over her. I'll go look for an exit so we can—"

Splat!

Suddenly, something round and skin-colored fell from the roof of the cavern onto Bisco's face.

"Mmmppph?!"

"Bisco?!"

"Pfah!" Bisco pulled the strange blob off and looked at it. "What the hell is this?!"

It appeared to be made of some fatty substance, and had no eyes or nose, but instead little legs like a pig's. These it wriggled fiercely in a desperate attempt to escape Bisco's grasp and reattach itself to his face.

"What the hell is it, Milo? Some kinda monster?!"

Milo's face paled in an instant. "It's a redbaby!" he shouted. "Get rid of it, quickly, or it'll melt your bones!"

"What?!"

Bisco looked back at the creature, which had already turned red and swelled to twice its previous size. Bisco could see that it was beginning to tear, and bright-orange light flowed out from within.

"Whoa, no thanks!!"

Slam!! Bisco's swiveling kick launched the mimic far off into the air, and a short while later, *Kaboom!!* The explosion scattered a hot red fluid that looked an awful lot like the magma that made up the pools and rivers nearby.

"Shit, that was close. That thing's a bomb!"

"The redbaby is a type of fungus that lives inside the stomach of *Mollusca evolutus*," Milo explained, considerably less carefree than before. "It helps to digest their food by clinging to whatever it can find and exploding... Bisco, look at that!"

Milo pointed to the spinal bug and car, which fell down with them. A group of redbabies had gathered around it, and one by one they all leaped into the air, bursting and scattering their digestive fluids over it. The fluid ate through steel and flesh alike, reducing everything to a murky sludge in a matter of moments.

"Geugh!" said Bisco, recoiling in disgust.

"They'll come for us once they're done," cautioned Milo. "We can't let them catch us. Let's go!"

"Damn, if it ain't one thing, it's another!"

Bisco helped Chaika back onto Milo's back, and the two of them set off in the opposite direction, without making a sound.

"All right, that should be far enough…," said Bisco, glancing back at the herd.

"B-Bisco, look!"

Bisco turned to see something else that left him lost for words. It was the other spinal bug, the one that had crashed into them. The redbabies had already been at it, leaving only its tough skeleton sprawled out on the ground.

But that carcass was not what Milo was pointing to. They crawled out from beneath it. A couple at first, but more and more crept from the shadows to join them. There were dozens, hundreds of redbabies, their attention trained on the two boys.

"…What now, Milo? Turn back?"

"It's too late. They're behind us, too! There's no way out!"

"Grrr. Then I guess we got no choice but to fight!!"

Interpreting Bisco's yell as a declaration of hostility, the redbabies all leaped toward the two Mushroom Keepers. Bisco and Milo went back-to-back and, conferring only through their eyes, took out the same arrows and aimed them at the floor.

Pchew! Gaboom!!

The arrow they had chosen to use was the silveracid nameko, the same mushroom exploited in their past battle with the oilsquid. The pungent stalks burst from the floor in two fan shapes, radiating outward from the boys, and intercepted the redbabies as they attacked from both sides.

Pchew! Pchew!

Any of them that touched the mushrooms were torn open by the powerful acid and burst. The fungal creatures lacked the intelligence to walk around the mushrooms, and simply kept on throwing themselves into certain death. The plan was a success, but…

"Dammit, there's too many of them!"

"They keep coming… There's no way out!"

…the redbabies climbed across the bodies of their fallen comrades, using sheer fungus-wave tactics to advance. The boys found themselves at the center of a rapidly closing skin-colored ocean of foes.

"Guess this is it," admitted Bisco. "What a rotten end for the Mushroom Keepers who saved Japan three damn times!"

"That's just the way it is!" replied Milo. "But I don't mind how I die, so long as it's with you!"

Fully out of nameko arrows, the two resigned themselves to their fate and smiled at the approaching wave of redbabies.

"...All right. Let's get on with it. Our life force should be enough mushroom food to keep them away from Chaika."

"Right, Bisco!"

Milo laid the girl down on the floor, and the two boys stood on either side of her. Drawing their bows, they leveled them at each other, at the heart, and stared deep into each other's eyes. Bisco's jade-green met Milo's starlight-blue, and glimmered.

"...Milo! Before we die, there's somethin' I wanna tell you!"

"What is it?"

"I..."

"..."

"I'm really glad I..."

"..."

"...Huh? What's that over there?"

"You're really glad you what?! Don't stop there!! Keep going!!"

"Shut up, Milo! Look! There's something...no, *someone* coming!"

Milo turned to see a small human figure deftly leaping across the swarm. Their silver hair danced in the orange light, and they moved with a force and agility that put even the two Mushroom Keepers to shame.

"Bisco, look!"

"Won! Shandreber! Shed! Snew!"

The figure's voice rang out loud and clear throughout the stomach, and with a *Thud!* they landed in between the two boys. A transparent dome of mantra energy engulfed the whole area, which the redbabies crashed into like birds into a window.

"Kusabira sect tenet number one..."

The silver-haired figure twirled; a glimmer of sweat glistened.

"A threat to life must always be answered with peace in one's heart."
Watching the hundreds of redbabies scratch at the barrier with their little legs, the figure exhaled sharply.

"And tenet number two…"

The young girl revealed her face and offered a sweet, angelic smile.

"…If that don't work, then beat the crap outta them! Isn't that right?"

The girl snapped her fingers, and part of the barrier exploded, blasting every last one of the creatures away. Those that weren't torn to shreds immediately still burst when they fell onto the nameko mushrooms underneath. A series of further explosions worked their way across the barrier, which must have completely spooked the redbabies, for they scattered in all directions without any sign of the dogged persistence they had been showing so far.

"Phew, that was close!" the girl said, watching them flee. "If you're going to die, at least do it in a holier place. Mr. Bisco *is* the founder of our sect, after all."

"Ah… Ahhh!!"

"It's you!"

"I picked up your signal using my Mantra of Detection. I didn't believe it at first, but I came to check, and here you are. I must say, sirs, I never thought we'd meet again in such a curious place!"

"'Amli!!'"

The girl, Amli Amlini, high priestess of the Kusabira sect, brushed her sweaty hair out of her eyes and readjusted the belts around her glass eye. It was her favorite one, jade-green like Bisco's.

"A-Amli!" Milo exclaimed. "Wh-what are you doing here?!"

"I should be asking you the same thing, Mr. Milo, sir," Amli replied. "How on earth did you end up inside the belly of an enormous whale?" Then she looked around curiously and asked, "But where is Mr. Bisco? I thought I sensed him as well. Was he not with you?"

"…Erm, well, about that…"

"I'm down here, Amli! It's me, Bisco!"

Amli turned to the prepubescent voice calling her name. She stared for a few moments in what seemed like horror, and slowly began to shake.

"A-Amli, there's no need to be afraid," said Milo in an attempt to reassure her. "This is Bisco. He's just a little...different...at the moment..."

"H...he..."

"Hello? Amli?"

"HE'S SO CUUUUTE!!!"

In an extraordinary display of might, Amli scooped up Bisco and squeezed him so hard he almost burst.

"Gyaaaah!! S-stop it, Amli! Let me go!!"

"Whatever happened to you, Mr. Bisco, sir? No, do not answer, for it matters not! I simply cannot believe how adorable you've become! Your face is all pudgy, your voice all squeaky, and you're even smaller than me!"

"G-get over it already! This isn't the time!"

"Well! I can hardly keep calling you my elder brother, now can I? What a wonderful reversal of fortune! You must take care to refer to me as 'Big sister' from now on, you hear?"

Amli continued to choke the life out of Bisco while Milo stood, eye twitching, a short distance away. It was only when Bisco's face began to turn a peculiar shade of purple that he stepped in to rescue his partner.

"You're going to kill him, Amli! Bisco's technically the god of your sect, remember!"

"What were ya just standin' around for, dumbass?! I coulda died!"

"...*Phew.* I do believe I lost myself there for a moment. You were just asking to be hugged, that's all." Amli coughed as if to put her shameful display behind her. "As for why I am here, that is because this creature devoured Shimane, including the head temple of the Kusabira sect."

"The head temple? You mean the Rust-Eater tower? That was eaten?!"

"Yes. Along with all the faithful, I might add. Then I sensed the two of you were already here, so I set out hoping I might find you. Mr. Bisco is the only one who can help save them."

"I'd love to help," Bisco replied, before looking at the floor, "but I've got my hands full with Chaika. She needs to get home first."

The three turned their gaze downward, to where the girl still lay, panting, with a flushed face.

"My goodness! Who might this young lady be?"

"She seems to be the elder's daughter of a tribe that lives inside Hokkaido," said Milo. "But I can't bring down her fever any further. Is there anything you can do, Amli?"

"So Amli Healing is to take on a case that stumps the great Panda Clinic, is it? Very well. It has been a while since I practiced, but I shall see what I can do." Amli cracked her neck and popped out her glass eye. "Mr. Bisco, sir, could I ask you to please open her mouth for me…? That's it; now hold it there."

"How's this?"

"Perfect! Now I shall proceed to suck the heat out of her body. Are you ready?"

"Y-yeah!"

Bisco held Chaika's head between his knees, using his fingers to pry her lips apart.

"*Won-shad-hulki-had-snew. Won-shad-had-hulki-snew…*"

Amli leaned over Chaika, peering into her mouth with the empty socket, and suddenly Chaika began screaming and crying as a column of steam rose out of her mouth.

"Chaika!"

"It's okay!" Amli shouted. "Keep her still!"

Chaika belched steam like an overworked car exhaust, which found its way into Amli's socket. Just as Chaika's face started returning to a more reasonable shade, Amli's flushed, and she began sweating bullets.

"That's enough, Amli! You're turning into a damn tomato!"

"It's okay—I can take it…! *Won-shad-hulki-snew!*"

With that, the last of the heat left Chaika's body, and Amli immediately ceased her mantra.

"Haah…haah…haah…"

Chaika slowly returned to normal. Her face, creased in discomfort, relaxed, and her breathing slowed. Even the ivy spreading across her shoulder was slower now.

"Chaika!" Bisco shouted. "...Whoa, she looks way better!"

"Haah...haah...haah...!!"

"Amli, what's wrong?!" cried Milo.

"This is nothing compared to clearing out Bisco's stomach!" she declared, popping her eye back in and giving herself a few sturdy whacks on the head. "It has been a while, but it's nice to see that I haven't gotten rusty, so to speak!" She turned and gave a dazzling smile, face dripping with sweat.

"Thanks a ton, Amli," said Bisco. "You saved her life, and ours!" He took a look around at what little remained of the redbabies and nodded. "We owe you one. You said you need our help, so take us where we need to go."

"We must be cautious," Amli replied. "Once I let down the mantra barrier, the heat out there will come rushing in. We don't want little Miss Chaika there to be afflicted with heatstroke again, or we'll be right back where we started."

Milo nodded in response, then turned to Bisco. "Let's split up. I'll take Chaika and get us somewhere cool. You go with Amli and see if you can help her out."

"Right, good idea!" replied Bisco.

"Be safe, Mr. Milo, sir. This way, Mr. Bisco, sir!"

Amli created a bridge of mantra energy, which she used to cross the pools of digestive fluid. Milo watched her leave alongside his partner until both were out of sight, then took off with Chaika to find a place to continue her treatment.

Come to think of it, it's far hotter in here than I expected. There were an awful lot of those redbabies running around, too... Perhaps it's to do with Hokkaido's latest diet?

Milo wiped off the sweat dribbling into his eye and continued following the walls of the stomach. A stray pack of redbabies attacked, but Milo blasted them away with his arrows without even breaking stride.

Usually, the stomachs of Mollusca evolutus *have specialized cooling organs. I should be able to find one of them if I just follow the wall.*

"...Aha! There it is!" said Milo with delight.

Just ahead was a pale-blue tunnel that stood out against the deep-red walls and seemed to lead elsewhere. From the mouth of the cave came a bunch of tiny, almost imperceptible little lights, and when they touched Milo, he suddenly felt a refreshing chill that caused all of his energy to return.

"This is it, the refrigerator sac...! But..."

Mollusca evolutus possessed many of these refrigerator sacs, dotted around the stomach in order to cool it and protect it from overheating. If the body was functioning correctly, these sacs could also keep the breeding population of redbabies in check. However...

"It's too late. Shishi's flowers are already here!"

...the exhaust port, as it were, was blocked by thick ivy, preventing the organ from fulfilling its required function. This explained why the rest of the stomach had been left in such chaos.

"I've never operated on an Island Whale before, but... Ggh!"

Milo's starlight eyes twinkled, and he summoned up what little mantra power remained, channeling it through the cube in his hand to create a large emerald ax.

"It is I, the glorious leader! *George's Tomahawk!!*"

Slammm!!

Milo's ax sundered the ivy, and it fell apart like sliced rope. As it drifted to the ground, Milo's emerald motes burned it up from the ends inward, until there was nothing left.

"Surgery complete! Too bad there was nobody around to see it... Wh-whoa, that's cold!"

Now unhindered by the ivy, cold air spilled forth from the organ and over Milo and Chaika. When the wind finally died down, the tunnel was filled with a cool, refreshing breeze, keeping the oppressive heat of the stomach at bay.

"All right, this should do it! You're going to be okay, Chaika!"

As the cool air washed over her, Chaika's breathing became more and more natural, eventually returning to normal. Milo continued down the tunnel until he reached the core of the refrigerator sac, and there he laid Chaika down on the floor.

"You should be safe here. Rest and recover."

"...Mmm... Fa...ther..."

As Chaika mumbled in her sleep, Milo stroked her soft blond hair and gave her a couple of emergency shots. Feeling that her pulse was steady once more, he psyched himself up and rose to his feet.

"All right. Chaika will be safe by herself. I need to catch up with Bisco and Amli. Those two are a pair of loose cannons; I hope they don't do anything too reckless while I'm not there!"

"Oh my god, it's even worse than I imagined!!"

Milo had just retraced his steps and laid eyes on the enormous Rust-Eater tower on the other side of the stomach when he heard *Boom! Boom! Gaboom!* and a number of Kusabira sect devotees came flying through the air toward him.

"O-our lord and savior!" "How could you do this?!" they screamed.

Milo drew his bow in a flash.

At this distance, a bamboo fungus should do the trick!

He fired his arrow into the stomach floor, and it exploded into a mass of weblike filaments, stretching like a net to catch the falling faithful before they hit the ground.

"Bisco!!" Milo yelled toward the tower once they were safe. "You can't just fling people around and not care about the consequences!"

"That's your job!" Bisco roared back. "I thought you'd get here five seconds ago!"

"You were counting on me arriving now?! What if I tripped or something?"

"Well, you didn't, did you? Here, got some more comin' your way!"

Gaboom! went Bisco's Rust-Eater arrow, tossing the Kusabira followers high over the magma pools and into Milo's fungal net. With only six or seven more, Bisco managed to get all roughly fifty of the adherents off the tower and into safety. The only ones left at the tower were Bisco and Amli and Raskeni.

Milo signaled over to them, and Amli returned his wave. Then she turned to Bisco with uncontained glee. "Serves them right! They should have listened to you. You only wanted to have some words with the shrine."

"What do you mean, *serves them right?*" said Raskeni, marching over to Bisco and glaring angrily into his eyes. "You were supposed to persuade them to leave quietly, not blast them away with mushroom arrows."

"Well, what was I supposed to do?!" Bisco growled back. "They didn't think I was really me 'cause of how young I look. You shoulda taught 'em better, Raskeni! You're lucky I didn't smite 'em all down for their disrespect!"

"What do you expect? A child appears before them, claiming to be their god…"

"And what's age gotta do with it, huh?! Gods can look like whatever they want!"

"Grh…"

"If you're only thinkin' about the present, you'll never grow as a person. You gotta be thinkin' about the future, your soul always growin', just like a mushroom does!"

Raskeni felt ashamed. Not only at hearing a child lecture her about her own teachings, but also at the fact that Bisco was absolutely correct. Amli looked at the two in turn, her smile indefatigable.

"Go easy on Mother, Mr. Bisco, sir. She has a lot to learn. Besides, we mustn't linger here any longer; the magma is still rising."

"Then let's get outta here," Bisco replied. "Grab on, you two!"

Gaboom!

Bisco's arrow launched the three of them far away, leaving the mushroom tower and the redbaby swarm far behind them. As they twirled helplessly in the air, Milo leaped up to catch them, and the four went rolling across the stomach floor.

"Nicely done, Mr. Bisco, sir!"

"Gruuh! It's hot! You're crushing me!"

"A-Amli! Get off him at once!"

"No, Mother, I shan't!"

"Amli!! Now!"

"No! Let go of me! I want to spend some quality time with him!!"

Raskeni lifted her struggling daughter into the air, letting Bisco crawl out from beneath, sweating and gasping for breath.

"Fuck, it's hot out here," he cursed. "We're all gonna melt."

"No, it's okay!" Milo replied. "I came across a refrigerator sac in the wall of the stomach! That's where Chaika is!"

"A refrigerator sac? What's that?" asked Amli curiously.

Milo bent over and adjusted her straying glass eye. "It's an organ that cools the stomach down when it gets too hot. It's cool and safe in there! Let's bring everyone over!"

"Got it!" said Bisco.

"Ye faithful!" shouted Raskeni, addressing the crowd. "Our god has revealed to us a way out! Follow us, and we shall ensure no one perishes!"

""Yes, ma'am!"" they replied.

The two boys nodded to each other, and everyone followed Milo's lead, marching across the stomach to safety.

"Whew... So cool..."

"At last, I can feel my humanity returning..."

Bisco and Amli looked greatly relieved to enter the cool environment of the refrigerator sac, and so did the rest of the Kusabira sect. They basked in its bluish light and allowed the cold air to bring solace to their overheating bodies.

"At last, the worshipers are safe," said Amli. "Now we can... Mother! Your clothes! Fasten yourself up!"

"Oh, who cares?" the slovenly dressed woman replied. "It's way too hot for that."

"I care, Mother! And do up your chestwrap! I am trying to ensure

Mr. Bisco grows into a proud and upstanding gentleman, and you are not helping!"

"Well, he's got to learn the temptations of the flesh somehow, and he's not going to get it from you."

"And what is that supposed to mean, Mother?! I'll have you know I'm a growing girl, thank you very much!"

"Akaboshi, Nekoyanagi." Raskeni addressed the two boys as her rambunctious daughter retied her clothing. "I'm glad the faithful are all safe, but there's a long way to go yet. We need to get them back to the surface."

Milo glanced over at the bustling throng and nodded. "As much as I'd love to lead a fifty-man expedition into the belly of an Island Whale," he said, "I think I'd better pass. Chaika says the pancreas—her village—is nearby. Bisco and I will head there and see if her tribe can help us. You stay here with the sect until we come back."

"By Chaika, do you mean that girl over there? She's been busy handing out food to everybody."

"Yes, that's her. She—? She what?!"

Milo looked all over for the girl. He eventually spotted her, handing out pieces of something pink and soft that she was tearing off from a lump in her hands. The Kusabira sect followers would examine it curiously, pop a piece into their mouths, and wolf down the rest as quickly as they could. By now, they were treating Chaika like their savior, bowing down to her in reverence.

When Chaika ran out of the substance, she closed her eyes as if in prayer, and placed her hands to the fleshy floor. When she did, specks of something began to rise out of the ground, coalescing in her hands, forming more of the soft, pink, mystery food item.

"The hell's that?" asked Bisco. "Can Chaika use mantra as well?"

"That's not mantra," said Milo, eyes wide. "That's Hokkaido's nutrients. She's sucking them out of him!"

Hearing their shocked voices, Chaika came jogging over, the lump of whatever-it-was still in her hands.

"I am not sucking them out, thank you. I simply ask, and Hokkaido agrees to share them with me."

"Chaika… You really *can* speak to—?"

"Here."

Chaika held out both hands, offering the two boys their portions. They shared a cautious glance, whereupon Chaika sensed their apprehension and sighed.

"It's called *pokpok*," she said, "and it's a holy food only an oracle like me can produce. Eat it. He wants you to. You haven't had any food or drink since you got here, have you?"

"Hold on," Bisco said. "You mean to say…you're feedin' us?"

"Well, somebody's got to. A-and I do know how to pay my debts…" Chaika's face reddened a little as she said it. "You've saved my life, how many times now? I have to show my thanks somehow… Or…don't you like the look of my *pokpok*?"

Bisco and Milo must have been the first to look so hesitant, as Chaika seemed a little worried that her kindness would go to waste. The two boys stared at her for a moment, then…

"Grrrrr…"

…both their stomachs rang out at once, and all of a sudden, they threw themselves at Chaika's *pokpok*, eating it out of her hands.

"Eeep?! W-wait! Slow down…! Ah-ha-ha! That tickles! C-careful; don't bite my fingers! It's okay! There's lots more where that came from!"

The two boys only pulled back once all of the *pokpok* was gone. Then Bisco let out a loud belch, while Milo managed to restrain himself.

"Y-you were like a pair of hungry wolves!" said Chaika, astonished. "I expected such rudeness from Bisco, but not Milo, too! My father shall hear of your crass behavior; mark my words!"

"That was lovely, wasn't it, Bisco? Tastes a bit like shrimp."

"A bit bland for my likin'," Bisco replied. "Needs soy sauce if you ask me."

"I—I cannot believe you! I let you partake of my *pokpok*, and that's all you have to say?"

"I dunno what you're talkin' about. More, please."

"Forget it!"

Milo wasn't quite sure how they had offended the girl to the point that she had tears in her eyes, but he held her in his arms in an attempt to smooth things over.

"I'm sorry, Chaika," he said. "I thought it was very delicious. It's just Bisco; he has the taste of a child, you see."

"Is that supposed to make me feel better?!"

"Anyway, we're nearly at the pancreas—the *pektika*, as you call it. I'd like you to introduce us to your village. Could you do that for me?"

"…Hmph."

Chaika puffed up her cheeks and was of half a mind to refuse, but Bisco and Milo had saved her life. Reluctantly, she acquiesced. "…Fine. They won't let you in without me anyway. I'll make sure they treat you with respect. You'd better be grateful."

"Thank you so much, Chaika!"

"Hey, can I get another helpin' over here?"

"Let's just go already! Follow me, you two!"

Chaika ran away, irritated, but as she did, she held her hand to the wall, drawing out more *pokpok* and tossing it to Bisco, who caught it in his mouth like a dog. Munching it down, he fell in alongside his partner, and the two followed Chaika to her village.

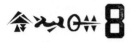

"Ouya! Back to the *pektika* at last!"

"I'm just glad we made it before your infection spread any further," said Milo.

"Look at these passages," said Amli. "There are man-made objects all over the place. There really are people living down here."

"Hold on a second…," grumbled Bisco from the far rear. "There's one person with us who ain't supposed to be here!"

"Huh?" said Milo.

"My, how scary. Where are they?"

"Right in front of me, you sneaky little troublemaker!" yelled Bisco, prodding Amli's pale cheek with his finger. Amli suddenly broke out in a cold sweat and let out a very unladylike *"Erk!"* "We told ya to wait in the coolin' sac or whatever!"

"But you don't understand! I was bored!" Amli shot back in a flare of defiance. "Mother can take care of the flock by herself, and I might never get another chance to go on an adventure with Mr. Bisco and Mr. Milo!"

"Listen, you! This ain't a game! One wrong step out there, and you'll—!"

"Oh, this is perfect!" Chaika interjected. "Amli also saved me from the redbabies in the *chaktika*! She must receive a reward as well! What would you like? I shall see to it that my father grants you any wish!"

"Truly?! Oh, wow. Well, I would like a new glass eye…"

Bisco found himself completely shut out of the two girls' conversation, and so instead of pressing Amli further, he simply fell back into line, a deeply unpleasant scowl on his face.

Just then…

"…Huh?! Milo!"

"Yes! I sense it, too!"

…the two boys suddenly drew their bows and stood to protect the two girls from the front and rear. Seeing this, Amli also adopted a Rustspeaker stance, making a sign with one hand.

"Mr. Bisco, sir! Are we under attack?!"

"*Oooou-yaaaaa!!*"

Before Bisco could answer her, a loud yell rang throughout the passage.

"Y've come, *deivo*! Release te oracle before te count a *eeda*, or we'll split open y'r *hedama*!"

"I can't make out a word. What's this guy sayin', Milo?"

"He says we have until five to release Chaika or he'll shoot us."

"Five? That's pretty generous. Don't they normally say *three*?"

"*Eeda! Velo! Bam!*"

"Whoa, whoa, whoa! That's way too fast! Don't you know how to count?!"

"*Ouya!* Wait, *sporko* of the north, protectors of the Ghost Hail!!"

"*Deno, Am…*"

The deep-throated voice stopped counting. Even Bisco, Milo, and Amli were surprised to hear Chaika's clear, bold words, and all turned to look at her.

"These people are not *deivo*! They are *saushaka* heroes who have saved my life and escorted me home. Harming them will only bring the wrath of the Ghost Hail god upon you!"

"Th-that voice…"

"*Ouya!* It is the oracle child, Chaika!"

One by one, the hunters climbed out of their hiding spots. Chaika looked at them all and nodded.

"I am sorry for worrying you, my friends," she said. Then, in a loud voice, she declared, "The oracle is returned! For it is I, Chaika, daughter of Cavillacan, elder of the northern *sporko*—the Mushroom Keepers!"

"Northern…"

"…Mushroom Keepers?!"

The two boys shared a look of utter shock. Glancing at the hunters, they could see bows, cloaks, and daggers not unlike their own, though their clothing was slightly thicker and had fur trimmings to keep out the cold.

"I see now," said Milo. "So that *sporko* that Chaika kept saying means 'Mushroom Keepers.'"

"Well, that threw me for a loop," said Bisco. "I didn't expect to find Mushroom Keepers in the belly of a whale— Oof!"

Bisco was almost trampled as the Mushroom Keepers swarmed past him and crowded around Chaika.

"*Ouya!* I can scarcely believe it! It *is* Chaika! She is back, safe and sound!"

"Go te the village and sound te bell!" cried the leader. "Elder Cavillacan must kin o' his daughter's return!"

The Mushroom Keepers were overjoyed to see their oracle, and each offered a prayer to their god in a language the boys did not speak.

Then…

"So, Chaika. Who's this naughty *devika* y've brought back with ye?"

"Who you callin' 'little devil,' prick? I'll bite your arm off!"

"Ach! Precocious little child, ain't he? Y're welcome to try, laddie!"

"Stop! Bisco is a proud *sporko* who saved my life. Do not make fun of him!"

At Chaika's rebuke, the Mushroom Keeper backed off immediately, shamefully retreating to the rear of the crowd. Bisco, meanwhile, gazed at Chaika, blinking in wonder at her actions.

"Their names are Bisco Akaboshi, Milo Nekoyanagi, and Amli Amlini. They may be *saushaka*, but they have saved my life and escorted me home. They are to be treated as honored guests of the village."

"R-really? These *devika* saved you…?"

"Am I clear?!"

"*O-ouya!*"

The Mushroom Keepers still appeared cautious, but they led the group through the passages of the pancreas with their lanterns. Bisco could tell from their vigilance that while a little rough around the edges, these tribal warriors were highly skilled Mushrooom Keepers indeed.

"I thought all you could do was scream and cry, but you're actually quite good at talkin', aren't you?" said Bisco, running up to Chaika's side. "That speech back there was really somethin'. You shut them all up real quick!"

"If you're trying to say you're impressed, I think you can do a little better than that," Chaika replied. While she attempted to appear unflustered, the smile on her face was plain to see. She leaned over to Bisco, and with a wink and in her usual bratty tone, added, "As an oracle of the *sporko* of the north, and the daughter of a hero, it is only natural I should carry myself with dignity!"

"*Ouya.* We have arrived. I shall inform the others."

The lead Mushroom Keeper stopped on a mound overlooking the village. Below lay a huge, dome-shaped space, the ceiling of which stretched interminably high. Sunlight shone in from somewhere overhead, illuminating the various houses all made out of scrap.

"Wow," Milo gasped. "These people built a village inside the pancreas?"

"That's right," Chaika answered. "Many things pass through Hokkaido. Building materials and other useful objects."

"My, it is just like the story of Pinocchio," said Amli.

Then one of the Mushroom Keepers shouted down at the village, "*Hoi-hoi-hoi!* The oracle has returned! Miss Chaika is safe!" When he did, dozens of golden-haired Mushroom Keepers streamed from every door. They were all as pale as Chaika and wore thick cloaks.

"By the grace of Reibyouten, she is safe! It's a miracle!"

"We must inform Elder Cavillacan at once!"

"Prepare a *festivo*! Bring all the food and wine we have!"

"Ouya!"

"Ouya!"

The village was suddenly in uproar, and people hurried to and fro, setting up a feast with yells of *"Ouya!"* Milo approached Chaika and whispered nervously in her ear.

"A feast sounds lovely, but we must see your father at once, before the ivy spreads."

"I know," she replied. "Come with me, you three."

"Miss Chaika?! Where are you going?"

"Let's go! Last one back to the village is a rotten *pokpok*!"

Showing ample familiarity with the terrain, Chaika slipped past her protectors and slid down the hill, hopping across the rooftops into the heart of the village.

"She's cheered up a bit now that she's home, hasn't she?" said Milo.

"Seems like she's used to havin' her run of the place," Bisco agreed.

The two boys, along with Amli, set off after her.

"Hey! We're about to have a feast. Don't run off!" cried one of the Mushroom Keepers, but the trio ignored him, following Chaika as she ran toward the largest building in the village.

"Khooooo…"

The village elder closed his eyes in concentration and expelled a hot breath from deep within. The two boys watched nervously as silvery spores emerged from his body and gathered in his right hand, shining like moonlight.

"Those are mushroom spores, no doubt about it," whispered Bisco. *"But I ain't never seen spores like that before. What are they?"*

"Shhh. Look!"

Cavillacan brought his glowing hand over Chaika's shoulder as she lay on her side, head in his lap. As he did, the tough vines across her body turned into white petals and fluttered away on the wind.

"W-wow!" gasped Amli. *"I've never seen any medical technique like that before!"* The elder's magic put both her knowledge of mantra and Bisco's mushroom expertise to shame. By the time Cavillacan was

done, there was no longer any sign of the flowers and ivy at all, just harmless white petals.

"'Tis doun. Te flowers ere banished."

Cavillacan mopped his sweaty brow and turned to the others, a fierce grin visible through his equally fierce beard.

"Worry not, me cheild. Ye're beck in gould health noe."

"Oh, Father!"

As the crying Chaika hugged him tight, he patted her gently on the back, and once he was done, he turned his attention to the three new-comers. Cavillacan was old, and his vision was starting to go, but his stout frame and thick arms showed that he was not ready to give up the bow just yet. The only bad thing Bisco and the others could say about him was that his accent was rather thick, far more so than Chaika's, and as a result it was almost impossible to discern what he was saying half the time.

"'Tis thanks tae ye'ses me Chaika be safe. I'd 'ave ye kin me gratitude."

""""What?"""""

"He's saying he would like to thank you all," said Chaika, throwing her arms around her beloved father's massive shoulders. "Father is a hero who once saved Hokkaido from assassins of the old Benibishi king, Housen. He doesn't bow down to others very often, so you'd better be grateful!"

"Wait a minute—did you just say 'Housen'?! Housen sent assassins to attack Hokkaido…?"

Cavillacan slowly sipped a mug of tea, and nodded.

"'Tis reight. Housen wis e'er a kinnin foe. We feought beck, yet the bleight stuck his flowers in te breign o' Hokkaido."

"Why would that old geezer do that?!" said Bisco.

"Remember who we're talking about here," replied Milo. "I think he wanted a bargaining chip in the negotiations with humankind. If push came to shove, he could absorb Hokkaido's power to put him on equal footing with humanity."

"Damn, and all the while he was preachin' peace… That sly fox!"

Cavillacan drained his mug, almost as large as his own face, and nodded again. Chaika leaned over and refilled her father's drink with nameko tea.

"In those daes, we cid stand against the Benibishi," the elder went on. "Bit te new king, Shishi, be a fae moa stubborn foe. Wit te power o' Hokkaido, she'd be indefeatable. Te whorl weorld y'd be in danger."

There was a solemn silence. Cavillacan sensed the tension his words had introduced and laughed, clapping his burly hands together.

"A sorrowsome tale for te eve o' me daughter's return! Come, tell us ye *saushaka* stoeries! How goes leife in the outer weorld?"

"Who cares about us?!" yelled Bisco. Unable to bear his curiosity any longer, he leaned over and pressed the elder for an explanation. "What was that technique you used on Chaika, Chief?! I ain't never seen white spores like those before!"

"The Hand of the Ghost Hail," Chaika explained proudly. "My father houses the spores of purity within his body. They come from the Ghost Hail mushroom, found only here in Hokkaido. It has the power to purify anything that has evolved into a twisted form."

"En auld, Ay were oracle, simma Chaika…"

What the hell is he saying?!

"Father was once an oracle, as I am now," Chaika said, translating her father's words. "That was when he was granted the power of the Ghost Hail."

"Ghost Hail mushrooms…"

The explanation sounded a touch more spiritual than what the two Mushroom Keepers were used to. Bisco was finding it hard to keep up, but he couldn't stop thinking about the mysterious mushroom variety they had mentioned.

Milo, meanwhile, was similarly lost in thought, when suddenly he remembered what they came for and clapped Bisco on the shoulder. "Elder," he said. "Could your power heal my partner? It was Shishi's flowers that made him young, cute, and adorable like this…"

"Was 'cute' and 'adorable' really necessary?" Bisco sulked.

"Aye, Ay ken see plein te flowers in ye, boye."

Oddly enough, Cavillacan didn't seem too surprised by Milo's words. He turned to Bisco and beckoned him over.

"Bisco. Ay kin nae if me auld power be fill tae cure ye, yet Ay must treigh."

Bisco looked around at Milo and Amli for support. His two friends nodded, so Bisco nervously approached the elder.

"...Mrgh."

Cavillacan placed his large hand over Bisco's face and neck and made a strange "*Gurm...*" sound. Bisco could not endure waiting for long, and soon asked, "Hey, Elder! What's goin' on? Can you cure me or not?"

"Ay see te flowers. They be nae too strong fir me, yet..."

"You can cure him? That's great!" said Chaika. "But, Father, what's wrong?"

"Bah-ha-ha! Y'r plen fill o' surpreises, Bisco. Ay see te Heaven's Leight dwells wittin ye."

Bisco, Milo, and Amli all looked confused, but Chaika almost ran to her father's side.

"I...I knew it! So those *were* Heaven's Light arrows I saw Bisco using in the *hartika*! I thought for sure I must have been mistaken..."

"What's this Heaven's Light you keep talking about?" asked Bisco in confusion. "You mean the Rust-Eater?"

"Aye, te *saushaka* calle it be thet name. Tae me people, 'tis called Heaven's Leight. Thegither wit te Ghost Haile, it foerms half o' te legendary pair o' mushrooms. Yet te two be leike night and daye. Wylle it dwells wittin ye, it blunts te power o' me own mushroom, stoppen me from purifeen te flowers."

Cavillacan's words were hard to understand at times, but Bisco understood the general gist. The elder would usually be able to purify the flowers, but the Rust-Eater spores inside Bisco's body opposed those of the Ghost Hail and prevented him from doing so. It seemed the only way to turn Bisco back to normal after all would be to take down Shishi.

"Damn," Bisco cursed. "After all that, we're back to square one!"

"Werry nae," Cavillacan bellowed, tousling Bisco's hair with his thick hand. "Ye shell see y'r reward fe saving me preicious Chaika."

"Father is preparing to lead the other *sporko* into war against the Benibishi," Chaika explained. "We'll make that bony young lady turn you back yet!"

"Let us help, Elder!" said Milo.

"The Kusabira sect shall lend its assistance as well," added Amli.

"Bah-ha-ha!" Cavillacan exploded into uproarious laughter at their youthful vigor. "Calm ye, calm ye... Todae be a dae o' celebration. Ay wender if te feast be prepayred yet...?"

Just as Cavillacan got up to check, there was an explosion outside, and a rumble shook the entire village. It was followed by a second, and a third, and each time the air quivered.

"Eeek! What's happening, Father? I'm scared!!"

"I'm guessing this ain't no festival performance," said Bisco. "What's goin' on out there?"

"Gurm..."

Cavillacan closed his eyes and twitched his nose, before hurriedly walking over to the wall to retrieve his longbow.

"Ay smell...pollen."

"Pollen?!"

Bisco and Milo rushed to the window and saw bright-red camellia flowers covering the walls and ceiling of the pancreas. The Mushroom Keepers who had been preparing for the feast were suddenly running to and fro, collecting their weapons while the clang of an alarm bell rang incessantly in the background.

"I don't believe it... In all these years, we've never known an attack on our village before!"

Chaika was beginning to panic. Cavillacan patted her firmly on the shoulder.

"Leive the village, me cheild. Shed aught happin tae ye..."

"No! Father! I cannot leave you to—!"

But before Chaika could finish, a booming voice rang out over the village.

"ATTENTION, CRIMINALS! SURRENDER THE MUSH-ROOM KEEPERS! DO NOT ATTEMPT TO RESIST!"

It was so loud, the very air seemed ready to burst.

"WE ARE PREPARED TO BEGIN DRAINING THE LIFE FROM HOKKAIDO. IF YOU WISH TO LIVE, THEN HAND OVER THE CRIMINAL CAVILLACAN, HARBORER OF THE ABOMINABLE GHOST HAIL SPORES!"

"Bisco! Do you recognize that voice?!"

"How could I forget? It's Satahabaki! The big guy's come here at last!"

In the center of the village stood a giant man, poised atop the ruins of a watchtower, illuminated by fire. There was no mistaking his bare, gleaming teeth. Just like Bisco said, it was the Iron Judge, Satahabaki himself.

"*Ouya!* We will never bow down to Benibishi!"

"We'll turn you into mushrooms and serve you up as tomorrow's dinner! *Ouya!*"

The tribal warriors fought bravely back against the Benibishi forces. Knowing their mushroom arrows would be ineffective, they instead focused on close combat, using their daggers to slice apart the thick vines of their enemy's weapons.

However, when it came to Satahabaki, their skills were not enough.

"That big one's their leader! I'll take him down!"

"RIDICULOUS!!"

When one woman leaped at him, Satahabaki picked up a log from the ruined tower and swung it effortlessly at her, sending the brave warrior flying high over the village and into the pancreas wall, where a huge camellia flower exploded out of her.

"O-ouya! He's too strong! Is he even Benibishi?"

"I AM HELL'S SCEPTER. THE BANE OF EVIL GODS. I WILL NOT BE SLOWED BY MERE FOOLS. ANY MAN WHO WISHES TO DIE..."

Cha-chang!

"...STEP FOOORTH!!"

"Even brainwashed, the big guy's still got a flair for the dramatic," noted Bisco.

"Now's not the time! We need to go!" yelled Milo, swiftly drawing his bow from his back. "Remember, mushrooms won't work on him! Amli and I will take him on with our mantra!"

Milo cast a glance at Amli, who returned an indefatigable smile.

"I shall be glad to assist, Mr. Milo, sir. That bothersome enforcer shall soon know the might of the Kusabira sect's high priestess!"

"All right," said Bisco. "And what should I do?"

"They're after the elder and the power of the Ghost Hail," replied Milo. "Take him and Chaika and leave the village. Can you do that?"

"Sure thing." With a nod, Bisco hopped over to Chaika, who was cowering with fear in a corner of the room, and flicked her on the forehead.

"Ow!! H-how dare you treat the oracle so roughly?"

"Now's not the time for hidin', Chaika. Get up! I need your help. You know this area better than anyone, and we need to get your old man to safety!"

"Me…? Protect Father…?"

Chaika could not respond at first. She was used to being protected, not protecting others.

"I—I cannot. I am still just a…"

Before she could say *child*, her eyes met Bisco's, and the word caught in her throat. She gazed into Bisco's sparkling, jade-green irises, then shook her head as if to banish her fear, and firmly latched on to Bisco's outstretched hand.

"I…I'll do it! I shall do everything in my power to protect him…! So please, Bisco. Help me. Let us bear my father from this place, together!"

"Nicely said," replied Bisco. Then, turning to Cavillacan, he added, "You're a lucky man, you know. Not many people can afford the protection of the world's greatest Mushroom Keeper, but today's on the house!"

"There's an escape chute we use for emergencies," said Chaika. "Follow me!"

"Right! Milo, Amli, thanks for bein' the bait!"

The two boys exchanged one last glance and nodded to each other. Then Bisco took the elder and left via the front door, while Milo and Amli leaped out the window, toward the crimson glow that marked the burning village square.

"There he is! That's the village elder, Cavillacan!"

"Don't let him escape! Use your ivy to capture him!"

"Time to put a stop to the detestable Ghost Hail spores!"

The Benibishi guards cried out, spotting Cavillacan and Chaika making their escape through the intricate mix of passages leading out of the village.

"They've found us! This way, Father, quickly!"

"Chaika. Me eyes be weak. Ay kin Ay be sloughin ye daun. Leive me beheind... Safe yeseilf..."

"You can't give up now, Father! I will be your eyes! Hurry up! We're almost at the escape chute!"

As Chaika stopped to urge on her father, a Benibishi warrior spotted the pair from a rooftop and sprang down upon them, wielding an ax formed of vines.

Chaika turned and screamed.

"Aaaiiieee!!"

"Cavillacan, Hand of the Ghost Hail!" yelled the Benibishi warrior mid-flight. "Your head shall make a fine offering to my king!!"

But just before the ax found its mark, a small figure leaped out of the darkness, bounced off a nearby wall, and delivered a mighty kick into the Benibishi's side.

"Shaddup!!!"

"Gah??!!"

The child's kick was as sharp and heavy as the swing of a greatsword, and it sent the Benibishi flying off, blasting through several buildings and landing in a crumpled heap. Then he swung his bow like a staff, beating away the other warriors before they could come close.

"Bisco!!"

"Chaika! There's a whole load of them on our tail! Are we at the escape route yet?"

"Nearly there! But there's more of them blocking our way! Bisco, can you do something about them?!"

"On it!"

Bisco broke through the ranks of Benibishi like a red-hot wrecking ball, knocking them all out in a single blow from either his bow, his dagger, or his martial arts techniques. He was such a storm of magnificent violence, it was as if his miniaturized frame was no impediment at all.

"Gadd! Te boye be leike a god o' fire!"

Cavillacan stopped to gaze at Bisco's works, entranced by the dance of destruction before him.

"Sae mighty a *sporko* has nae bin seen in a thousand…nay, ten thousand yeirs!"

I've never seen Father so impressed!

Even Chaika had to admit, the way Bisco tore through the Benibishi ranks like a stray firework was nothing short of astounding. But to hear her father acknowledge his talent peeved her for some reason, and she puffed up her cheeks and shot back:

"Well, men can't just be fighting all the time. They need to be wise, like you, Father. He could never lead our village! He is too stupid, too vulgar, and he calls me names all the time!"

"Bah-ha-ha! Ye alweis hed a sharpe tongue fe those ye liked! Yet Ay afear ye cennae be wed, nae till y'r bothe seventeen!"

"Wh-wha—?!!"

Chaika went from pale-white to cherry-red in an instant, and she flapped her lips wordlessly. Before she could come up with a decent response, the two arrived at the escape chute.

"We made it, Father! Come on, let's go!"

It was a peculiar-looking place. A low hill rose out of the ground, peppered with holes. Behind each hole was a chute, and the chutes appeared to lead to different organs of the island megabeast, as indicated by the signs that hung over them: LIVER, SMALL INTESTINE, LUNGS… The names went on.

"Ay cennae leive yet! We mest weight fer t'others!"

"It's okay, Father. I'll take care of them. You take refuge in the *puktika...*"

Chaika led her father to the passage labeled LIVER. But just as the elder was about to make his escape, a pair of joking, mocking voices caught their attention.

"Not so fast, fools. Where do you think you're going?"

"I'm afraid the liver's off-limits. Hokkaido's on our twelve-step program."

"Who's there?!" yelled Chaika, when suddenly Cavillacan moved his stout frame in front.

"Git beck, cheild!"

The *Clack! Clack!* of their heels rang out as two women stepped in front of the escape route. One was dressed in red, the other in blue, and both folded their arms across their chests, sneering powerfully at the elder and his daughter.

"Hee-hee-hee... We knew you'd show up sooner or later if we just kept an eye on the exits."

"We know all about your little escape route, fools. And now the two of you have fallen into our laps. We can eradicate the Hand of the Ghost Hail *and* his successor in one fell swoop."

"B-but how?!" Chaika yelled, despair creeping into her voice. "How did you find the village?! We have been safe from the Benibishi here for generations!"

"Hee-hee-hee!" The blue one chuckled. "Why, that's all thanks to you, Princess. Thanks to your stupidity, that is."

"B-because of me...?!"

"It's simple. We knew if we infected you with flowers, you'd have to return home to get it cured. Then all we needed to do was follow you."

"We didn't count on you taking the scenic route, though," added the blond one in the red dress with some chagrin. "We lost a lot of good men following you through the main artery. What fool came up with that plan?"

"N-no… It's my fault… It's all my fault…"

"Now it's time to end this," the red one said, manifesting a whip of ivy in her hands. "Submit to my whip, Cavillacan!"

"Ye kids er aul te simm. Nae respect f'yer elders…" Cavillacan drew the meat cleaver at his belt, which glistened in the light of Hokkaido's viscera. "Ay shell streik ye daun, witch, e'en if it costs me me *hartika!*"

"Father!"

"Oh, please. Whipping you is no fun. Old men don't scream nearly as much as children. I'll make this quick. Your daughter, on the other hand, will suffer. Slowly."

"Ye *deivo…!*"

"Time to die, old man!"

The woman in red cracked her whip, slicing a deep cut into Cavillacan's flesh. Just then, a blazing red arrow came out of nowhere, piercing the snakelike lash and tearing it clean in two.

The force of her weapon breaking sent the blond woman reeling backward, and a young boy landed between her and her target, like a small ball of flame.

"The mighty sure have fallen, huh?" he sneered. "Gone from vice-wardens of Six Realms to whatever this is!"

The boy's jade-green eyes clashed with those of the blond, who let out a small *"Tch!"* of frustration.

"You used to treat Shishi like shit, and look at you now…takin' orders from her like a couple'a lapdogs! What happened to you? Where's your pride? Answer me, Gopis! Mepaosha!"

"Oh great, here's the runt. Looks like even Shishi's power can't shut you up, Akaboshi. Hee-hee-hee…"

It was the blue-clad, bespectacled vice-warden, Mepaosha, who first answered to Bisco's taunts, but the look on her face was unflustered and gleeful. Gopis's anger, on the other hand, was clear as crystal.

"Barbarians like you Mushroom Keepers couldn't begin to understand. Shishi has seen fit to share her power with us. See?!"

Gopis pulled down the front of her dress, revealing a mass of writhing vines implanted in her chest, with a bright-red camellia flower at its core. Bisco looked across at Mepaosha to see a similar mass on her exposed thigh.

That's Shishi's flower! So these two are brainwashed as well!

"With Shishi's gifts at our disposal, there's no way a kid like you can stand in our way!"

"How long will you last, I wonder, protecting that kid and her father? Time to find out, Akaboshi."

Gopis narrowed her eyes and flashed a sly grin, and the ivy whip re-formed in her hands once more. Meanwhile, Mepaosha stuck her finger in her ear, pulling out a similar lash of vines.

"You two are all talk, same as usual," Bisco shot back. "If you're gonna fight, then let's do it."

"As you wish!"

"Take this!"

The two flicked their whips, but struck only empty air as Bisco rolled to the side. Bisco had dodged the attack by a hair's breadth, and yet he felt the rush of air and a cold sweat form. Gopis and Mepaosha were far stronger than before. It had to be Shishi's flowers, bolstering their physical capabilities.

"Hands off Akaboshi, Mepaosha!" Gopis roared. "He's mine! You take care of the old man and his child!"

"Hee-hee-hee. You sadistic cow. Can't you keep your fetishes in check?"

"Shut it, you four-eyed fool! If they escape, I'm telling Shishi it was *your* fault!"

"Yes, yes, all right. Keep your tits on."

The *Crack!* of Mepaosha's whip flicked the carving knife out of Cavillacan's hand. As Bisco looked over in concern, Gopis's next attack sliced at his skin.

"Ha-ha-ha!! Oh, Akaboshi. You know how much I love torturing children. Now I get to fulfill that need and take out my nemesis at the same time!"

"Shaddup! You don't get to act all high and mighty on borrowed power!"

"Oh, it's so lovely hearing that in your adorable voice! Oh, please, I can't wait to hear your tortured wails, your desperate screams!"

Shishi's flower seemed to have heightened Gopis's innate sadistic streak, for now she seemed at the very height of pleasure, and the precision of her whip-strokes was deadlier than ever.

Damn, I can't just keep dodging. I need to strike back!

Reassessing the threat that Gopis posed, Bisco switched tactics and prepared to take a hit.

One strike won't kill me. I'll take that opportunity to counterattack!

"I'll slice you to ribbons, Akaboshi!"

Now!

Just as the whip connected, Bisco released his arrow, a crimson streak that landed solidly in Gopis's shoulder.

"Grrh! Wh-what?!"

The elation of feeling her attack land nearly blinded Gopis to her own wound, and her expression of pleasure slowly changed to one of despair.

"I-impossible. My whip should tear a kid like you apart!"

"Don't believe everythin' you see…," said Bisco, grinning even as blood erupted from his lips. "You lost 'cause you forgot one important thing. You're fightin' the Man-Eatin' Redcap."

"Gbluh!!"

Gaboom!

Bisco's red oyster mushrooms exploded from the tip of his arrow, blasting Gopis back, skimming her across the ground and into a wall.

However, Bisco was hurt, too. He fell to his knees, clutching the cut across his shoulder and coughing up blood onto the floor.

Dammit… I was too weak after all…

Taking a hit and using the opportunity it presented to deliver a finishing strike was one of Bisco's signature tactics, but it only worked because Bisco was almost supernaturally robust. With his body regressed to that of a child, Gopis's flower-enhanced whip was too powerful to shrug off, and the damage dealt to him was quite severe.

Still, I took out one of the two... Now for the other one...!

Bisco clenched his teeth and lifted his heavy, bloodstained limbs, when...

"Noooooo! Father!"

...he heard Chaika scream and the slash of Mepaosha's whip. Her relentless attacks had finally succeeded in disarming Cavillacan and leaving a deep gash across his chest.

"Gg...rh... Ye sweine..."

"My, oh my, my hand is beginning to ache. You're a stubborn old geezer, I'll give you that, but unlike my witless protégé over there, I don't find this pleasurable in the least. You're only wasting my time..."

"Grh... Ye be fae too young te best me, cheild..."

"No matter. It'll all be over soon. Now, become nothing more than rust on my whip!!"

"Stop!!"

With all the courage she could muster, Chaika stepped in front of her father, arms open wide.

"Put away your whip, servant!" she declared.

"...What?! What's this crap about, kid?"

"I shall not allow you to lay another finger on my father, the elder of our village! Brandish your whip again, and my soul will become a bolt of lightning that strikes you down!!"

"Wh-what? Your soul will *what*?" replied Mepaosha, staring in amazement, before doubling over in laughter. "Ah-ha-ha-ha!! That's the funniest thing I've ever heard! That's rich! Little Miss Chaika, hiding behind her daddy. What makes you think I'll be scared of you?"

Chaika began to cry, but still she stood fast before Cavillacan's hunched-over form.

"Let me tell you something, kid. I'm an atheist. I ain't afraid o' no ghost. It doesn't make one blind bit of difference to me if I gotta kill you or your daddy first."

"Kh...rrrgh!"

"You still don't get it, do you?"

Mepaosha moved. Her horseshoe earring swayed, and the whip of ivy lashed.

"I'm going to carve up your cute little face! Every time you look in the mirror, you'll remember how you failed him this day!"

The whip came down. Chaika looked away.

Crack!!

She heard the slicing flesh, but Chaika felt no pain.

"...Huh?"

Gingerly, she opened her eyes...and saw...

"Gr...rh!!"

"Bisco!! No!"

Bisco had leaped in the way, taking the blow meant for her. He was covered in blood, but still he stood, undefeatable.

"You can't...! You're so small! You can't keep taking hits for us, Bisco!"

"Shut...up...Chaika... This...is...nothin'...!"

"Erk. Akaboshi?! Damn, you took Cow Tits out quick."

Mepaosha was taken aback by Bisco's sudden appearance, casting a glance over to the far wall where her partner lay in a crumpled mess. Still, she recognized that Bisco's wound was deep indeed, and the boy was barely hanging on by a thread. A wicked grin slowly spread across her face, and she readjusted her spectacles.

"Hey now, Akaboshi. You're not looking too hot. Do you really think you can save the princess and earn your happily-ever-after like this? You can barely stand! Why, with just one more crack of my whip, I'll—"

"...Try it. I dare you."

"...What?!"

"Try it and find out once and for all if Chaika's tellin' the truth."

Bisco's bloodshot eyes shone bright. He smiled, allowing a tiny pointed tooth to peek from the corner of his roguish grin.

"She says if you kill her, her soul will strike back at you like lightning. If you don't want that to happen, then I suggest you take your shitty little whip and go."

"...You little brat. If only your words were as sweet as your face."

Nothing got on Mepaosha's nerves more than the taunts of puny weaklings like Bisco and Chaika. Something snapped inside her, and she raised her whip high.

"Let's see you act so smug without a nose, Akaboshi!"

"I warned you, Mepaosha. Now you're gonna see why people are scared of ghosts."

Crakkkk!!

Mepaosha's whip struck Bisco cleanly across the face. An evil grin crept across her lips, and then...

Fwoop!

...Mepaosha was lifted into the air as if by an invisible giant. She swung round, centered on the tip of her whip, over Bisco and down into the ground on the other side.

Bang!

"Gg...ghah?!"

It all happened so fast, Mepaosha had no time to figure out what was going on. She was flung up and over again, hitting the ground back where she started.

Bang!

"Whoa?! Ghheh!!"

"Count the thunderbolts, glasses. One, two. Seems like the oracle's prediction came true after all!"

Bisco bit off the end of the ivy whip and spat it aside. In a desperate gambit, he had caught the lash between his teeth, and he swung Mepaosha around, using only the muscles in his neck.

"Im...impossible... You only have the strength of a child... How could you...?" muttered Mepaosha as her weapon disintegrated. Then her lips curled up in a grin. "...No. That's just like you...Akaboshi. Hee-hee-hee. What a relief..."

Mepaosha managed to say nothing more before coughing up blood and collapsing, unconscious. Bisco, too, could stay upright no longer and fell to the floor, bleeding profusely.

"Bisco!!" yelled Chaika, and she ran over to help him up, but her hands became slick with his blood. "Oh no, you're hurt…!"

Bisco seemed to pay his injuries no mind. He spat out a broken tooth onto the floor.

"Bisco. Are you going to be okay?"

"I'm fine. It's a baby tooth. It'll grow back."

"I don't mean your teeth! You're hurt! And it's all because you stood up for us!"

"You were pretty cool yourself."

"Huh…?"

"You were like a bow. And I was your arrow, goin' wherever you pointed."

Bisco messily tried to wipe the blood off his face and smiled a simple-hearted smile.

"You'd make a great archer. You ever think about takin' up the bow?"

"…Good grief. Whatever shall we do with you?"

Chaika made it difficult to tell whether she was annoyed or relieved, but out of reverence for the hero who saved her life, as well as for her father, Chaika tore off a piece of her holy garb and used it to wipe up Bisco's blood.

"Bisco!!"

Just then, Milo and Amli bounded over. Milo spotted Bisco's wounds from the air, and by the time he landed, his bag was open and the medicines were in his hands.

"You've taken a real beating again," he said, injecting them into Bisco. "You get ambushed?"

"Yeah. Took care of it, though. They're over there."

"I've got painkillers. Strong, regular, or weak. Which would you like?"

"Weak."

"Regular it is, then. You always downplay it, Bisco."

"Father is hurt, too," said Chaika. "Bisco risked his life to help."

Milo quickly finished wrapping Bisco's bandages and moved over to the unconscious Cavillacan.

"Are you two okay?" asked Chaika with a twinge of panic in her voice. "What's become of the village?!"

"I shall attempt to explain, Miss Chaika, ma'am." Amli looked uncharacteristically serious. "You may want to be sitting down... I'm afraid the village has been utterly destroyed, and an enormous camellia flower erected in its place. The troops were scattered, and barely managed to escape with their lives."

"N-no..."

"What about Satahabaki?" asked Bisco. "Did you kill him?"

"It took the two of us just to hold him back," said Milo. "We used a mantra to freeze his legs, so I don't think he'll be going anywhere, but..."

Just then, as if on cue, a deafening voice rang throughout the pancreas.

"FOUL CONJURERS, YOU HAVE MET YOUR MATCH!"

And not a second later, the ground quaked as the Benibishi giant landed before them.

"Your tricks cannot bind me, sorcerers. Surrender and accept your fate!"

"Satahabaki!"

Bisco and Milo went back-to-back and drew their bows, ready to protect the other three. Satahabaki reached down and smashed the layers of Rust stuck to his legs with his fists, before rising to his full, terrifying height.

...However, strangely, he did not attack. Instead, he cast a look across the battlefield, spotting the fallen forms of Gopis and Mepaosha and scooping them up in his hand.

"Fools. You have failed me again."

"L-Lord Satahabaki... Please forgive me... Cavillacan still lives..."

"It matters not. We have what we came for. The Ghost Hail Stone."

Saying this, Satahabaki held up a silvery cube, ornately engraved. It glimmered in the dim light of the pancreas and cast off glittering spores that seemed drawn in a particular direction, like a compass point.

"Oh no!" exclaimed Chaika. "Our village has protected that treasure for generations! It marks the way to the Ghost Hail Node!"

Satahabaki gave the stone a shake and, trying not to crush it with his massive strength, tucked it safely underneath his armpit.

"With the stone in our possession, we have no further need of this village. If we are to absorb all of Hokkaido's nutrients, we must make our way to the node."

"L-Lord Satahabaki. You can't possibly mean to leave them alive?" protested Gopis from underneath one of Satahabaki's massive arms. "Look! They are exhausted! On the verge of defeat! This is our chance to take out Cavillacan *and* Akaboshi once and for all!"

At Gopis's words, Satahabaki slowly turned and looked at Bisco. Beneath the bandages, those jade-green eyes flickered like flames.

...Akaboshi. The warrior who earned a thousand blooms.

Muttering something imperceptible under his breath, he turned and walked away.

"L-Lord Satahabaki!"

"To slay Akaboshi, I must be prepared to lose my life in return. The time is not yet right."

"Wh-what?! He's just a kid! Just step on him!"

"If you think ability stems from physical strength...then you still have much to learn."

With that, and guided by the light from the Ghost Hail Stone, Satahabaki tore open one of the escape chute entrances and disappeared down it.

After he was gone...

"Th-that..."

"That was freakin' CLOOOSE!"

...Milo and Bisco put away their bows, and all four of them collapsed to the ground, by now far too exhausted to put up a decent fight.

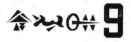

"Blegh! *Cough! Cough!*"

"Amli!" Chaika chided. "Try to be more ladylike, won't you?"

"But this is too much! I know we're in a hurry, but did we have to take the artery? Ugh, I feel like my lungs are coming up…"

"I'm sorry, Amli, but we're almost at the node. Just bear with it…"

After leaving the wounded Cavillacan in the sanctuary of the kidney, Chaika became unwontedly concerned with pursuing Satahabaki, and so the four set off down Hokkaido's bloodstream in the direction of this mysterious Ghost Hail Node.

When they arrived, Chaika took the lead, charging ahead while wiping the sweat off her brow. Milo caught up to her and, helping her along, took the opportunity to ask a question.

"Hey, Chaika? What kind of organ is this Ghost Hail Node? I've never heard of anything like it in *Mollusca evolutus* biology."

"I'm not surprised you haven't," Chaika replied. "That's because only Hokkaido has it."

Chaika ran out of breath and fell to the floor. Milo helped her up onto his back, and the two set off again, with Chaika resuming her story.

"The Ghost Hail Node is where all the energy that moves Hokkaido is generated and stored," she explained. "To Hokkaido, it is even more vital an organ than the *bretika* and the *hartika*."

"More vital than the brain and the heart…?"

"So that's what Shishi's after?" Bisco piped up.

Chaika nodded. "You saw the garden they produced on the surface. The power of the Ghost Hail Node could allow them to create thousands of those. I couldn't even begin to imagine what power they could wield if they absorbed all of Hokkaido's energy… Wait, this is it, the entrance!"

At Chaika's words, everyone stopped and looked around. The red floor was netted in white, fibrous material, like the surface of a cantaloupe, and all throughout the space echoed a soft heartbeat that caused the fibers to glow with a dazzling white light.

"It's beautiful!" exclaimed Amli. "We're deep in the bowels of some creature, and yet it's almost…ghostly."

"This must be the Ghost Hail Node! Wow, it's like nothing I've ever seen—! No, nothing any doctor has ever seen! Isn't that amazing, Bisco?"

"Don't ask me. As far as I'm concerned, you seen one internal organ, you seen 'em all."

"Oh, sorry. It's just because I went to school…"

"How the hell do you always bring that up?!"

Leaving the boisterous trio behind, Chaika approached the entrance to the node and stepped inside. When she saw what awaited her there, she let out a pitiful cry and slumped helplessly to the ground.

"Chaika?! What happened?!"

The others ran over and followed Chaika's trembling finger with their eyes…

"We're too late," she said. "The Benibishi…they've already been here!"

"M-Milo, look at that!!" Bisco shouted, pointing to a bright-white light emanating from deeper within the node. Its source was an enormous silvery mushroom, growing tall out of the organ floor. The mushroom itself seemed full of life, and as if to prove this, it shook and let out a cloud of white, hail-like spores from its cap with a *Ba-fwoom!*

"It's the Ghost Hail mushroom," said Chaika. "The source of my and Father's powers, and the engine that drives Hokkaido."

"That thing's almost as big as the Rust-Eater...," said Bisco. "And it looks fine to me. Whaddaya mean we're too late?"

"Look closely, Mr. Bisco, sir," said Amli, directing his gaze to the surface of the mushroom. As his eyes adjusted to the light, Bisco realized what had provoked Chaika's dismay. The mushroom was tangled in brutal, thorn-covered roots that sucked the very life out of it.

"I see," he said. "Shishi's plants are drainin' that thing dry!"

"You can see the roots going up through Hokkaido's back," said Chaika, her voice trembling with grief. "The rest of the plant must be aboveground. We ought to destroy these roots and burn the whole thing, but now..."

It was obvious that the plant and the mushroom were now deeply entwined. Even the Benibishi must have been confident nothing could be done, for there wasn't a single guard defending the place.

And yet...

"We can't give up now, Chaika!"

...Milo's determined words came as he gazed at the trapped Ghost Hail.

"Flowers may be strong against mushrooms, but they're weak to the Rust. Amli and I can command the Rust with our mantra. There might be a way to get rid of these roots without harming the mushroom."

"With...mantra?"

"Leave this to us, Miss Chaika, ma'am. I may not look like much, but I am the high priestess of the Kusabira sect, don't forget!"

"Thank you, you two... Yes, you are right. Your divine Rust power shall be a powerful boon!" Chaika's eyes glittered with hope...but then she looked down and shook her head. "But I fear it shall be of little use. Even if we clear away the roots, the flower up top will just attempt to regrow them. We need to somehow destroy both at the same time."

"What's so difficult about that?" said Bisco, wrapped in bandages, his cloak flapping, extending a hand to Chaika. The girl looked into his jade-green eyes and took it without a thought, and Bisco pulled her to her feet. "We got *two* mantra users here: Milo and Amli. One of 'em can take the roots, while the other goes up top. Sounds like a plan to me."

"B-but, Bisco…!"

"Milo! I think the roots'll be toughest! I'll leave 'em to you. Take care of Chaika as well, will ya?"

"You got it, Bisco!"

"If the flower's up top, then that's where Shishi'll be. Amli, you're with me. Time to do a little lawn surgery!"

"Right you are, Mr. Bisco, sir!"

Chaika looked between the two boys, and their determination lit a fire in her heart as well. She nodded deeply and took hold of Bisco's arm with both hands. "Bisco, Milo, Amli!" she entreated. "This moment decides whether Hokkaido lives or dies. Please help us!"

"You got it. Don't worry. We're the strongest Mushroom Keepers in Japan. When we mean to do something, we succeed."

"…"

"Still not convinced?"

"…No, I believe you. After everything I've seen…"

Bisco flashed his canines and grinned at Milo, who returned a pleasant smile.

"All right, we're off!" said Bisco, lifting Amli and tucking her under his arm. "Hold on tight!"

Bisco then fired a wire arrow into the air like a grappling hook and reeled the two of them up and away toward the far roof of the cavern.

"Eep! How majestic, Big brother!" cried Amli, and Chaika watched as the two of them disappeared amid the light of the Ghost Hail and the sun shining in from above.

Chaika kept her eyes focused on them even when the two were no longer visible.

"Are you worried about him?" asked Milo. "About Bisco?"

"No, I'm not," replied Chaika, shaking her head. "He'll…he'll be fine."

"…"

"He proved to me it's not your size that matters. It's what's inside."

She spun round to face Milo, and her golden hair fell about her brilliant smile. Milo gave a satisfied nod, then took a deep breath and glared at the writhing mass of roots ahead.

"Milo!" Chaika cried out after him. "…Are you going to be okay by yourself? Do you need my help?"

"Chaika. If you trust Bisco, then that implies you trust me, too."

"Huh?"

"That's because there's nobody Bisco has more faith in than me!"

Milo stood and grinned a wicked smirk at the threat ahead, like his partner always did. Then he spoke the words, and a brilliant green cube appeared in his hand.

"It's time to start this!" he declared. "Chaika, stick close to me!"

"Okay!"

As if waiting for that very moment, the vine-like roots of Shishi's flower sensed the power in Milo's hand and lashed out at the pair.

"Won/shandreber/alhad/snew!"

Milo's mantra produced an emerald blast of wind that shot toward the roots, cutting them apart. Where the roots were torn, the stumps were infected with Rust, so that they could not grow back but instead crumbled into green dust.

"Wow! Milo, that's amazing!"

"Stay still, Chaika! This mantra is a lot of work!"

The roots seemed extremely perturbed by the presence of Milo's zephyr blade, and one by one they peeled themselves off the mushroom and lashed out at Bisco and Chaika like a relentless storm of whips.

Damn! They're faster than I thought!

"Milo, look out! Above us!"

"Oh no! *Won/shad/shed/snew!*"

Thanks to Chaika's warning, Milo was able to produce a mantra shield in the nick of time that protected them from the sudden assault. As he watched the vine whips dash themselves on the barrier and crumble away, Milo felt the sweat bead on his neck.

Uh-oh. After all that, this might be trouble after all…

More and more of the roots peeled away, some of them even striking at Milo through the wind. Each time, Milo's power was redirected to the barrier, causing the gale blasts to wane in strength.

"Oh no. At this rate…!"

Even Chaika could see that Milo was fighting a losing battle. She made up her mind and clapped her hands, rubbing them together and praying.

"If my father could do it…then so can I! All of you have given me the courage to try!"

"Chaika! It's too dangerous! Stay behind me!"

But the girl looked into Milo's eyes and spoke louder than the wind. "I need to touch the Ghost Hail, Milo. If there's anything left of Hokkaido…we need his strength. I am his oracle; he will not refuse me."

"The mushroom?! You can't! The roots are too thick! They'll tear you apart!"

"Please."

Chaika looked deeply into Milo's starlight eyes. Her pink lips moved softly.

"Trust me, Milo. Keep me safe until I can touch the Ghost Hail. You saved my life. Now it's my turn."

Milo paused, unsure of how to respond. And then…

"Okay!" he said, channeling all his energy into the emerald wind. It parted the roots like the Red Sea, forging a straight path to the mushroom.

"Now, Chaika! Go!"

…without even wasting time with a response, Chaika dashed into the space, but the roots sought to impede her progress. Milo cast a mantra barrier on her, keeping her safe until she could reach the mushroom at the core of their twisted mass. Soon, however, he could keep up his strength no longer, and the barrier faded, while dozens of roots prepared to rip him limb from limb.

However, it was at that moment that Chaika reached the base of the Ghost Hail. She looked up at its full, towering height and raised her hands, and her palms began to glow with a silvery light, just like the elder's had done.

"Hokkaido!" she yelled. "Listen! I need to save my friends! I need to save you! Please help us!"

Then she plunged her hands into the soft skin of the mushroom stalk.

Shlop.

Shlop! Shlop! Shlop!

One by one, white, furry beasts leaped out of the mushroom and landed around Chaika. They all lacked eyes or a nose, each possessing only a single pair of jaws that took up their entire face. They immediately began snapping at the roots, tearing them to shreds. One of them assisted Milo, ripping the vines off him as the boy doctor fought them off with his blade. Freed from their grasp, Milo took a look around, failing to conceal his shock.

"It's...the white hair antibodies! You summoned them, Chaika! You called them here to save us!"

"Eat them! Eat them all up! I am Chaika, your oracle, and I declare these roots an enemy of Hokkaido! They must all be eradicated!"

Astride one of the white bears, Chaika barked her orders to the herd. She sounded so regal that, for a second, Milo forgot she was quite so young. When at last he remembered himself, he readied his dagger and began slashing away at the flower roots.

Directly above Hokkaido's most important organ stood its tallest peak, Ghost Hail Mountain.

Its apex commanded a three-hundred-sixty-degree view of the surrounding landscape, and a young Benibishi girl stood there alongside her towering assistant.

The girl wore a gown that used to belong to her father, and as it caught the wind and fluttered, she gazed at the sight before her with a face like ice.

"I see…," came the soft and quiet voice that issued forth from her crimson lips. "So this is the spot."

In front of her, a ring-shaped vortex of white light, like the eye of a tornado, emanated from the ground at the very peak of the mountain.

"Indeed," answered the colossal protector at her side. "We are now directly above the Ghost Hail Node, the source of Hokkaido's power. Allow your great flower to take root, King Shishi. Then all we Benibishi who bathe in its pollen shall receive a power far surpassing that of any human."

…A power far surpassing that of any human.

The flame of ambition glittered in Shishi's cold gaze.

This time, they shall be forced to know the tyranny and oppression we have endured.

"Our roots already control the Ghost Hail Node below. Now, Your Majesty. The time has come to plant your flower and fulfill our wish!"

"...Yes."

Shishi nodded and closed her eyes in focus. As she did, the vines coalesced in her hand, creating her trusty ivy sword, glowing gold. She walked past Satahabaki, who bowed his head, and she stood at the center of the ring of light. Taking a breath, she lifted the sword above her head and cried...

"...Flourish! Lion's Crimson Sword!"

Shnk!!

Shishi stabbed the blade into the ground at her feet, and immediately, the white light of the vortex turned a deep crimson, like her flower.

The entire mountain trembled as if in fright. The wind picked up, becoming an incredible blizzard that swirled around Shishi, and the flower behind the girl's ear opened wide to scatter its glowing pollen. The power of Shishi's Bountiful Art began drawing energy out of Hokkaido and into the creation of the camellia flower.

Soon a magnificent ivy pillar broke up through the ground and stretched into the sky, as if to pierce the heavens themselves. Satahabaki raised his arms in defiance of the powerful storm winds.

"Wh-what an impressive display of Florescence!"

The tower of vines continued rising out of Hokkaido's tallest peak. Shishi was sweating slightly. She turned and called out to Satahabaki. "Once the flower blooms, our victory is all but assured. Pay close attention, Someyoshi."

"M-my!!"

An ever-so-slight grin of triumph spread across Shishi's face, the wind from the rushing vines beating back her violet hair. The tower grew to a hundred meters tall, when at last, a crimson camellia bud appeared atop it, throbbing as if ready to blossom.

Shishi's eyes flared red with ambition once more, and the sword in her hand glowed with a golden light. She pulled it free of the earth and readied herself to plunge it in again.

Soon humanity...life on this rock...all will be slaves to the Benibishi!

"Flourish! Lion's Camellia!!"

Gathering up all her power, Shishi channeled it into the blade. But just before she could stab it into the roots of the tower...

"Not so fast!"

Pchew!

"What?!"

Ka-ching!

Shishi swiveled and parried the mushroom arrow with her blade, breaking her concentration mere moments before the flower bloomed.

This arrow... There's only one man it could belong to!

Her once-frigid expression was consumed by rage. She looked up at the sky, toward the arrow's source, and there she saw...

...amid a cloud of glittering spores, a young boy, eyes gleaming like twin jades.

"Think you can just ignore Milo and me and skip right to the endin', huh, Shishi?!"

"Bisco. It's you...!!"

"You should know that if you wanna get what you're after, you have to go through me first!"

Why must you always stand in my way, Brother?!

The once-feared Mushroom Keeper was now naught but a little child, yet still his soul seemed to shine through his eyes, causing Shishi to recoil in fear. She took one step backward.

...How can he still fight back at this size? And how did he get out of Hokkaido?!

"Take thiiis!"

Bisco's second and third arrows flew at extraordinary speed. Shishi moved fast, dodging the projectiles in the nick of time, but...

Gaboom! Gaboom!

"Hrh?! Krhh!"

...after the arrows stuck into the snow at her feet, they exploded into red oyster mushrooms, blasting Shishi far backward.

You…you dare show up now, when I'm just one step away!

"So you've come, Akaboshiii!" came a bellowing voice as, tagging in for his royal charge, Satahabaki stepped out of the blizzard and swung one of his thick arms at Bisco. "I shall not let you interfere with my liege's mission!"

"There you are, judge man!" Bisco shot back. "Where's your self-respect gotten to these days?"

"Stand aside, Mr. Bisco, sir!"

Showing up a little after Bisco, Amli entered the vortex of energy and began chanting a mantra, calling together the Rust into a hefty boulder.

"Won-shad-bagow-snew!"

Amli made a motion like a baseball pitcher, hurling the enormous Rust rock at Satahabaki. It collided with the Iron Judge head-on, sending him rolling across the snow and off a nearby cliff.

"NOOOOOO…!"

"How's that for a strike? That's the Kusabira special, the fireball straight!"

"Thanks, Amli!" shouted Bisco. "We'd have had a tough time facing him in a fair fight!"

"Mr. Bisco, sir! Up there!"

Amli landed softly in the snowfield and pointed to the apex of the ivy tower. The camellia bud was still pulsating, tiny motes of pollen spilling like light from between its furled petals.

"We don't have much time before the camellia finishes absorbing the energy it needs!" she said. "We need to prune that oversized climbing plant, or Hokkaido's in danger!"

"And how're we supposed to do that?!" Bisco shouted back.

"Just leave it to me, Mr. Bisco, sir."

Amli popped out her glass eye and stashed it away in her pocket. Then she gathered all her mystical energy in the empty socket…and a violet arrow emerged from the hole.

"Hey, Amli! You sure you wanna be doin' that in front of other people? A little indecent, don't you think?"

"Oh, shut up! Now's hardly the time!"

Amli slapped Bisco around the head and placed the arrow in his hand.

"This arrow is formed of pure Rust. It is a blasphemous technique… but it's the only way to destroy a plant of that size. You must strike the bud at its heart, Bisco, quickly! There's not a moment to lose!"

"All right, got it!"

Bisco began climbing the tower of vines…then stopped and turned back.

"Wait, Amli, what about you?"

"There is something else I must do."

Amli's voice was oddly resolute. Bisco followed her gaze to a figure standing in the snow, sword in hand—the ice queen herself.

"Shishi!"

"If she attempts to use her Bountiful Art again, the flower will surely bloom. I cannot let that happen."

"You're gonna fight her by yourself? Don't be crazy. That's—!"

Before Bisco could finish, Amli spun around, placed her finger to his lips, and smiled gently.

"The mushrooms are powerless against flowers—you must know that by now. Yet my Rust powers are perfectly positioned to take Shishi on, are they not? Surely you do not mean to say that you lack faith in my abilities? After all this time?"

"No, Amli. But…!"

"Mr. Bisco, sir. If you truly care so much for me, then promise me one thing."

Amli's gaze met Bisco's in the midst of the howling blizzard.

"Shishi shall be my most formidable foe yet. I may need to use…a forbidden technique. If I should do that, and should the mantra become too powerful for me to control… If wickedness should overtake me, I pray that you, Bisco, be the one to put me down."

"You can't—"

"Please, Big brother. Promise me this."

The girl before him was a far cry from the happy-go-lucky Amli whom

Bisco knew. He could see the resolution in her eyes, and swallowed any protests he might have been about to say.

"All right." He nodded. "But it ain't gonna come to that. Gimme three minutes, and I'll have this flower tower brought down faster than you can say 'lawn mower.'"

"I do not know about you, but it does not take me three minutes to say 'lawn mower,'" Amli retorted. "Besides, I have no doubt that Shishi shall be brought low in that time. Just you wait and see!"

With that, Bisco grinned and began making his way up the tower.

"That fool...! He seeks to injure the bud!"

Shishi broke into a run, forming a javelin of ivy in her hand, which she tossed at Bisco as he climbed. It hurtled through the air, unerringly closing in on its target...

"*Won-shad-shed-snew!*"

Amli's chanting threw up a shield of mantra power, which the plant-spear bounced harmlessly off before falling back to the ground.

"Hrgh! You would stand in the way of a king?" Shishi growled. "Tell me, who are you?"

Amli twirled on the spot and daintily lifted the sides of her *hakama* like a skirt.

"Pleased to meet you, Your Majesty. Amli Amlini, at your service."

Her introduction complete, Amli placed her hand to her empty eye socket...and drew out a long spear of Rust, cloaked in a violet glow.

"In the name of our god, Bisco Akaboshi...I shall oppose you!"

Amli's stance was tall and proper, nothing like usual when she was playing around with Bisco. The violet aura grew until it enwreathed her entire body, casting a purple light onto the snow around her. She looked so strong and brave that even Shishi had no choice but to take her seriously.

I cannot let down my guard.

"I see you are skilled," Shishi said. "It will be a shame to cut you down, but the time for talk is past. If you continue to stand in my way, I will show no mercy, girl or not!"

"Why, what a coincidence."

A violet flame flickered in Amli's one remaining eye.

"I was just thinking the very same thing about you, Princess Shishi."

"You make light of the king. I shall have you know the weight of your sin!"

Shishi leaped into action, and Amli caught the blade on her spear. The sound of clashing metal reverberated across the snowy mountaintop.

It seems my taunts worked! thought Amli. *But...*

The two flitted here and there, clashing their weapons again and again.

Sh-she's quite strong for a girl!

It seemed that Amli's Rust spear was indeed quite effective against Shishi's ivy sword, as every time the two weapons clashed, the blade became chipped and damaged. However, Shishi did not let up for a moment, twisting and thrusting as though nothing had happened, gradually putting Amli on the defensive.

"I see, a spear of Rust... Troublesome."

Spotting the damage to her blade, Shishi only clicked her tongue, launching a kick at Amli and blasting her back. Then she began focusing the Florescence in her right hand.

"An inconvenience...but nothing more. The Rust may be anathema to the flower, but even the mightiest daisy cannot fell an oak!"

Amli staggered to her feet and watched as Shishi channeled the Florescence into her sword, making it sharp again.

"One with the power to slay flowers could make for a potent ally. Join me, Amli Amlini, and while the whole world will be forced to kneel at my feet, you alone shall be permitted to stand by my side, your mind intact."

"Do you really think a follower of Mr. Bisco could acquiesce to those demands?"

Amli wiped the sweat from her brow and shot back in a voice like poison.

"It is you who should stand down, Miss Shishi, ma'am. Give up this fool's errand, and we would be happy to welcome you back to our side."

But Amli's words only seemed to put a crazed grin on Shishi's lips.

Her crimson eyes went wide, and she sprang at Amli like a panther, swinging her ivy sword.

"Then so be it!" she yelled. "Offer your blood to my blade, Amli!"

Amli barely managed to block the overhead blow on her spear. She was sweating all over, trying to match Shishi's speed. Blood spilled from between her clenched teeth, and yet somehow she managed to persist, fending off every last strike successfully.

I shall not last...much longer...

   ...However!

   I shall show Mr. Bisco...just how brave this spirit fights!

"Won-ul-hibaki-snew! Hi-yah!"

   Clang!

A spear of Rust shot up from the snow, brushing Shishi's sword aside.

"Mrgh!"

And in that opening...

"Take this!"

...channeling all the life energy she could spare into her mantra, Amli drove the Rust spear's point toward Shishi's chest in one desperate, last-ditch thrust.

"Goddammit, how high is this thing?!"

Bisco looked up toward the top of the ivy tower as the raging blizzard threatened to wrench him off it. The main vine stretched up and away, into the sky, and the great camellia that sat at its peak was still a fair distance off yet.

Luckily, Bisco's new size was a boon here. Through skillful use of his wire arrows, he could leverage his reduced mass to make progress at incredible speed. The higher he went, however, the stronger the winds blew, and soon they threatened to snatch him clean off the vine and blow him away.

"Grrr... Gotta stop usin' the arrows and just climb!"

Bisco glared up at his goal and replaced his bow on his back before taking his knife in one hand and braving the rest of the climb on his own. The wild gales caused his cloak to flap like a flag in the wind.

"Just you wait, Amli! I'm nearly there…," he growled, throwing himself into the ascent. Suddenly, however, he heard a dark, spiteful voice echoing up from far below.

"…kaa…ooo…shii…"

"Hrgh?!"

"AAAKAAABOOOSHIII!!!"

"When will you learn to give up, you big bozo?!"

The voice was so loud it blocked out the howling wind, even at this height. Naturally, the only possible owner was the former Six Realms warden, Satahabaki. Though Amli had knocked him off a cliff with her mantra, it seemed that by means unknown, or perhaps through sheer force of will, he was back with a vengeance, making his way up the giant flower stalk after Bisco.

"No criminal shall escape my GRAAASP!"

"How the hell is he so fast?!" exclaimed Bisco, wiping the sweat from his brow. "I gotta get movin'! If he catches me, that's it!"

All of a sudden, Bisco's climb had turned into a two-man race. Bisco had a respectable lead to begin with, but all his skill and dexterity came to naught when matched against the three-meter mountain of a man that was Someyoshi Satahabaki. By the time Bisco looked back to gauge the distance, the Iron Judge was already close enough to make eye contact.

"Akaboshi! Our victory is inevitable! Cease this fruitless struggle and surrender with dignity!"

"Shaddup! We Mushroom Keepers don't know the meanin' of 'surrender,' so why don't you make like a cherry tree in the Rust Wind and get the hell outta my sight!"

Just as Satahabaki launched a weighty fist, Bisco unhooked the bandolier of vials around his waist and flicked it like a whip, causing it to wrap around the plant stem and stay there.

"What?! What are you scheming, knave?!"

"You're about to find out!"

Bisco hopped onto a leaf sticking out from the stem and launched a punch at the vial belt...

Boom!

A coil of flame erupted from the belt, causing a ring of fire to spread around the main vine.

"Nrrrgh! You...!!"

The shattered vial scattered infernoshroom spores onto Satahabaki beneath, enveloping him in hellfire.

"Grrgh! Chemical attacks are against the rules of warfare!"

"You sure you want to bring that up? You're fightin' a damn child!"

The camellias screamed as Satahabaki's enormous body began to burn. Satahabaki roared, seemingly not out of any fear for his own life but for that of the flowers.

"You rat! How dare you!"

"If you wanna live, you'd best let go. The snow'll cushion the fall *and* put out the fire! It's a two-for-one deal!"

As the blizzard claimed Satahabaki's form, Bisco coughed on the smoke of the explosion and began climbing once more, driving his knife into the stem to get a grip.

"...That's it! Almost there!"

The storm meant Bisco could only see a few meters in front of his nose, but at last the enormous bud of the camellia came into view.

"Peh! Peh! Geez, all this pollen!"

The bud itself was more like a mass of camellia petals, and whenever they gently parted, a cloud of pollen emerged from the center. From the way it was pulsating, it seemed ready to blossom at any moment.

"Made it just in time! I'd better hurry up and use Amli's Rust arrow to—"

But just as Bisco drew his bow, he heard another loud noise from down below.

"RRROOOAAAHHH! AKABOSHIII!"

"Whaaat?! Again?! The guy's insane!"

He looked down to see Satahabaki stubbornly scaling the tower, his body wreathed entirely in flame. He looked like a Malebranche of Hell emerging from the inferno.

How does he still have the fight in him?!

The sight of the burning giant clawing his way up was enough to root Bisco to the spot in terror, but...

No! Keep it together! You know the big guy's as stubborn as a mule. And you still got a couple more tricks up your sleeve!

...Bisco was sure not to lose his cool. He calmly pulled a few more arrows from his quiver and fired them off at the giant flower stalk beneath.

Goom! Goom! Gaboom!

This slightly sticky sound announced the growth of Bisco's special slime nameko mushrooms. Immediately after growing, they melted into a slick oily substance that dripped down the vine and onto Satahabaki's hands.

"Rrrgh?! Whaa—?! Nooo!!"

It was all Satahabaki could do just to cling to the stalk. He glared up at Bisco, who took one look back before making for the bud again.

"Ain't nothin' special, but it's more than enough to take down a giant like you!"

"Nrrrgh! Akaboshi, you coward! Face me without your tricks!"

"You kiddin'? You'd squash me flat! I'm the size of a kid; I gotta even the playin' field somehow!"

"Still, I cannot...!"

As Satahabaki lost his final grip on the stalk and began to fall back, he extended both arms toward Bisco. From his wrists came quick-growing vines that shot toward Bisco in a last-ditch effort to block his ascent.

"I cannot let you go any farther, Akaboshi!"

The ivy latched on to the tower like a rope and pulled Satahabaki's massive frame up, directly toward...

"I've been waitin'... Waitin' for ya to slip up and do somethin' like that!"

With both legs wrapped around the stalk, Bisco pulled his bow tight.

"Nrgh!!"

Seeing Bisco glitter golden with spores, Satahabaki realized his fatal mistake. If Bisco's mushroom arrow hit its mark while he was in midair, he'd have nothing to hold on to.

"Y-you've been waiting for me to let go of the stalk...ever since we started!"

"My body may be child-sized...," said Bisco, tapping the side of his head, "but my mind ain't. In a battle of wits, it's clear who outta us is the winner."

"Curse you, Akaboshiii!"

"I ain't got the calories to fight you! Now, go wait down at the bottom till I'm done!"

Pchew! Gaboom!

Just as Satahabaki threw his weighty arm, Bisco's Rust-Eater arrow hit him square in the chest.

"Aaakaaaboooshiii..."

Satahabaki's voice became fainter and fainter as he fell to earth in a pillar of thick black smoke.

"Geez, dealin' with that guy gives me heartburn..."

Bisco watched him fall, then suddenly remembered his mission and cast his eyes upward.

"Awoooaaahh!"

A sound like the howling of many dogs came from the bud, which slowly began unfurling its petals.

"Shit!"

Bisco summoned all the strength his tiny body could muster, clambering up to the mass of petals, scaling them one by one before finally arriving at the entrance to the bud.

"So I just gotta jam this in there, I guess!"

Taking Amli's Rust arrow in hand, Bisco began prying apart the petals, making his way deeper into the pollen-filled core of the bud.

Gruh... The pollen's so thick here!

The inside was uncomfortably warm, and so full of pollen it started clinging to him, almost like it was trapping him, interfering with his mind.

Obey.
  Obey us, humans.
  Bow down to your masters.

Grrr! This is…Shishi's Bountiful Art! The power of her Florescence!
The voice pounded in Bisco's head like a drum. Bisco yelled, trying to force it out of his mind.
"Shut…uuup!!"
Clenching his teeth, he forged deeper into the bud, and at last Bisco reached the center, where he found the stigma, the germination site for the pollen.
"Hah!! That's gotta be it!"
With heavy breaths, Bisco nocked his violet Rust arrow and pointed it toward the flower's reproductive organ.

Don't do it.
  Don't shoot.
  Be our slave.
  Bow down to us.

Bisco ground his back teeth, forcing the flower's voice out of his mind. His jade eyes glimmered.
"Your plan ends here, Shishi!"
Pchew!
The crack of Bisco's bow sounded like a rifle shot, and the Rust arrow struck the flower's core like a streak of light.
Gaboom! Gaboom!
Mushrooms made of Rust exploded from the stigma, a most paradoxical sight.
"Awoooaaaahh!"

The bud howled in pain and spat Bisco back into the cold air outside. Twirling through the air, drenched in pollen, Bisco announced his victory with a yell.

"How'd you like *them* mushrooms, asshole?! How the hell're you supposed to take over Japan when you can't even handle one little kid?!"

"Awooohh!"

Gaboom! Gaboom! Gaboom!

The Rust mushrooms tore through the flower bud like paper and, without slowing, spilled out onto the tower itself, making their way down toward its roots. Meanwhile, the upper reaches of the tower turned to rust, blown away on the raging blizzard winds.

Bisco could do nothing but surrender his body to the storm as he plummeted toward the ground.

"All right! It's done…!"

He began to relax, but just then, he felt a strange wind from down below and tensed up again.

"What's this?! It's…not Amli…?!"

It was an evil wind that tormented Bisco's keen senses and chilled his spine.

"I got a bad feeling about this… Amli! Amli!!"

Bisco didn't know what was down there, but he knew it couldn't be good. He straightened his body like a pencil, building up speed, aiming for the spot where he had left Amli and Shishi to conduct their bloody battle.

Ching! Ching! Ka-ching!

Shishi stood over Amli, relentlessly swinging her sword over and over again, which Amli only barely managed to deflect with her spear.

"Look at you!" Shishi jeered. "You're only delaying the inevitable…!"

"Krh…!"

"Now die!"

Clang!

"Ahh!"

Shishi swung hard, knocking Amli's spear aside and out of her grasp. "This is the end, Amli!"

Shishi lunged, hoping to finish off her disarmed foe, when…

"Won-shad-varuler-snew!"

"What?!"

…dozens of Rust spears materialized in the air and launched themselves at Shishi. Shishi fended them off, leaving herself open to a thrust from Amli's Rust knife that landed in her shoulder.

"Hmph," Shishi grunted, hopping back a step. "You have plenty of tricks, I'll grant you that." She grabbed the knife and tore it free. "And to survive so long against my attacks…is truly impressive."

Shishi brandished her sword, the faintest trace of regret visible in her features.

"However, there is only so much a little girl can do. My next attack shall end you…Amli Amlini."

"Haah…haah…haah…!"

Shishi was right. She was prepared to continue the fight for hours if necessary, while Amli was at her limit already. The brilliant spear techniques of the Kusabira sect's high priestess had kept her safe from Shishi's deadly strikes, but keeping up with her superior speed was a fatiguing task, and Amli's defenses had slipped. Deep slashes covered her shoulders, arms, and legs, dyeing the snow crimson.

"I suppose so," said Amli, coughing up blood. "I must have misjudged you…Shishi…"

"So you are ready to accept your fate?"

"Oh, I wouldn't say that…"

Her lips were stained red, but they bore a grin still.

"You haven't seen all of my tricks yet. I have a very special ace hidden up my sleeve. I think you shall find it is you who will be accepting her fate today."

"…So be it, then."

Shishi swung her right arm, and a brand-new ivy sword appeared in her hand.

"I shall have to finish you off before you can use any more tricks!"

Shishi kicked off the snow, launching herself in a straight line toward Amli.

"Won-ul-shad-snew!"

At the very last second, Amli threw up a Rust barrier to deflect Shishi's lunge. However, the blow was so forceful that it drove the blade into the shield, opening up a large crack in spite of the Rust's supposed advantage.

"Some ace that was. You are still just stalling for time," Shishi said.

If I stay on the defensive, Miss Shishi will surely strike a killing blow sooner or later.

Amli held out her arm, focusing on maintaining the shield, and began muttering a new mantra under her breath.

…I shall have to switch to the offense. Risky as it may be…

"Won-culvero-kelhasha…won-halcuro-kelhasha…!"

What?!

Across the barrier, Shishi watched as the flame in Amli's eye socket flared, and she knew something big was coming.

She…she wasn't bluffing!

Shishi quickly channeled her Florescence into her blade, sending dark-green ivy throughout the shield. The ivy ate away at the mantra barrier from within, causing it to crack apart.

"Won-kon-zen-muto-amli-kelhasha…!"

"We mustn't let her complete her spell! Come, my blade, destroy her feeble barrier!"

With a great *Smash!* the shield crumbled, and Shishi raised her sword, ready to bring it down on the now defenseless Amli.

Big brother…please… Remember our promise!

"So long, Amli Amlini!"

"Won-ulhilseva-kelshinha-snew!"

Shnk!

Shishi showed no mercy, even against a young girl, and sliced Amli cleanly in two…

…or at least, she would have.

"…Wh…what?!"

Shishi's slice, with all her power behind it, landed directly in Amli's shoulder…and stopped. A small line of blood ran from where sword met flesh. Amli's other hand gripped the blade, holding it back, preventing it from reaching its fatal target.

"Kheh-heh-heh-heh…"

Amli lifted her head, but on her face was a barbaric, wicked smile the young girl should not have been capable of.

"My loathsome child. It seems you finally require my strength. Had you just called upon me from the beginning, this battle would already be over."

"How strange," Shishi said. "You had a mantra capable of granting you such power, and yet you kept it hidden all this time?" She retracted her sword and leaped back, watching Amli rise to her feet. "Wait. I see now. You're not Amli. Who are you?"

"Kheh-heh-heh-heh… Trying to take over Japan without me? I have heard many tales in my time, but none so ridiculous as that."

Amli drew another Rust spear from her eye socket and swung it, emitting a powerful gale that cleared away the snow in a wide circle around her. It was a force unlike any she had wielded in the battle so far.

"You face Mashouten, the Rust Lord. To ask who I am is the greatest blasphemy ever known."

What manner of shamanic art is this? thought Shishi. *It is as if I face someone else entirely!*

"Listen well, inferior life-form, for I shall teach you. I…am the Rust Lord Kelshinha! Let my holy spear bring the wrath of god upon the vain and withered king!"

"I listen not to the words of dead men!"

Shishi steeled her gaze once more and brandished her blade aloft, swinging it down on her foe.

"Killing Slice: Lion's Crimson Sword!"

"Kheh-heh-heh-heh! Fool! You cannot kill a god!"

Ka-ching! Ka-ching! Ka-ching!

Shishi's golden sword, and Amli's spear of deepest violet. Each time they clashed, it threw off sparks that lit up the mountaintop.

How is she so strong compared to a moment ago?

"It matters not how much you clad your sword in embellishment!" Amli roared, as she swung with deadly force, knocking Shishi's blade aside. She wasted no time in following up, lunging into Shishi's unguarded opening.

"You are weak of arm…"

Ka-ching!

"…weak of mind…"

Ka-ching!

"…and weak of spirit, child!"

Ka-chinggg!

"Grhhh?!"

The final swing of Amli's three-hit combo snapped Shishi's sword at the hilt, and sent her flying backward. Shishi hit the moutaintop multiple times before pushing off the ground, regaining her balance in the air, and landing cleanly on her feet.

"You would call a king a child?!" she barked back. "The dead should hold their tongue!"

Shishi was made of sterner stuff than to quail at a single broken sword. The blade grew back in an instant, and Shishi focused all her power into it.

As much as I despise relying on my father's move, it must be done!

"Offer your heart to my spear, foolish girl!"

Amli leaped nimbly across the snow and up into the air, aiming the point of her spear downward. But Shishi's eyes glimmered, a crimson flash in the icy white.

"Many others called me a child," she said. "Many others called me a girl. They mocked me, and all of them met their end. With this!"

"Mrgh?!"

"Bountiful Art: Revelation!"

At Shishi's words, the golden glow of her sword turned a fiery crimson. She growled and poured all of her Florescence into a single sweeping blow.

"Finishing Move: Balsam Blaze!"

Shishi swept her blade, slicing apart the blizzard, leaving a crimson trail that hovered in place for a moment before shooting toward Amli.

"No mewling brat's blade can touch me!!"

Amli extended one hand and summoned a mantra barrier. Shishi's phantom blade collided with it, running a crack straight through the shield. Amli reeled at the surprisingly powerful force of the blow, but with the attack held successfully at bay, she grinned a smile of relief.

"Behold! None can destroy my—!"

Amli's words caught in her throat. She couldn't believe her eyes. Shishi's blade became cloaked in crimson flame once more, and this time she held it up, above her head.

"None can destroy your shield? Is that what you wanted to say?"

"I-impossible! How do you have any energy left after that last attack?!"

"Then I am the first man to destroy it! Remember that when you're rotting in Hell, dead one!"

Shishi threw her sword downward with all her might.

"Finishing Move! Balsam Blaze: Cross Slash!"

Shishi's second blade of crimson light overlapped with the first, forming an X-shaped energy blast that shattered Amli's mantra shield completely.

"Grrh! Impossible... How could a mere girl...possess such power...?!"

Swish! Swish!

"Groooaaahhh?!"

The cross-shaped beam of light pierced Amli, sending her flying far backward. She attempted to regain her balance in midair, but...

Bwoom! Bwoom!

...camellia flowers appeared all over her body, blasting her down into the snowy earth once more.

"Grh..."

Amli struggled to her feet, covered in flowers.

"How could a child like you...possibly hurt a god like me...?"

The camellia has taken root. It is time to end this.

As Amli barely managed to prop herself up with her spear, Shishi leaped in to deliver the finishing blow. Her hidden art had used up nearly all her power, and so she needed to draw the battle to a close as soon as possible.

"Begone, spirit of the dead! Let my sword lay your soul to rest!"

Shishi gripped her golden sword and brought it down with all her might. At the same time, Amli readied her Rust spear and made a desperate thrust.

The two weapons clashed...

Swish!!

"..."
"..."

A silence reigned. There on the snowy mountaintop, only the sound of the blizzard filled the air.

Then, at last, one of the combatants spluttered hot crimson onto the fresh white snow.

"Gblgh...?!"

It was Shishi.

Impossible... The Balsam Blaze... Nobody could have avoided that...!

"Kheh-heh-heh. Kheh-heh-heh-heh-heh!"

Amli let out a deep chuckle. The bloodstained spear ran straight through Shishi's right breast. At the last second, she had deflected Shishi's fatal strike while delivering a lethal blow of her own.

"Children are so easily deceived. Did you really think you could kill me with that pathetic attack of yours?"

"But how...? I saw the flowers bloom...with my own eyes!"

"Khah-ha-ha. You mean *these* flowers?"

Amli waved her hand over herself, and the camellia flowers that had seemed to grow from Shishi's ultimate technique simply turned to Rust and disappeared on the wind.

"An illusion…!"

"Yes, one measly illusion. And you licked it up! How could you possibly hope to stand against me, you gullible fool?!"

Amli pulled back on her spear and kicked Shishi's body off it, sending her flying far across the snow and out of sight completely.

"Hmph. What a petulant brat she was."

Amli staggered to her feet, breathing heavily. Then she slowly began walking over to where Shishi had fallen.

"She was young, but her body was full of life regardless. Her organs will make fine additions to my own. Khah-ha-ha-ha."

"Khah-ha-ha…"

Just then…

"Khah-ha… Mmrgh?!"

All of a sudden, Amli stopped. A rain of golden spores fell softly in front of her face.

"…It cannot be!"

Amli wheeled around and looked up into the air, to see a child shining brilliantly like the sun.

"Kelshinhaaa!!!"

"You!" Amli's eyes flared wide. "You've come. You've come at last! Akaboshi! Akaboshiii!"

"Get out of her body, you shriveled-up asshole!!!"

Pchew! Pchew! Pchew!

"W-won-bada-shulk… Wh-what…? I cannot… Gbluh!"

Bisco loosed his sunlight arrows toward Amli, leaving glimmering trails. Due to the wounds sustained in her battle with Shishi, Amli could not complete her mantra quickly enough, and the arrows perforated her body in a pattern like the stars of Orion.

"Grrrrrgh…"

Goom! Goom!

Bisco's Rust-Eater arrows grew with just enough force to leave Amli alive. She coughed up blood and glared at Bisco with rapidly unfocusing eyes.

"I knew it was you, old man. I could smell you from up there!"

"You whelp, Akaboshi! If I had my old body back, and not this girl's…"

"So this is what Amli was talkin' about…"

Bisco bit his lip, a bitter look on his face. Then he shook his head and glared down at Amli…or, Kelshinha, with all the hatred he could muster.

"Usually I'd offer to join forces with an ancestral spirit…but it seems you ain't got no respect for your daughter's body. What kind of father are you?!"

"Die, Akaboshi!"

"Rrrraaaagh!!"

Kelshinha lunged for his bitter foe, spear in hand, and at that very same moment, Bisco grabbed a Rust-Eater arrow and countered.

"Aka…boshi…"

"…"

The spear stopped a mere centimeter from Bisco's windpipe, pressing into the flesh of his neck. Bisco's arrow, on the other hand, was lodged deeply into Kelshinha's chest, just in front of the heart.

"I have wished for your power…for so long, Akaboshi…," came the old man's voice.

Bisco wrenched the arrow free. Thanks to his unparalleled finesse, there was no mushroom growth like usual. Instead, only a cloud of Rust-Eater spores entered Amli's body. The spores forced out the violet Rust, making it pour like smoke from the arrow holes. At first, the flow was gentle, but it grew and grew until the Rust was shooting out of her like a geyser, rising into the sky.

"Aka…boshi…"

"I'll see you in Hell, old man, and we'll have all the time in the world to fight. Until then, don't let me see your face in the land of the livin', you hear?"

The last of Kelshinha escaped through his daughter's eye socket, and the flow suddenly stopped, leaving Amli herself once more.

"…Haah! Haah! Haah…!"

At last Bisco was able to catch his breath, and he ran over to the fallen Amli, calling her name and helping her up.

"Amli! Amli! Amli, open your eyes. Goddammit! If I knew you were gonna pull this shit, I never woulda let you fight alone!"

Bisco rummaged through the vials at his hip and took out a glowing blue lurkershroom medicine. After a moment's hesitation, he slammed the needle into Amli's chest.

"Gbh..."

Amli jerked as the shock caused her to resume breathing...

"...Phaaaah?!"

...Then suddenly she opened her mouth and gulped down a deep breath.

"Amli!! Thank the gods, I thought you were a goner!"

"H-how...? The Mantra of Soul Transfer should have erased me completely..."

"Don't worry; I took care of your old man. He'll be roastin' in Hell by now."

"Y-you 'took care' of him?! How on earth—?!"

"Don't try an' talk! I wanted to go easy on you, but you still took a real beatin'. It's a good thing you're a lot tougher than you look, or you'd be dead."

Bisco had never been so grateful to have the strength of a child. To weaken Amli enough to drive out the Rust from her, without killing her, was a formidable task. If Bisco had been at full strength, he probably would have blasted her to pieces.

Bisco grinned apologetically and plucked the Rust-Eaters from Amli's body. In truth, Amli was so surprised to be alive that she wasn't sure how to respond, but as Bisco bandaged up her wounds, she managed to muster an awkward smile all the same.

In her most desperate hour, Amli had turned to the Mantra of Soul Transfer, a forbidden spell that surrendered one's body to another personality lurking within. The thing was, it was meant to be irreversible, with no way to free Amli's soul from the evil Kelshinha's clutches.

* * *

"*I thought that was it,*" Amli whispered, Bisco's hand on her cheek. "*I thought I was saying good-bye. How is it, Mr. Bisco, sir, that you seem to do the impossible as a matter of course?*"

"You say somethin', Amli? I didn't quite catch that. Anyway, you're all healed up. Can you try to stand up for me?"

"Of course! Why, I feel better already, Mr. Bisco, sir...! Wait, look at that!"

Amli pointed over Bisco's shoulder at the sky beyond, to the enormous flower that bloomed atop the tower.

"*Awoooahhh!*"

The flower and its stalk were becoming Rust, dissolving from the top down. Partially disintegrated chunks fell to the earth like boulders, and Amli threw up her Rust barrier.

"Yeah, we did it, Amli! Your Rust arrow did the trick, just like you said!"

"The Rust is falling like a landslide! I should have told you this would happen! Stay by my side, Mr. Bisco, sir, and don't move!"

The rumbling continued as rubble fell from above, cloaking the land in dust, Rust, and snow. And when it finally settled...

"...We won!" Bisco yelled. "Hell yeah!"

...Amli dispelled the barrier, and she and Bisco looked up at a clear blue sky. The raging blizzard had calmed, and there was no sign of the colossal flower stalk that had existed just moments before. All that remained were a few rusted chunks, scattered across the snow.

"You did it," said Amli. "Truly, there is none who can best you in spirit. The madness of these 'Benibishi,' as you called them, has come to an end."

"Don't say it like it was all me! You nearly died, don't forget!" Bisco gave a childlike grin, only amplified by his cherubic features. "*We* did this. Together. I gotta thank you, Amli... You really pulled through for us."

"...Why...Mr. Bisco...!!"

Amli was uncontrollably elated by Bisco's kind words and lovable face. She threw her arms around him, squeezing him tightly.

"Nnnggwaaaah!!!"

"It's not fair! You can't just say something so...kind and innocent! If you really want to show your thanks, then there's only one thing to do! Come and give your big sister a kiss!!"

"Says who?! G-get off me! How the hell are you so strong?! Erk! S-stop! You're hurtin' me!"

Amli's almost superhuman strength seemed to come at the strangest times. Bisco found himself unable to extricate himself from her, and his face slowly turned pale.

"Mr. Bisco, sir? What's the matt—? Ahh!!"

Feeling Bisco's heartbeat waver, Amli released him before it stopped completely.

"Ahem. I do apologize. It seems I let my emotions get the better of me a little."

"A little?! Bullshit! You almost squeezed the spores outta me!! Look at 'em! They're actin' like my life's in danger again!"

"Mr. Bisco, sir," said Amli, suddenly becoming awfully serious. "I do believe we should go back down now. With the tower gone, there is no reason to stay here, and Mr. Milo could be in danger. We must hurry back and help him at once!"

"All right, you got it! We'll want Milo to take a look at you, too. I did all I could, but he's the expert when it comes to doctor shit."

"It seems the hole the flower made when it came through has been blocked... We shall have to open it again."

Bisco nodded in affirmation, and Amli began muttering a mantra. At the green energy vortex where the tower once stood, the ground began to rumble and crack apart.

I have used up almost all my power... I can feel the mantra fading!

"Hey, Amli! You're not lookin' too hot. Don't force it!"

"Won-shad-velow-snew!"

There was a *Crack!* as the earth split open, and a small hole appeared at the eye of the vortex. Bisco held up Amli as she coughed and spluttered, and began pulling her toward it.

"Stay with me, Amli…! Dammit, you used up too much power already. Let's go see Milo. He'll know what to do."

"D-do not…worry…about me. Are you ready to go, Bisco?"

The pair nodded at each other and prepared to leap into the hole. But right at that moment…

Whoosh!

"What?!"

…from out of nowhere, a sharp ivy whip came flying toward them. It homed in on Bisco like a serpent lunging for its prey, and just as it was about to strike…

"Mr. Bisco, sir! Out of the way!"

Slash!!

…Bisco heard the sound of slicing flesh and saw a spray of fresh blood.

"Uh… Ah…"

"Mr.…Bisco…sir…"

The one the serpent took…was Amli. She had jumped in front of Bisco at the last moment, and the whip impaled her front-to-back before coiling around her.

As Bisco stood, open-mouthed but unable to scream, Amli smiled back, showing the same roguish grin that Bisco always used.

"…It is…a good…trade. I should already be dead…Mr. Bisco, sir. If my sacrifice…can allow you to go on…then we have already won."

"Nooo! Amliiii!!"

"Go! Mr. Bisco, sir…find Milo…and save Hokkaido!"

Amli threw off Bisco's hands and, with a kick, sent him flying back, into the hole leading beneath the earth.

"Amliiii!!"

"*Won-shad-varo-snew…* Rgh!"

As she watched him vanish, Amli muttered a spell, and the earth sealed over once more. But before she could see it close completely, the ivy whip pulled her away, dragging her across the snow and over to the feet of its wielder.

"Cough! Cough! Cough!!"

The blood from Amli's lungs stained the snow. Gasping for breath, Amli looked up into the blinding sunlight and the silhouette of the person standing there.

I thought...he killed her.

It was Shishi, standing tall in the sun. The flower behind her ear swayed, and her long eyelashes fluttered. The blizzard from earlier was completely gone, and now the mountaintop was bathed in warm, radiant sunlight, and a cool breeze rustled Shishi's hair.

But it doesn't matter... I've won. I've protected Mr. Bisco...

Amli gazed up into Shishi's crimson eyes and mustered a weak smile. Then she fell forward, face-first into the snow, unconscious.

You let him escape. Amli Amlini. To the very end, you stood up for my brother.

Shishi looked down at Amli's sleeping face, peaceful despite the large amount of her own blood decorating the surrounding snowfield, and she clenched her teeth hard. She looked out at the ruins of her tower, squinting as though the sight were too bright to bear.

"I...I lost..."

The scar from Amli's spear was almost completely gone now, healed over by the camellia's incredible regenerative capabilities. The bitter taste of defeat, however, was not so easy to cure.

"I've been beaten... One single child thwarted all the grand designs of the Benibishi race."

A breeze blew across the mountaintop, and the rusted-up ruins of the flower tower crumbled into nothing.

"How can I show my face before my people now...?!"

Shishi bit her lip, glaring into the clear blue sky.

"Shishi...

"Shishi.

"Shishi!"

Suddenly, the flower behind her ear unfurled, spilling glowing pollen, and Shishi heard a whispered voice.

"It is not over yet.
"You must not give up hope."

At first, Shishi could not tell where the voice was coming from. She looked around, surprised, but there was nobody else with her on the mountaintop. She heard a light chuckle from behind her left ear, as though whoever was watching her found her actions deeply amusing.

"Who's there? Reveal yourself!"

"I am the camellia. Your flower."

"The...camellia?"

"I have always been with you. I know everything about you."

Shishi felt a sudden and overwhelming sense of dread. She tried to shake off the voice, pretend it was only a hallucination, but it persisted, whispering sweetened words directly into her mind.

"It matters not if one flower is plucked. Together we have the power to plant so many more. Far larger...and far more beautiful."

"You lie! My power is spent. I can no longer—!"

"Then take hers."

The ivy crept out of Shishi's back unbidden, lifting Amli's unconscious form and suspending her before Shishi's eyes.

"Take her. Absorb her power, and together we shall create the perfect flower."

"You want me to absorb Amli's power?!"

"An unfathomable strength lurks within this girl. The strength of the Rust. All flowers fall to the Rust, save you and I. We alone may command this power, and bring our evolution to its ultimate stage."

"..."

Shishi listened to the soft, entrancing whispers of the camellia flower.

"Do you not wish for such power? Enough to grant the Benibishi their freedom, forever..."

"...Rhh."

"You cannot give up here. Not when victory is so very nearly within your grasp. Shishi. Remember what you have sacrificed to come this far. A happy, peaceful life. A quiet succession. A father's love and acceptance. You cast all that out for one chance at freedom. Don't you remember?"

Shishi gulped. Her face was a mixture of exaltation and dread. She couldn't turn back. So she parted her lips and with a raspy voice answered:

"Let me have it..."

The camellia chuckled, but Shishi was no longer listening.

"I have spilled blood upon the path. There is no going back now. So let me have it...the power. The power to lead my people to freedom!"

"Hee-hee-hee-hee-hee. Very good. I knew I was right in choosing my host, Shishi..."

With that, the vines from Shishi's back moved again, bringing Amli's face right up to Shishi's.

"Now, drink."

"D-drink?"

"A lover's kiss. Between you and the power you crave."

"A lover's...kiss...?"

The vines cradled Amli in a soft embrace. Shishi pursed her lips and brought them closer and closer to the unconscious girl, when she suddenly felt an unnatural hunger. She gripped Amli's face and kissed her hard.

"Hmff?! Mmmmfff!!"

Shishi's wild kiss brought Amli to her senses, and she attempted a strangled scream. Shishi, meanwhile, could feel the power that dwelled within Amli's lungs, like water under an unimaginable amount of pressure. It welled up, launching itself up through the girl's throat and into Shishi's body like a tsunami.

A-amazing... So this is the power of the Rust... The power of mantra!!

"Feel it! Quake in fear! Bear witness to the Rust's power! A sweet, intoxicating power! Hee-hee-hee-hee! Now I am immortal! The camellia cannot be destroyed!"

I feel…hot. The power…it's tearing me apart…!!
Bwoom! Bwoom!

A pair of petals sprouted from Shishi's back, like wings, glistening in the sunlight.

"Aaargh! It…it hurts…!!"

Shishi threw Amli to the ground and doubled over, clutching herself, trying to hold back the burgeoning power.

"Y-you! Camellia! Wh-what have you done to meeee?!!"

"Tee-hee-hee-hee. I have allowed you to be reborn…as a god. A flower god, Shishi."

"Urgh! Aargh! Aaaaaaghhh!!!"

Shishi fell to her hands and knees and watched in horror as vines sprouted from her fingertips. They crawled across the ground, bursting with bright-red camellia flowers. An unimaginable pain racked Shishi's body, and she screamed as a whirlwind of pollen enveloped her.

"M-Milo, hold on! This is dangerous! How reckless can you get?!"

Thanks to the combination of Milo's mantra and Chaika's summoned beasts, the Ghost Hail Node was completely free of roots. The Ghost Hail mushroom looked none the worse for wear after having its energy sucked out of it, and it still stood tall and proud in the center of the space.

"We don't know what this *greity deivo* can do if he gets back up! We ought to finish him off while we have the chance!"

"Shhh!" said Milo, placing his finger to his lips. "Silence in the operating room, Chaika. I need you to be my assistant, so focus."

Then Milo turned his attention downward, back to the surgery he was performing. The patient had fallen from up above, wrapped in ivy vines and camellia flowers. It was none other than the former warden of Six Realms, Someyoshi Satahabaki himself.

I thought for sure we were in for another fight when he showed up...

After his drubbing at the hands of Bisco, Satahabaki had fallen from the plant tower, straight into the hole that Bisco and Amli had come through, and had landed with a *Plumf!* on the Ghost Hail cap, before bouncing down to the feet of Milo and Chaika.

Just like with Gopis and Mepaosha, the camellia seems to be brainwashing him. If I can just remove it...!

Ignoring Chaika's worried look, Milo searched Satahabaki's muscular frame until he found a small glowing flower hiding just behind the neck.

"Found it! Chaika, can you use the Hand of the Ghost Hail on this flower here?"

"What?! I can't possibly purify all this! There's too much!"

"It's okay—you just need to make a start. Come on!"

Milo guided her hand to the plant, and Chaika's fingers closed around its base before glowing with a silver light that made the flower wriggle and shake uncomfortably.

"It's off the nerve. Now!"

Dr. Panda placed his hands over Chaika's and pulled, ripping the plant free of Satahabaki's spine. All in all, it was roughly two meters in length, with roots more vicious than any the boy doctor had ever seen.

"All right, it's off!" Milo smiled, pleased at the successful surgery.

Suddenly, Chaika let out a scream. "Eeek! What is that?! Milo, watch out!"

Milo looked to the plant in his hand, to see that the root had taken on a life of its own and coiled up, as if to strike him unawares.

"Oh no!"

Milo brandished his dagger and fought back, but even after he lopped parts off it, the root seemed to feel no pain and did not die. The flower opened up its petals like jaws and lunged for Milo's windpipe, but at that very instant...

"Hmph!!"

Snatch!

...an enormous arm shot out, grasping the flower just centimeters from Milo's neck. The giant man rose to his feet, casting a shadow across Milo and Chaika, and brought the flower before his eyes.

"How dare you...?!"

"Uh-oh!"

"Milo, run!"

"How DARE you...pervert my sense of JUSTIIICE?!!"

Chaika leaped to protect Milo, but he was not the Iron Judge's aim. Satahabaki threw the flower against the ground and stomped on it with one of his huge, treelike legs, after which the parasitic plant completely stopped moving at last.

"Grrr... You have failed," he said. "You have failed, Someyoshi Satahabaki! You were supposed to uphold the law, and yet you allowed the camellia to enter your mind, manipulating you..."

"Y-Your Honor! It's okay! We've destroyed Shishi's flower! It's over!"

"YOU! Nekoyanagi!"

"Y-yes?!!"

"I...am deeply grateful. I shall not forget this debt."

Satahabaki took Milo's hand and shook it so hard, he came off the ground. Still, Satahabaki seemed to bear no grudge against the pair, so Milo and Chaika breathed a collective sigh of relief.

"Your Honor, can you tell us what's happening up there? What about Bisco? Is he okay?!"

"Ah, Akaboshi..."

Satahabaki opened his mouth as if to speak further, but he suddenly seemed to realize something and looked up toward the ceiling.

"It seems there is no need. He can tell you himself."

"...What?!"

Milo followed the judge man's line of sight, to the roof of the cavern...

"Waaaaaaaaaghhh!! Milooo!!"

""Bisco?!""

Milo and Chaika cried out in unison. Framed by his billowing cloak was Bisco, falling headfirst toward them.

Milo fired a clamshell mushroom at the ground and catapulted himself upward, catching Bisco mid-fall and rolling across the floor.

"Phew... Climbin' up, fallin' down... It's been a busy day!"

"Bisco! We took care of the roots. How did things go up there? Did you manage to get rid of the flower?!"

"Sure did! Me and Amli took care of that... Oh shit, Amli! Shishi's got her! We need to save her!"

"Shishi has Amli?! Oh no...!"

Milo helped Bisco to his feet and rubbed his back as he coughed. Suddenly, Satahabaki strode up to them.

"I see," he said. "So Shishi has taken the Kusabira high priestess."

"Yeah. Damn Shishi. She's— Wait! What the hell are you doin' here?!"

"It's okay, Bisco! We removed the brainwashing! He's back to himself again!"

"Say what?! I'm even *more* scared of him now!!"

"Worry not!" came Satahabaki's booming voice. "The situation has progressed far beyond the law. I cannot hold you responsible for anything that has happened here."

Satahabaki folded his massive arms and seated himself down where he stood. Chaika took a seat next to him, scowling at the Iron Judge with suspicion.

"I fear the fate of the nation is still at stake," Satahabaki continued. "You may have felled that tower, Akaboshi, but Shishi possesses a power a hundred times stronger."

"What? Whaddaya mean by that?!"

"Before my treatment by Dr. Nekoyanagi and the Ghost Hail girl, I was linked to the camellia. I witnessed Shishi's thoughts."

Everyone leaned in close to listen to Satahabaki's unusually quiet words.

"Just before the connection was severed, I felt a mighty torrent of Rust energy flowing into Shishi. I can only assume that the mantra user, Amli, fell into Shishi's hands, and Shishi extracted the Rust energy from her."

"Wh-what?!" Milo and Bisco both moved closer, pressing Satahabaki for an explanation. "You mean to say Shishi absorbed Amli's power?!"

"The old king Housen used to say something very similar. The flower could only achieve ultimate evolution by appropriating the power of the Rust. Of course, many flowers would simply perish when exposed to the Rust, but perhaps Shishi could—"

A rumble shook the cave, cutting off what Satahabaki was going to say.

"Mrgh! Could it be...?" he said, grinding his enormous teeth and uncrossing his legs. "It has begun. Shishi is advancing to the next step of the Benibishi evolution. She is becoming a god!"

"You jinxed it, you great oaf! You shoulda kept your big mouth shut!"

"It can't be… We worked so hard to save Hokkaido! Isn't there any way to stop her?"

"There is!" Satahabaki replied. "We must defeat her physical form before the sky flower manifests." He got to his feet and stared at the cavern roof, from which debris was already beginning to fall. "However, if Shishi has already obtained the power of the high priestess, then neither Rust nor mushroom will be enough to harm her. Even with all our forces combined, we stand little chance."

"Well, there's only one way to find out!" said Bisco. He readied a wire arrow and was about to fire it into the roof of the cave when Chaika stopped him.

"Wait…! Hold on a second, Bisco!"

"What good's waitin' around gonna do us?! You heard the big guy— Shishi's gonna eat Hokkaido for breakfast unless we do something!"

"Courage without direction is foolishness! Listen to me! We still have a trick up our sleeve!"

"What…?!"

"This!"

Chaika closed her eyes for a moment and prayed, and white spores gathered in her hands, sparkling with a silver light. It was the light of the Ghost Hail, the hidden mushroom of Hokkaido.

"Th-that's amazin', Chaika! I didn't know you could do that as well!"

"Do my eyes deceive me?!" Satahabaki exclaimed. "It is the light of the Ghost Hail, the only mushroom pure enough to combat the Florescence!"

"But, Chaika," said Milo, "surely you don't mean you're going to fight Shishi alone! It's too dangerous!"

Chaika broke her focus and gently shook her head, allowing her golden hair to sway from side to side.

"Of course not! The Ghost Hail is far too frail. Not even Father could purify that…creature."

"Then why the hell did you show it to us?!" yelled Bisco. "You tryin' to get our hopes up?!"

"Shush! What I mean is, every oracle so far has been too weak, even my father. But what if the power dwelled within another, one with the strength and courage to supplement the mushroom's gentle grace?"

Bisco stopped and shared a glance with Milo. Then the two of them looked to Chaika again.

"There is a legend handed down among the *sporko* of Hokkaido," she said. "It says that when an oracle possesses both the powers of sun and moon—of the Heaven's Light and the Ghost Hail—they will be able to ward away any calamity."

"You puttin' stock in fairy tales now? We're tryin' to be serious here!"

"I *am* serious! I'm super-duper, ultra-mega serious!! Now shut up and listen!!"

Chaika turned and looked Bisco dead in the eye as she explained.

"Bisco Akaboshi. I shall appoint you to be Hokkaido's newest oracle. By the power vested in me, I shall grant you Hokkaido's power...the power of the Ghost Hail."

"Wh-whaaat?!"

"Give Bisco...Hokkaido's power?! You can *do* that?!"

Bisco's and Milo's incredulous shrieks echoed throughout the cavern. Chaika seemed to be getting tired of the way the boys lost their minds at each and every revelation, and she quickly moved on to her next statement.

"We must hurry, or that accursed creature of flowers will spell our doom. We need to get to the ritual chamber as quickly as possible!"

"B-but! I ain't from your tribe, kid! You sure your land's god is gonna talk to me just like that?!"

"He'll have to! Beggars can't be choosers! Anyway, why are you so stubborn? You're supposed to be the rule-breaker here, not me!"

"O-okay, okay! So where is this ritual chamber of yours?!"

"In the *chiltika*—the womb! That's where we need to go!"

""Th-the womb?!""

The two boys cried out in surprise once again. Chaika tried her best to calm them down.

"Bisco I can understand, but why do you sound so surprised, Milo?! You know Hokkaido is a living creature! What's so strange about a living creature having a womb?"

"Y-yeah, I guess so, but why...?"

"Well, to make babies, of course. Furthermore, Hokkaido is currently with child— Well, I say child, but it's actually a bunch of Ghost Hail spores that Hokkaido will use to create a new island in the seas of Japan."

Bisco and Milo could barely keep up with the astonishing information coming from Chaika's mouth. However, they quickly understood that they couldn't waste time expressing their surprise at every little thing.

"O-okay, so...we need to go to the womb so I can ask to borrow the Ghost Hail's power, right?"

"Not borrow. You will become it. We oracles are part of the sporestream, and all new mediums must be reborn as a child of Hokkaido."

"The *what* stream?" Bisco yelled. "It just keeps comin'! You sure you're not just makin' all this up?!"

"There is no time for questions!" Chaika replied. "We must hurry!"

But just as Chaika finished speaking, there was an enormous *Crash!* from the roof, and a huge length of ivy stuck into the cavern floor like a spear. Bisco and company managed to jump aside, when out of the smoke came a second and third spike, which Satahabaki held at bay with his massive arms.

"Nrgh. So Shishi has begun her assault. It is only a matter of time before she finds this womb you are after. I shall hold her off. Go! Chaika of the Ghost Hail!"

"You can't hope to fight her off by yourself!" said Bisco, drawing his knife. "We'll settle things here together, *then* go!"

"Bisco!"

Milo suddenly threw his arms around his partner. With eyes of starlight-blue, he stared straight into Bisco's twin jades.

"I'll help distract Shishi. You and Chaika need to reach the womb.

But Shishi will stop at nothing to prevent that. If she shows up, Bisco, you need to protect Chaika. You're the only one light and nimble enough to do that."

"…Milo…!!"

Bisco found his usual complaints were swallowed up by his partner's starlike eyes. He stared into them wordlessly.

"…You sure you can do it, Milo? You're not gonna be dead by the time I get back, are you?"

"Who knows? Maybe if my partner gave me some encouragement…"

"Ha!"

Bisco hopped up to his partner's height and, taking the boy quite by surprise, wrapped his arms around Milo's neck, holding his whole head to his own chest.

"You are the shining star that lights up the darkest night, Milo. You're strong. No matter who or what stands in your way, you'll find a way through…"

"…B…Bisco…!"

"…"

"…"

"You understand?"

"…"

"Hey! Do you understand?!"

"Y-yes!!"

"All right!"

Then Bisco turned and sprinted over to Chaika, who for some reason had turned a rosy shade of red.

"Sorry for the holdup, Chaika. Let's get moving!"

"…I can't even be mad at that," said Chaika, turning away, before grinning and snatching Bisco's hand. "I'll show you to the womb! In return, you have to keep me safe until we get there. Deal?"

"You don't even have to ask!"

Milo watched the pair go and stood there with a blank look on his face. It was only when Satahabaki intercepted Shishi's vine attack with his stout arms that Milo snapped back to reality.

"Do not let down your guard, Nekoyanagi! Remember they are counting on us to hold off Shishi!"

"Ah...sorry. It's just... It's been a while, that's all."

"I cannot say I understand that which you are referring to," said Satahabaki, snapping the vines on his knee, "but the threat Shishi poses to humanity is incalculable. You will need to keep a stout heart to face her! Do you really think you're in the correct frame of mind?!"

"Yes!"

"What?!"

Satahabaki was taken aback by the directness of Milo's response and the beaming smile upon his face.

"I'm the shining star that lights up the darkest night. No matter who or what stands in my way, I'll find a way through. It doesn't matter how strong Shishi is. In the end, the last man standing will be me!"

"Wh-what a preposterous claim! And where, pray tell, is the evidence to support it?"

"Oh, I don't have any evidence," Milo replied, grinning, as he drew the bow from his back. "But Bisco said it, so it must be true."

"I fear in court, that would be inadmissible— Hooh?!"

Gaboom!

Before Satahabaki could protest further, Milo fired a King Trumpet at their feet, launching the two of them high into the air.

"Your Honor!" he shouted. "I'm taking us over ground! Hold on to me!"

"Next time, instruct me before you take action, NEKOYANAGIII!"

As Satahabaki floundered for anything to hold on to, Milo took his hand and pointed his cube at the fast-approaching ceiling.

"Won/shad/velow/snew!"

The roof of the cave opened up in response to Milo's mantra, allowing sunlight into the cavern and forming a hole that the two passed through on their way to stop the newly ascended Shishi once and for all.

"Oooaaaahhh?!"

The King Trumpet catapulted Satahabaki out of the underground cavern and sent him rolling across the snow-covered surface, coming to a stop only after amassing a sizable ball around him like a snowman.

"...Truly, the inner workings of these Mushroom Keepers' minds are an enigma..."

Satahabaki rose to his feet and brushed the snow off himself. Milo appeared, hopping nimbly across the snowfield and up onto Satahabaki's shoulder.

"Wow...look at that!" said Milo, marveling at the blinding light that shone down from above. "I never expected to see something like this...!"

"Indeed. There is little we can do now..."

A single, enormous plant dominated the sky. But miraculously, there was no stalk or roots whatsoever, just a flower, hovering in midair. What kept the plant afloat seemed to be the many petals around the rim of the flower, shimmering with warm colors. Each time it flapped these winglike appendages, a gust of pollen blew across the land.

"This form...! Shishi has ascended to the ultimate level of Benibishi evolution! Her Florescence has transcended mortal nature and made her a god!"

"Shishi?! You're saying that flower is Shishi?!"

"Behold!"

Satahabaki pointed a thick finger toward the center of the petaled wheel. If Milo strained his eyes, he could just make out an enclosure of some kind containing a shining humanoid form.

"Ahh! Shishi!"

Shishi's cold gaze was recognizable even at a distance, and unreadable as ever. Squinting further, Milo also noticed a second figure lying at Shishi's feet.

"That's Amli! Shishi has her! We need to do something!"

"But the question is how... Mrgh! Nekoyanagi! Watch out!"

Suddenly, dozens of vine spears the size of towers shot out from the sepals of the sky flower and stuck into the ground, causing Milo and Satahabaki to jump aside at the last moment. Coughing as the smoke cleared and gazing around at the destruction, Satahabaki grunted in surprise.

"What power. How can we hope to stand against it?!"

The spears spread out from the flower in a fan shape, spaced at regular intervals and all piercing Hokkaido's back. Soon they began glowing with a soft light and pulsating as though pumping something up their length.

"What's happening, Your Honor?! The vines have lit up!"

"Shishi has begun absorbing Hokkaido's essence," Satahabaki replied. "Not content with merely usurping the power of the Ghost Hail, she has turned to drawing every last drop of life force from this isle to fuel the flowering."

"The...flowering?"

"Once the sky flower has absorbed enough nutrition, it shall commence the flowering," Satahabaki explained, as he watched the plant drain the land dry. "It will scatter the pollen all throughout the nation, and all humans—nay, all living things—will become its mind-slaves. Perhaps this has always been young Shishi's scheme from the very beginning."

"We need to stop her!" Milo yelled, breaking into a run. "What are we standing around for?!"

"She cannot BE stopped!" Satahabaki called after him, causing Milo to stop and turn around. "She is no longer even Benibishi; she is a god! What human can fell a god? It is impossible!"

"You know, Your Honor, for a judge, you're awfully indecisive!" said Milo, hopping atop one of the ivy spears and flashing Satahabaki a grin. "There's no such thing as impossible; Bisco has proved that to me time and time again! Whenever I think he's reached the limit of human capability, he powers on through it. That's how I know...we can do this!"

"Nekoyanagi...!"

Then Milo set off running, up the vine that led to the sky flower, leaving Satahabaki to ponder his words. He turned them over in his head, contemplating their meaning, before finally slapping himself in the face with the massive iron weights he called hands.

"Khaaaah!" he screamed, powering himself up with a yell. "Bravo, Nekoyanagi! Nine-Tenths Bloom! I, too, shall stake my life on your admirable creed!"

He hopped up on the vine, nearly crushing it beneath his weight, and began jogging after Milo, heading for the center of the flower and the Benibishi god who dwelled there.

...

...
My path...
...I have stained my path in blood.
But still.
If my life can buy a future for my people...
Then all is well.
All is...
...
...Hmm?
I feel...strange. What has become of me?
Shishi's eyes flickered open, as if rousing from a dream, and she looked down at herself.

"...Wh-what's happening?!!"

She had become a giant flower, hovering above Hokkaido, using her petals to stay afloat while scattering pollen into the air. The ivy spears that extended from her body appeared to have a mind of their own, mercilessly draining the life from the land below while Shishi could do nothing but watch powerlessly.

"Wh-what's happening…? What's going on?!"

"Hee-hee-hee-hee…"

She heard the voice of the camellia, echoing in her mind.

"A most pleasant view, don't you think? We have conquered the Rust, you and I, and achieved the final step of our evolution. You are now a god. A plant god absorbing all life from this worthless earth."

"A…god?!"

Shishi was struck speechless by what she heard. The giant vines shot out against her will, plucking the fearful Benibishi soldiers from the ground and dragging them to the flower's center.

"Wh…what?! Those are our people! Let them go!"

"Why, Shishi? All life should be put to use powering our Florescence. Isn't that what you want?"

"I… No! I never wanted…!"

Crack-crack-crack!!

The next moment, Shishi felt warm blood flowing over her body through the flower. Then she heard the screams. The screams of the people she had sworn to protect.

"Gwaaah! Graaaaagh!!"

"Please, Shishi! Our king, pleeease!"

"Spare my child, I beg you…! Ghhh!"

"Cough! Cough…! Gbluh…"

"Waaaaagh!! Aaaaagh??!!"

A morbid chill ran through Shishi's body. It was the taste of death, of her comrades being turned into nutrients and becoming part of her. Shishi screamed until her throat felt like it would tear apart.

"Waaaaaaghhh!!! Stop it!! Make it STOPPP!!"

Shishi, held in place by the winglike petals sprouting from her back, jerked and wailed as the power flowed into her, before finally vomiting up the contents of her stomach.

"*Ho-ho-ho-ho. There is no need to be upset. What greater fate could there be for your people than to become your strength? The weak must die and become food for the strong; it is the natural way.*"

"I…I never wished for this. The only reason I sought power…was to protect my people! Not to destroy them! I wished to grant them freedom! Not…this!!"

"*…*"

"If you really *are* my flower, then you must listen to my commands. Put them back now! And if you cannot, then kill me!"

All of a sudden, the voice took on a icy, affectionless tone.

"*…It seems you misunderstand your place in all this, Shishi.*

"*I am the camellia. The subjugation. I am not yours, Shishi. You are mine. You are my soil. My plant pot. The executor of my will. That is all there is to it.*"

Shishi felt another chill run down her spine. The camellia chuckled in her mind.

"*In fact, all the Benibishi are nothing but our vessels. Pots to nurture us until we are strong enough to manifest by ourselves. For that to happen, we require blood. We require struggle. And so we needed a new king who would bring these resources to the nation.*"

"Flowers…require blood? A new king? Wh-what are you talking about?!"

"*We needed you, Shishi. We needed you to take us down the blood-drenched path! And we worked hard to ensure that you were in a position to do so…*"

The coldhearted whispers of the camellia caused Shishi to break out in a cold sweat.

"*We may exist together, two minds in one body, but the distinction between us is not easily drawn. Which of us was it, I wonder, who wished to sit upon the throne? Which of us sought a man's strength? And which of us sliced off our beloved father's head?*"

* * *

"Where do you end, and I begin?"

"Wah…aah…! Aaaaaghhh!"

Shishi turned a ghastly shade and emitted a half-crazed scream.

"Lies! You lie, flower! I am…! I am…!"

"Ho-ho-ho. Don't struggle. You mustn't damage the flowers."

"No! No! You're not the boss of me! *I'm* the master of my own fate! *I* control my own life! It's all me! Me! Me! Meeee!!"

"Ho-ho-ho-ho-ho… Now the time for talk is over. Taste it. Fresh life, sweet and tantalizing as nectar…"

Crack-crack-crack!!

"Nooo!! Not this… Please… They're dying…dying inside me!! Make it stop! Make it stoppp!!"

"They are happy. You exist wholly to feed us. To help us grow. Together, we shall flourish and create a kingdom to last for a thousand years. One ruled by us, the flowers, and you, our loyal mulch.

"Ho.

"Ho-ho-ho.

"Ho-ho-ho-ho-ho-ho-ho-ho-ho-ho-ho…"

The ringing laugh of the camellia echoed in Shishi's mind. Again and again, she tried to bite off her tongue and choke on the blood, but her detached body part only grew back, and the blood poured from her mouth like a waterfall.

She wept, and tears of blood streamed from her eyes. She felt the pain of all she had consumed, Benibishi and Mushroom Keepers alike, pressing on her mind, suffocating her with despair, and in her helplessness, she cried out the only name she could.

Brother…

Broth…er…

Then, in her mind, she saw him, at the center of the dazzling flower. It was only a vague image, but there was no mistake. Her long eyelashes fluttered, scattering the pollen that had built up on them.

"It is time to sleep, Shishi. Leave everything to me. Ho-ho. Ho-ho-ho-ho…"

Shishi felt a wave of tiredness overcome her. She was to wait, sleeping, like a bud, devouring her countrymen, all to become food for the flower. She couldn't bear such a thought. She began panting heavily, but she could not fight it. The drowsiness hit her, and she gently closed her eyes…

"…shi…"

…Mmm?

"Shishi!"

A familiar voice, calling her name. She opened her eyes to gaze at its bearer.

"Mi…lo…… Help me…… Help me, Milo!"

She stretched out her hand, but the sky flower denied her salvation. The petals closed around her, dragging her off, along with Amli, into the heart of the plant.

"Shishi!!"

Milo reached the end of the ivy pillar, but just as he reached out toward Shishi's glowing body, the flower pulled her back in, closing its petals protectively around her.

"Don't you…dare get in my way!"

He pulled his knife from his hip holster and tried to cut away the petals, but something sharp and shining parried his blade.

"Wh-what the…?!"

Milo had no words. What he saw was Shishi's weapon, the Lion's Crimson Sword. Dozens of them, growing out of the plant's core. All were wielded by twisted vines, which haphazardly slashed and jabbed at Milo.

Ka-ching! Ka-ching!

"Ggh… Grrgh?!"

Each swing was as powerful as Shishi herself, perhaps even more so, and Milo found himself on the back foot. Proficient though he was with short blades, he couldn't hope to defend against so many skilled foes at once.

"Gh…ahh!"

At last, one of the blades knocked Milo's dagger up into the air, creating an opening into which the other blades converged to strike a killing blow…

Oh no!

"Nrrrrrghhh!!"

At the very last moment, Satahabaki landed before Milo, receiving each and every merciless blow on his hardened armor of muscle.

"Your Honor!" Milo yelled.

"There is nothing more to do here. Let us retreat for now, Nekoyanagi!"

Satahabaki then took Milo and launched himself off the ivy pillar toward the ground below, while the sky flower sought to block his escape. Little flowers on the ends of the vines fired a stream of seeds at him, which struck the ground he left behind, causing colorful flowers to sprout.

Satahabaki hit the earth and swiftly moved to avoid the machine-gun seeds, sliding into the shelter of a nearby cave, where he put Milo down at last.

"Thank you, Your Honor. You saved me… Ah, you've been hit! Let me take a look!"

"I'm afraid we cannot afford to waste any time," said Satahabaki, tearing the flowers off his body and casting a solemn gaze back at the sky flower. "We can only pray that Akaboshi and the girl are successful. We cannot hold out for a minute longer."

"If only it wasn't flying," Milo pondered. "Then it would be way easier to get to. Or if we had wings…"

Suddenly, he spotted an orange streak of light, high up in the sky. A thin, wispy cloud marked its trail, like an airplane, and from its direction it appeared to be moving directly toward the sky flower.

"What is that…a shooting star?"

"This is no time for stargazing, Nekoyanagi! The fate of the world is at stake!"

"I'm not! Look! Look at that!!"

The object passed into Hokkaido airspace and raised a gleaming orange claw that glinted in the sunlight.

Slash!

With a single swipe, it severed one of the thick ivy towers rooting the flower to the ground. But it didn't stop there...

Slash! Slash! Slash!

It spun like a top, slicing another, and another, and another.

"Actagawa!! It's Actagawa!!"

There was no mistaking the silhouette of the sky flower's assailant; it was none other than that of the boys' staunch and stalwart steelcrab steed, Actagawa. As for how he crossed the sea, it seemed the jetpacks attached to his back and several of his legs were responsible. Even now, he put them to use, dancing through the air like a maverick fighter pilot.

And when Milo saw who was in the saddle, he did a double take, for it was none other than the jellyfish girl grifter, Tirol Ochagama, clutching to Actagawa's reins for dear life!

"How's that, ya oversized beanstalk?! My new-and-improved jet-powered Actagawa's gonna cut ya down to size!"

"T-Tirol?!"

"Milo!! Why didn't ya tell me you were here?! Get up here and take over! I can't...hold on much longer!!"

"Tirol! You came to save us!"

"I wouldn't have bothered if I knew this thing was waitin' for me!!"

Actagawa sliced at the ivy roots, while the enormous flower attempted to knock him out of the air with its vines. Each time the crab swung his trusty greatclaw, Tirol leaped in the seat, emitting wild and terrified yelps of all pitches and tones.

"Tirol!"

"Nekoyanagi," said Satahabaki, guessing at Milo's aim. "You wish to be taken upon that giant crab, is that correct?"

"Please!"

Satahabaki lifted the relatively light boy off the ground. Then he swung his massive arm, launching Milo high into the air.

"Ngyaaaaahhh!! I can't hold on! I'm gonna fall! Aaaaaghhh!!"

Tirol's grip weakened and weakened, until finally she was thrown from the reins and into Milo's arms. Milo continued to soar through the sky, landing back in the beast's saddle.

"That was close!" he said. "Are you okay, Tirol?"

"This big jerk doesn't listen to a word I say! An' after all the work I put into upgradin' him, too… He oughtta be grateful!"

"It's okay! The Mushroom Keepers are here! Leave Actagawa to me!"

Milo swiftly installed Tirol in the passenger seat and picked up the reins. Sensing his master's presence in the saddle, Actagawa prepared to show off his full potential, and his greatclaw glinted in the light.

"Now it's time to strike back! Come on, Actagawa! We gotta buy time until Bisco gets back!"

"H-hold on, doctor boy… I think I'm gonna hork…"

"It's okay! I won't look!"

"That ain't the problem! I mean…ugh… Bleeegh…"

Milo drew his bow and pointed it at the sky flower, which seemed to be growing brighter by the second. Actagawa sensed his urgency and reignited his jetpacks, taking off once more toward their flowery foe.

Thud!

"Eek!"

"Gugh!"

"Ow...! Wait, I think we lost them! I don't see those vines anymore..."

"Okay, great, just get off me! You're crushin' me!!"

After leaving the Ghost Hail Node, Bisco and Chaika had been dashing through the maze of passageways that made up Hokkaido's innards. Along the way, the vines of the sky flower attempted to pursue them, but thanks to Chaika's quick-wittedness and knowledge regarding the lay of the land, the two managed to dive down a long passage and secure their safety. At the foot of this passage, however, Bisco was met with the hard meat floor, while Chaika received a relatively softer landing atop him.

"Oh, I'm sorry...! Wait, did you just call me fat? It's my clothes that are so heavy, you know, not me!"

"I wasn't callin' you anythin'! I just wanted you to get the hell off!" Bisco yelled, rubbing his back, when suddenly he felt a cool chill that seemed to cloak the entire floor of the cavern. It was strange, especially when considering the uncomfortable warmth of the passages they had just been lost in.

"What the hell...? Spores?"

"They are immature Ghost Hail spores. Look, aren't they beautiful?"

The source of the cold was a thick cloud of white spores that clung to the ground like a layer of mist and came up to about waist height.

"When Hokkaido is about to give birth, half of the spores generated in the Ghost Hail Node make their way here," Chaika explained.

"I can feel some kinda wind blowin' this way."

"Yes. We are almost at the womb. Stay close to me, Bisco. You mustn't anger the unborn child, whatever you do."

How am I supposed to know what'll anger it??

Bisco accepted Chaika's hand, muttering under his breath, and she led Bisco into the direction of the wind, forging a path through the mist of spores.

Then, eventually, the pair reached the core of that holiest of organs—a huge, dome-shaped space containing a large round body, shining like the moon itself. When Bisco saw the mysterious orb, he shouted in disbelief.

"Wh-what...? What the hell is that?!"

The orb was roughly spherical, but it did not stay the same shape and constantly shifted, as if alive. Sounds of *Gaboom! Gaboom!* could be heard as mushrooms sprouted up all across the surface, but the roiling mass of the orb took each and every one of them and absorbed them into itself.

"We have arrived," said Chaika. "This is Hokkaido's child."

"The hell?! What's with all the mushrooms that keep growin' on it?"

"That is the raging stream of life. Like a baby kicking at its mother's belly. It's still spherical; that means the child has not yet decided what shape it wants to be."

Bisco gulped. Pious to a fault at the best of times, Bisco was left so awestruck in this solemn environment that he dared not speak a word.

"...So how am I supposed to become the next oracle or whatever?!" he asked at last.

"Be patient! I will try to commune with it now."

Chaika took a deep breath and raised both arms toward the moon-like orb. As she focused, the mist of Ghost Hail spores began gathering around her, causing her body to glow with a dazzling white light.

"...I beg of you. Open your heart...!"

Chaika summoned all her spiritual energy, entreating herself to become one with the orb. The orb, however, continued roiling and gabooming, roiling and gabooming, with no apparent change. Bisco watched as Chaika's expression turned pained and drops of sweat began to form on her forehead.

"H-hey, Chaika, you okay?! Is it listenin' to you or what?"

"It's no use. It is too angry. It can feel its mother's pain, and it is afraid. It needs to be calm before it will grant you the power of the Ghost Hail!"

Bisco, meanwhile, was growing more and more impatient. His partners were in danger, and if Shishi found this place, it could all be over. And so, unable to take any more waiting, he opened his mouth and shouted at the glowing orb.

"Hey! Snowball! You got guests down here! Ain't you gonna serve us tea or nothin'?!"

"B-Bisco?! Wh...wh...what are you thinking?!"

But just then, something very strange happened. Almost as if it had heard Bisco's words, the orb slowly stopped roiling, and the mushrooms stopped growing.

""Wh...whaaa—?!""

Bisco froze in shock. He had just been voicing his frustration; he didn't expect the thing to actually *listen* to him. The orb, meanwhile, only hung in the air as if awaiting Bisco's next words, the gentle breeze sending ripples across its surface.

"Th-the thing actually heard me?! That can't be right..."

"I think it did! Try saying something else!"

"Like what?! Uhhh..."

As he was pondering precisely what to say, Bisco felt a very odd sensation, as if the orb were staring at him, though of course it possessed no eyes or features whatsoever. Deep within his own body, Bisco felt a growing heat, and soon a golden mushroom popped out of his shoulder.

"Eeek!" yelled Chaika. "What on earth is that?!"

"It's the Rust-Eater," Bisco replied. "Somethin' about it's reactin' to the big guy!"

Bisco stared in shock as the orb responded. It rumbled, and...

Ga-boom!!

...a single large Ghost Hail mushroom sprouted out of it, as if copying Bisco. It felt like the orb was trying to express joy in some manner, as if...

The mushrooms are callin' to each other!

Though they had no proof or explanation, both Bisco and Chaika felt it in their bones. It was a primal, almost divine sensation, like witnessing some long-kept secret of the universe.

"...Crap! Can't let the euphoria distract me! I got a job to do!"

Bisco tore the Rust-Eater cap from his body and, though unsure of precisely how he was communicating with the orb, tried shouting out to it once more.

"Hey, Son of Hokkaido! I know you can feel it! Shishi's vines are suckin' your old lady dry! If we don't do somethin' about it, both you and her are gonna die!"

The orb remained silent, floating gently.

"You gotta give me your power, kid! If there's a price to pay, just tell me. You can take my arm or my eye or whatever you want, just let us get it done! My partner's in danger!"

The orb remained silent, floating gently.

"C'mon, dude! Say somethin', at least!"

Suddenly, the surface of the orb opened wide, revealing a hole into what looked like a boundless void. The sight shocked Bisco into silence, and then...

"ROOOOOAAAA"

"Whoooa?! Waaaaah! Waaaaaaaaahhh?!!!"

"Eeeeeeek!! Wa-waaaaaahh!!"

...an enormous gust of wind, like a hurricane, swept Bisco and Chaika off their feet and into the air. Bisco grabbed on to a ledge jutting out of the ground and hung there for dear life, his cloak flapping madly behind him.

"G…grrrr! Is he tryin' to eat us?!"

"No, Bisco!" cried Chaika, her arms wrapped around his neck. "He has accepted the Heaven's Light spores! You must let go!"

"You let go! If you're so sure, then you go first!"

"N-no! Not by myself! It's too scary!"

The gale-force winds picked up the layer of spores, causing a blizzard of white that seemed to grow stronger by the second. Soon enough, Bisco could hold on no longer, and both he and Chaika were sucked into the hole at the center of the great white orb.

""Waaaaaahhh!""

Plop!

Gulp.

The orb completely swallowed the two children, and immediately afterward, several Ghost Hail mushrooms sprouted across its surface. With the two noisy intruders gone, the womb fell silent once more…

…save for the orb, throbbing and quivering ever so slightly, as though preparing for something. It glowed with a silver light, and glittering spores danced in the air around it.

"A name?

"Of course I've chosen one.

"His father said to ask Enbiten to name him…

"…but I don't think a kid's name is the business of the gods."

"He'll be Bisco.

"Strong and sweet, to help kids grow up big and strong…"

"It's not a joke. I'm serious.

"Strength brings life, but…

"Strength alone brings only loneliness.

"Life needs a little sweetness, isn't that right?

"Bisco.

"My darling Bisco…"

It was a strange sensation, like grasping at mist. Something warm and enveloping, safe and secure…

Like a dream.

…

…Was that…my…?

* * *

The memories of the womb and the soothing ocean made Bisco want to stay there forever, drifting endlessly in the silence.

"...sco..."

Then, ever so gently...

"...Bisco!"

...from a place so far away, he heard a girl calling his name.

"Bisco! Wake up! Please!"

"...Whoaaaa?!"

Using the last of his mental reserves, Bisco tore himself away from the comforting illusion.

"Oh, phew! You're awake!"

"Chaika? That you? Where the hell are you?!"

Bisco opened his eyes, but all he could see was white. He was suspended in a milky sea of spores, unsure which way was up. However, for some reason, he didn't feel afraid at all. Instead, there was an enveloping warmth that seemed like it would wash all his troubles away.

"You're doing good, Bisco! You've passed the trial and gained the approval of Hokkaido's child!"

"Chaika? I can hear you, but I can't see you! Where's your voice comin' from?!"

"Don't worry about me! Hokkaido's child spat me back out after delivering you to him! I can see you; I'm outside, back in the womb!"

Chaika seemed excited to be witnessing the process in person, but her words did little to enlighten Bisco, stuck at the center of it all.

"We just have to wait and see what the child will do next," she said. "Just...stay there, and don't try to fight it."

"Well, how long do I have to wait? I've been floatin' here for—"

Suddenly, in front of Bisco's eyes, the milky clouds parted and a large silver figure came forth.

"Whaaagh?!"

The shock sent him reeling, and Bisco somersaulted in place a few times before flapping his arms to regain his balance and taking another look at the strange object.

"It…it's…"

As more of the white spores parted, Bisco began to see its true form.

"…the child…?!"

"That's the fetus itself," Chaika explained. "It has taken human form to speak with you."

The fetus drifted in the sea of white spores. It pulsated like a beating heart. Gently, yet Bisco could feel it at a distance. For a while, Bisco could do nothing but silently gaze upon the magnificent sight.

"It's amazing," Chaika whispered. "Bisco, look, it's moving!"

The giant silver fetus lifted one of its arms from across its chest and held it toward Bisco, palm outstretched. Bisco wasn't sure how to react, but the hand looked so inviting, he swam through the sea of spores to approach, paddling closer bit by bit.

"Now, Bisco, give him your hand."

"My hand?"

"He is granting you the Hand of the Ghost Hail! Place your palm to his!"

Facing down the enormous palm, Bisco looked at his own and hesitated. He gazed up into the child's eyes, pure and untainted. He felt the spores calling to each other, pulling them together, and Bisco obeyed. He placed his hand to the fetus's.

Just then, Bisco felt a searing pain in his mind, and ancient memories that were not his own flashed through his brain like a movie on fast-forward.

"Wh…whooooaaa?!"

The memories of the Ghost Hail mixed with those of the Rust-Eater lying dormant in Bisco's blood, and set off a chain reaction. The sun and the moon, together at last, unlocked a power of life so ancient it surpassed all human reckoning.

I'm…I'm turning back to normal!

As the power flowed into Bisco, he felt his limbs stretch. His arms, his legs, his torso, all reverted to their former size, and Shishi's curse was broken.

This is…the Ghost Hail. The power of the Rust-Eater and the Ghost Hail, working together!!

No sooner did Bisco realize he was fully back to normal again than a powerful current of energy swept through his body, rendering him unconscious. The twin powers of the Rust-Eater, awakening within his own body, and the Ghost Hail, flowing into him from outside, carried his mind away into sweet oblivion.

ᘛᗑᎾ᎐ **15**

"Gyaaaaah!! Ohmygodwe'reallgonnadiiiiiie!!"

"Actagawa! On your right!"

A thick whip of vines lashed out, which Actagawa deflected with his mighty claw. He had grown strong indeed since his last fights, now able to parry such heavy blows with ease, but there was no ignoring the crab's woeful unsuitability for aerial combat. Each block sent him spiraling away, and he struggled to keep his thrusters under control.

"Aiiiiiiiiieee! Make it stop! I lost my lunch once, and I don't wanna hafta do it again!"

"There's nothing I can do, Tirol! You'll just have to get used to it!"

"How the frick am I supposed to do that?! We're gamblin' with our lives just by bein' here!"

Tirol's remodeled "Jet Actagawa" fought bravely, and Milo steered him through the air like an orange meteor, slicing all the vines connecting the sky flower to the ground.

However, in the end, there was very little a single steelcrab could do against a foe of this size. Whatever life force the flower managed to absorb, it immediately put to use making itself bigger, growing large enough to cast a shadow over the very mountains themselves. Plus, each time a root was severed, the plant simply regrew another, and there appeared to be no end to the battle in sight.

By now, Hokkaido's landscape was beginning to look very dreary.

The glittering snow had melted, and all around stood withered plants and trees, as if a drought had swept the land.

"Shishi's trying to drain all the life out of Hokkaido!!" Milo yelled.

"She's just growin' the arms back! Milo, you gotta do somethin'!"

"I know!! But we just need more time. Once that flower blooms, it'll spread its pollen all across Japan!"

"What are you gonna do with more time…? Oh yeah! Where's Akaboshi?! Why don't you and Akaboshi do that weird thing with the bow you always do?"

"We're waiting on him now! And it's not weird!"

"HO THEEERE! NEKOYANAGIII!"

Looking down, Milo spotted Satahabaki uprooting one of the vines with his bare hands. In a voice even louder than his usual bellow, he called up to Milo in the sky.

"Behold the sky flower!" he yelled. "Its yellow flowers turn crimson before our very eyes!"

"What happens when they change color completely?" Milo shouted back.

"Then the flower is ready to bloom! That is when it shall rain its pollen across all the land!"

"Wait, then that means we got no time!" shrieked Tirol, looking to the flower. "Oh, I got it. This is one'a them unwinnable fights, ain't it? Best just give up while we still got our skins, I say. C'mon, Milo, let's get outta here. Leave Japan to die and find some other land to peddle my wares."

"Bisco will come. I know he will. We need to buy him time."

"Err… Panda Boy? You listenin'?"

"We'll head to the heart of the flower! You with me, Tirol?"

"Does it sound like I am?! You been listenin' to a word I just said?!"

Milo gripped the reins with newfound courage, and Actagawa prepared to charge. The jet booster on his back fired full throttle, blasting the three of them off toward the flower's central part. The flower attempted to intercept, launching its massive vines at them, but Actagawa dodged and evaded every last one on his approach to the core.

"Won/shad/viviki/snew!"

Actagawa raised his claw, and Milo's cube began spinning around it, granting it an enormous casing of crystalline emerald.

"Open it up, Actagawa!!"

Smash!

Actagawa drove his emerald claw into the petals defending the flower's core, and though they were as hard as steel, they yielded to his attack, exposing the center to the daylight sun.

Inside, they saw...

"Shishi!!"

...the god of the Benibishi. Her entire naked body constantly glowed crimson, so strongly that Milo couldn't look directly at her. Yet still he drew his bow.

"...

"...Ho-ho-ho.

"I am surprised you made it here. Human perseverance never ceases to amaze."

Shishi smiled. Milo froze in astonishment. This was not the Shishi he knew. It was a deeper threat, more unknowable. One that simply adopted Shishi's form.

"...What are you?!"

"What's the matter? I thought you were going to shoot me."

"You're...you're the one who's been controlling Shishi!"

"I see. So you cannot bring yourself to kill your dear friend... Ho-ho-ho-ho..."

"Get out of Shishi! I command you! Leave her alone!"

Milo bit his lip in rage, drawing blood, and loosed his arrow at full power.

Pchew!

"Ho-ho. How futile. You would take arms against a god, and that is all you can do?"

The arrow stopped mid-flight, snatched by an ivy vine right in front of Shishi's eyes.

And then...

"…Milo. Please…"

…a faint trace of the real Shishi started to return.

"Stop…me. Milo… Brother… You have to kill me…!"

"Shishi!!"

"…Still resisting, are we? You bony child…"

The other Shishi clutched at her own breast, digging her sharp nails into the flesh, driving away the real one.

"Do not come back here, mulch. Know your place."

It's not Shishi fighting anymore! It's this evil power, whatever it is!

"Now come to me. Lion's Crimson Sword."

Shishi muttered softly, and the glowing ivy sword appeared in her hands. Only this was much larger than any Shishi had conjured before, reaching nearly ten meters in length.

"Jeepers creepers, Milo, that thing's gonna slice us in half!! You gotta get us outta here!!"

"Actagawa, block!!"

Tirol's voice brought Milo to his senses, and he quickly ordered Actagawa to cross his claws to defend against the blow. The sword hit him head-on, sending Actagawa spinning vertically through the air for about a hundred meters, colliding and bouncing off the snow-covered ground several times before finally coming to rest.

"U…urgh… Aah! Actagawa!"

When Milo recovered from their crash landing, he saw that the sword had left a slash mark right across the steelcrab's shell, and Actagawa was still in a daze from the sheer impact of the blow. Tirol had not fared much better; she appeared to have passed out at some point during the fall and lay unconscious in the passenger seat, very much not in a position to move.

Milo looked up to see Shishi glowing crimson, framed against the floating camellia. She held her sword up high, and the petals of the flower disassembled, forming a shell around her. Eventually, the entire sky flower took humanoid shape, mimicking Shishi's sword-raised pose.

And the sword in its hands was monstrously huge. With all the mass of the giant flower making up its form, it was large enough to split the whole island in two. Even Milo trembled at the sight. And to make matters even worse, the giant seemed poised to strike the exact point where Actagawa and Tirol lay.

"Won/shandereber…"

Gravely injured, Milo began chanting one last mantra, one on which he would stake his very life, to protect Hokkaido and all who stood upon it.

Bisco will… Bisco will defeat you. He'll save all of them…even Shishi!

The cube spun in his hand, and its emerald gleam reflected in Milo's starlight eyes. He did not fear death; he believed in the power of life.

So I have to make sure Bisco has something left to come back to. Hokkaido, Chaika, Tirol, and Actagawa! Even if I have to die to protect them!!

The giant of petals began to swing its leafy blade.

"Won/shandereber/shed/shed!!/shed!!/sn…!"

The cube gathered speed, like a typhoon of green, as the fearsome sword came down right upon Milo's head.

Just then…

Booooom!!

…a noise like cannon-fire erupted, and the entire island shook.

"Huh?!"

Milo's concentration broke, interrupting his mantra. He looked toward the source of the sound to see a human figure rising into the sky like a rocket, expelling a white wisp of smoke behind him as the wind coursed through his bright-red hair.

"…It's him!!"

The figure reached maximum velocity and flew into the sky above Hokkaido like a firework, colliding with the colossal sword of the sky flower.

Ka-booom!!

A shattering impact rang out, and Milo looked up to see that the figure had stopped the blade with his bare hand.

"You made yourself the size of a damn castle," he snapped, "and this is the best you can do?!"

The silver light dancing around this man-shaped object flared to life, and he clenched his other fist tightly. The white spores he ejected immediately gathered in his arm, turning it brilliant silver.

"You're gonna need to go bigger than that to beat me, Shishiiii!!"

The figure swung a silver haymaker into the sword, causing it to instantly burst with a *Poof!* into a snowfall of white petals. The figure then jumped away, hair and cloak fluttering in the wind.

"Milo!!" he yelled. "You all right down there?!"

"Barely! Where have you been?! I swear you always come at the last minute on purpose!"

"Bullshit! You should count yourself lucky I got here at all, the shit I've had to go through!"

The figure smiled, a roguish grin that bared his canines. He was, of course, Bisco Akaboshi, adult-sized once more, thanks to the power he received at the hands of Hokkaido's child.

"H-huh…? Wraaaagh! What the hell is that?!"

Tirol, roused from her slumber at last, immediately let out a crazed scream. She tried to run to no avail, then, remembering she was still strapped into the saddle, she hurriedly twisted around to unfasten it.

"Tirol!" said Milo. "It's okay—it's just Bisco!"

"I can see that, bamboo-brain! I'm talkin' about that! Up there!"

Milo finally noticed the dark shadow forming over him and looked up. When he did, he let out a squeal of fright. Bisco's attack had snapped Shishi's sword in two, but it seemed the pointed end was still in the process of becoming white petals, and right now the fragment was falling directly on top of them.

"What the frick are you gawkin' at, Milo?! Shoot it! Shoot it!"

"Biscooo! Down here!!"

Milo called up to his partner, still flying in the air. "Save us! We're going to be crushed!"

"Are you crazy?! He's too far! Akaboshi's never gonna get here in—!"

Yet Bisco, responding instantly to Milo's call, began performing a very strange movement, like running in midair…and somehow, white mushrooms appeared beneath his feet for him to push off of, leading him in a straight line down to Actagawa and the others. Then…

Fwooom!!

Once again, Bisco stopped the smoking fragment of Shishi's sword with a single hand. It was the same old Bisco, and yet in his new form he possessed an air so majestic, so divine, that even Milo could scarcely believe this was the same man he knew so well. The white spores emanated like a mist from his body, and across his exposed skin ran a strange, glowing, silver tattoo.

But when the man returned his gaze, Milo saw those eyes, filled with the same old jade light, and there was no doubt in his mind just who it really was.

"Looking cool, Bisco! Nice ink!"

"Milo, look after Tirol! I still got no idea what I'm capable of!"

"Okay…! Oh, she passed out again."

"Rrrrraagh!!"

Bisco took a deep breath, and his arm glowed silver again. Then he punched the sword's tip, and it exploded into a shower of white petals.

The sheer beauty stole Milo's breath a second time.

"The Ghost Hail…the mushroom of purity. The power to purify anything that has evolved into a twisted form… But this is far stronger than anything Chaika or the elder could use!"

"Seems to get on pretty well with the Rust-Eater," remarked Bisco, looking down at his gleaming arm. "It's like the two mushrooms are helpin' each other grow. The Ghost Hail's normally weak, but with the Rust-Eater's help, it can be just as strong."

Milo gazed in wonder and nodded, while Bisco took a curious look over his shoulder at the unconscious Tirol.

"So what's up with Jellyfish and Actagawa? They here to see the sights?"

"They came to save us, obviously! Anyway, that doesn't matter! Right now, we need to stop that thing before it flowers!"

"Sure. We just gotta do a little weedin', huh?"

"Bisco, get on!"

With Bisco's return, Milo was full of life and optimism again. He hopped into Actagawa's saddle and took the reins, while Bisco lowered the sleeping Tirol onto the ground. Then he climbed up into the passenger seat.

"You ready for this?!" Milo asked.

"You bet your ass. Time to give that student of mine a spankin'!"

Milo nodded and lashed the reins, and Actagawa reactivated his booster rockets, jetting into the sky.

"Wh-whoa?! What the hell?! Actagawa, when did you learn how to fly?!"

Actagawa, of course, did not respond or even pay too much heed to Bisco's words. He simply turned his rockets up to full power and headed back toward the giant floating flower, eager for a rematch.

"*That Nekoyanagi. Was he a friend of yours? Perhaps it was rash of me to kill him so quickly. What a waste of good looks. I should have kept him, like a daffodil in a vase of water, preserving his beauty until he withered away at last.*"

"…ll you…"

"*What was that? I cannot hear you unless you speak up.*"

"I said I'll kill you! I'll take you down to Hell with me if I must!"

"*Khee-hee-hee-hee-hee… It's good you still have so much energy, Shishi. However, it appears you still do not understand. This was your wish, Shishi. This is the ultimate power we both sought. Accept that fact, and join me. Drain it all to your heart's content. You can taste how good it feels, can't you, Shishi?*"

"Urgh… Agh… Grrrrrgh…"

"*Ho-ho-ho… Feel it… Another human, drained of life… Hmm?*"

Through the tears, Shishi could just make out the form of a captured Benibishi…and of the silver whirlwind who cut through the vine, saving their life. The severed ivy transformed into a shower of white petals that fell to the ground like hail, while the helpless Benibishi was caught upon the back of some large-shelled creature.

"*…So that crab still lives. But it was not that animal's claw that cut through my vine. What was it? This is troubling. Very troubling indeed.*"

"…"

Shishi felt the severed vines at the far reaches of her senses, and she whispered:

"...It was...Brother..."

"*What?*"

"Brother is coming...to defeat you."

After tasting only despair for so long, at long last, a faint trace of hope crept into Shishi's voice.

"B-Brother...will stop you! He won't let you have your way!"

"..."

"When I wounded him, you were unable to control his mind. His soul was too strong! The best you could do was turn him into a child!!"

"..."

"Well, Brother's arrows *are* his soul. Your precious Florescence will not protect you from them! Brother will slay us both, and your plans will— Gaaah! Aaaagh!"

"*Quiet, child. I cannot think with this racket.*"

The camellia clamped down on Shishi's soul, tucked deep away within the body it had dominated. It bit Shishi's lip hard, drawing blood.

But Shishi's soul was not gone. Far inside her prison, she repeated to herself...

...I never should have dreamed of you.

...And you never should have accepted me.

This is your fault.

And so, you should be ready to end it, with your own two hands...

That singular hope kept Shishi safe from the swirling despair, and she held it tightly, praying with all her heart that it would come to pass.

"Seven! Eight! Two more! That makes ten!"

Bisco swiped his shining silver left arm through the sky, leaving a shimmering trail that sliced the vines of the sky flower and reduced them to white petals. Seeing their shining savior rescue them from the vines, the Mushroom Keepers of Hokkaido—the *sporko*—cried out in praise.

"*Ouya!!* Behold, our god! The Claw of the Ghost Hail! He has descended to save us!"

"*Ouya! Ouya!* We *sporko* are blessed by heaven's protection!"

"It took him a while to show up, though."

"Quiet! I'm sure he was just busy!"

"Hah!" Bisco looked down at the Mushroom Keepers quickly gathering beneath him. "Quick to entreat your gods when it suits you, huh? Look at me, you dumbasses. It's me! Bisco Akaboshi!"

"Isn't that nice, Bisco?" Milo called over. "It seems wherever we go, people treat you like a god!"

"What's so good about that, huh…?! Anyway, was that the last one?"

"Yeah! Now all that's left is Amli and Shishi! Let's take care of them before the plant grows any more vines…! Actagawa! Watch out!"

Milo jerked on the reins, and Actagawa engaged his jet boosters, spiraling out of the way just as one enormous vine shot past him. His orange shell danced in the darkening sky over Hokkaido, as Bisco's silver streak followed him.

"The sky flower is a mixture of evolved plant and Rust power," Milo explained. "Neither Rust nor mushrooms will affect it. But if we can use the Ghost Hail to rewind its evolution…"

"Yeah. I figure one shot of a Ghost Hail arrow from the Mantra Bow should sort that thing out."

"Whaaat?!! You can do that?! Then let's do it right away!"

"Wait! It'll mean using my full power. If the arrow hits the flower dead-on, Shishi ain't gonna survive that."

"You want to save her, don't you, Bisco?"

"Yeah. I can hear her. She's calling my name."

Bisco watched the sky flower, gently floating in the twilight, and his jade-green eyes glimmered.

"We have to get Shishi outta there first. Then we can kick that flower's ass. Any ideas, Milo?"

"I can do that!" replied Milo without a hint of thought.

Bisco was taken aback by his sudden response. "Y-you can?! How?"

"It's easy. Shishi's right in there, where the petals have closed. You just have to open them and let me get inside; I'll take care of the rest."

"You wanna go in there...with Actagawa?!"

"No, I already tried that. It didn't work. There's not enough room in there for both of us."

"Hmm? Then what are you...? Oh. No, no, wait, wait, wait!!"

But Milo pulled on the reins, and Actagawa raised his greatclaw, pinching Bisco and Milo off his back. From the raw power exuded by Actagawa's stance, Bisco could easily tell what was about to happen, and he began struggling, kicking his arms and legs to no avail.

"Sit still, Bisco. It'll be fine. You're not kid-sized anymore."

"It don't matter what size I am!! The Tornado Throw ain't meant for humans!! Ain't you usin' this strategy a little too much?! Think about me for a change!!"

"What are you talking about, Bisco? You're a god! Come on, let's get moving before the plant regrows! Take it away, Actagawa!!"

"Nooo! Make it stop! I'm gonna be sick!"

Actagawa began rotating, slowly at first, but gradually increasing in speed, even activating his rocket boosters to achieve the maximum rotational velocity imaginable. In just five seconds he was a blur, a miniature golden sun hanging in the sky, throwing off sparks.

"Let's go, Actagawa!!"

Ka-bang!!

Actagawa released the two boys, catapulting them far into the distance like a cannon.

"Perfect aim! Come on, Bisco, get ready!"

"Shut the hell up! I've never met a doctor with such a blatant disregard for life!!"

Bisco and Milo soared through the air like fighter jets, leaving a pair of wispy trails behind them. They powered through layers of thick petals that the camellia used to protect itself, breaking open the path to the flower's core.

"Awooohhh!"

The final protective layer exploded into a shower of white petals, a hitherto unimaginable number that scattered into the air as the flower recoiled and cried out in pain.

Meanwhile, Actagawa, now bereft of both riders, hovered in the air for a moment, watching his masters disappear into the flower's core. Then, seeing the flower lift its vines in an attempt to reach in and expel the intruders, he jetted off toward them, his greatclaw at the ready.

"Whooooaaaa?!"

With the power of the Tornado Throw behind them, Bisco and Milo punched through layer after layer of Shishi's petal defenses, finally arriving at the core of the sky flower.

"We did it, Bisco! We got here so fast, the flower had no time to intercept!"

"*Cough! Cough!* I think Actagawa enjoyed that a little *too* much, if you ask me!"

Bisco steadily picked himself up off the floor, then jumped to his feet upon realizing where he was. Behind all the enemy defenses lay the flower's core, a spherical space at the center of the curling petals. However, it was hard to make out much, for the air was thick with pollen that glowed the same vivid red as the petals, and the only light was the setting sun filtering through the entrance that Bisco had torn open.

"Shishi's gotta be around here somewhere!" he said. "Shishiii! Where are you?!"

"*...Ho-ho-ho-ho...*"

Shishi?! No...it's something else!

"*Ho-ho-ho... Ho-ho-ho-ho-ho-ho.*"

The ominous laughter seemed to come from everywhere at once, echoing off the walls of the spherical chamber. Bisco and Milo went back-to-back and drew their daggers, the fire in their eyes beating back the terror that lurked in the darkness.

"*What a reckless move, to come here without any plan at all. I can see why Shishi is taken by your courage.*"

"You're the flower that's been controllin' her! Let her go! Why did you possess her?!"

"I am Shishi's flower, the camellia. I did not possess her; we have always been one."

The spores flowing out of Bisco illuminated the darkness. The flower, meanwhile, only laughed.

"Ho-ho. Rest assured, it was Shishi who wished for power. All I did was give her a little push on the back."

"You bastard…"

"I have you to thank, Bisco Akaboshi. Imagine my disappointment upon learning this frail little girl was to be my host. But you gave her a soul to look up to. You gave her a desire. You planted the darkness in her heart, and all I had to do was make it grow."

"Bisco!"

"I know!"

Bisco could feel himself moved to anger by the camellia's words, but Milo pinched him rather roughly on the back of the hand, breaking him out of it. Shaking off the pain, he readdressed the flower.

"Sorry, but we didn't come here to chat!" he yelled. "We came for Shishi. We know she's in there! If you ain't gonna hand her over, then we'll just have to do this the hard way!"

"Ho-ho-ho-ho-ho-ho! Big words for one so small. What can you do, so deep within the lion's den? You may as well have delivered yourself to me on a silver platter."

As the camellia finished speaking, the whole flower trembled, and several sword-wielding vines appeared. Bisco scowled as they sealed off the exit, while the camellia only chuckled.

"I have decided. Bisco, you shall be my next host. I cannot wait to taste a body so rich in spores…"

"Bisco," whispered Milo, peering at the swords all around. *"You see that? At the back of the room…there's a tunnel leading deeper in. The swords are all guarding it carefully, so I'm betting that's where Shishi is."*

"The old panda sense tinglin' again, huh? And what happens if you're wrong?"

"I don't know. I've never been wrong."

"Ha!"

"I'll distract the swords, Bisco."

"...!"

"Only one person can save Shishi now, and that's you."

Bisco turned and looked in shock at his partner, and there met his starlight gaze. His eyes were clear, like a polished window into the boy's very soul.

"Bisco," he said, staring back. "You're like a magnet for life. You can pull precious metal from the deepest, darkest swamp."

Milo's voice was hushed, but full of love. Love...and the acceptance of whatever came next.

"You need to take Shishi far away from this place...just like you did for me in Imihama that day."

Bisco pursed his lips, wanting more than anything else to object to his partner's plan, but knowing he could not. Instead, he snatched Milo and pulled him close, and Milo's sky-blue hair fluttered as he surrendered himself to the warm, comforting arms of his partner.

"...Fools. Do you forget where you are?"

Annoyed, the camellia raised its swords, their tips all focused on the two boys.

"Allow me to put an end to this farce. Lion's Crimson Sword!"

The vines thrust, and the blades shot toward Bisco and Milo...

"...I'm havin' a bondin' moment with my partner..."

""Don't interrupt!!""

The two boys leaped into the air like a whirlwind, delivering a powerful pair of spinning kicks that blew all the swords away. As soon as he landed, Milo began chanting a mantra and held out the emerald cube in his hand.

"Won/ul/viviki/snew!"

Usually, Milo's cube transformed itself into the weapon he desired, but this time it first flew away and passed through Bisco, turning bright-silver as it did so. After returning to Milo's hands, it took the form of a staff.

"Yay, Ghost Hail Staff!"

"What the heck? Milo, what is that thing?!"

"I just borrowed the power Hokkaido gave you; don't worry about it. Get going! You have to save Shishi, remember?"

"...All right!"

"Foul and insipid dregs of humanity. Know your place!"

Bisco set off running toward the tunnel, and a bunch of Shishi's swords rushed down on him.

"Rrrraaaahhh!"

Tapping into the staff techniques passed down by his sister, Milo swept all the swords away with one swing of his Ghost Hail Staff. The power of the cleansing mushroom turned them all into clouds of pure-white petals.

"Let me guess. You think Bisco's the main threat here? Everyone always does."

"You... Nekoyanagi!"

"Nobody ever takes me seriously. I'm fed up with it!!"

Milo shook his head in disbelief, swishing his sky-blue hair. He stood in front of the tunnel, blocking any attempt to go after Bisco, and he laughed as the camellia regenerated its army of Lion's Crimson Swords.

"If you want to hurt Bisco, you'll have to go through me. So make a hundred swords. Make a thousand if you want! I'll turn them all into a bouquet of flowers to give to Pawoo!"

"Shishi!! Shishi, where are you?!"

Bisco ran down the long, dark tunnel, his voice disappearing into the depths of the flower. He sensed he was near the plant's core now, and the whispers of the camellia were no longer anywhere to be heard.

"Shishi?! Come on, answer me...! Whah?!"

Suddenly, Bisco placed his foot in empty air, toppling down an unseen step and planting his face in the floor. Through the darkness, Bisco could see dozens of glowing red camellia flowers lining the walls of the room. Then all of a sudden he heard footsteps, and a female figure slowly walked up to where he lay prone on the floor.

A splendid crimson aura emanated from her body, casting light on the walls. She looked otherworldly, divine, and it was only the flower behind her ear that still reminded Bisco of the Shishi he used to know.

"...So. You have come at last, Brother."

"..."

Her frigid gaze was as impenetrable as ever, devoid of emotion, and it was clear to Bisco that the dark roots extended deep into her heart. Still, he peered back into her ice-cold eyes without a quiver of hesitation.

"...I'm afraid the flowers have consumed me," Shishi said. "Your words cannot save me now."

"..."

"...Nothing can."

As Shishi spoke, the Lion's Crimson Sword appeared in her hand. Meanwhile, Bisco swiftly produced his knife and drew the blade across his own palm, whereupon the spores in his blood transformed his dagger into a silver staff.

The two readied their weapons and stared each other down. It was Bisco who spoke first.

"Shishi."

"..."

"...I've come to get you."

Shishi pounced like a crimson-eyed panther, but Bisco caught her sword on his silver staff. He delivered a kick to her wrist, knocking the Lion's Crimson Sword away and slicing apart the ivy that connected it to Shishi's wrist.

"You're as impatient as ever, Shishi. You just gotta... Whah?!"

Shishi did not relent. She slashed again with a second sword, secretly manifested in her other hand. Bisco barely pulled back in time, letting the blade slice his cheek before blocking the follow-up on his staff.

"A weapon made of the Ghost Hail, with the power to nullify the Florescence. You really are strong...Brother."

Their weapons locked, Shishi pushed, forcing Bisco backward with unthinkable strength.

"But it is futile. You are no match for the power of life I possess, siphoned from Hokkaido…and from my own people. It is enough energy to craft a hundred swords!"

"A hundred? Hah! A hundred, eh?"

"Die!"

Shishi knocked Bisco's staff upward, slicing his chest with her blade.

"Ow! Fuck!"

His blood sprayed from the wound, drenching the room in crimson.

However…he still managed to use his staff to sever the second sword from Shishi's wrist.

"You are holding back, Brother. Why do you aim not at me, but at my swords?"

"Two down, ninety-eight to go."

"…?!"

"After that, you're comin' back with me. So bring it on. I can do this all night."

Shishi's eyes quivered slightly, far beyond the icy facade, a telltale sign Bisco did not fail to notice.

"…Y-you…"

Her voice shook, as her heart, resigned to death, felt something warm it had not expected to ever feel again.

"…You… Still, even now… You're still trying to save me! Me! Stuck at the bottom of a deep, deep pit of blood!"

"I told you, Shishi. I've come to get you."

"Y…

"You're…

"You're too LAAAAAAAATE!!!!"

A scream, like all of Shishi's bottled-up emotions, exploded out of her at once. She flew into a rage, and Bisco defended against step after step of her lethal dance, rapidly becoming bloodied by a sheer flood of blows he couldn't hope to keep up with.

Crakk!

"Eighty-seven!"

"It's all your fault, Brother! It's all your fault!!"

"Seventy-nine."

"You accepted me! You allowed the darkness into me!"

"Sixty-eight... Grrh! Haah...sixty-three!"

"You ignited my courage. Saw me onto the blood-soaked path."

"Sixty-two!"

"You must have known where that path would lead. I killed my father! Slew my people! I cannot go back now! There's nowhere left for me to go!"

"Forty-nine!"

"And still you come, Brother?! To save me? Ha! What is there left to save?!"

She raised her sword up high, and that was when Bisco uttered his response.

"...Your tears, Shishi."

"What?!"

Though Bisco's face was caked in blood, his jade-green eyes gleamed. It was only now that Shishi realized she was crying.

"I don't give a crap how you live your life. But I saw you cryin', so I came to get you."

"..."

"...'Cause I care about you, Shishi. That's all the reason I need."

Krakk!!!

Bisco's staff collided with a threefold bundle of Shishi's ivy swords, and both parties' weapons snapped in two. Bisco turned to face Shishi. He was firm, determined despite his many injuries, while Shishi panted heavily without a single scratch.

"Now I'm all warmed up," he said. "Don't stop now, Shishi! We still got forty-six swords to go!"

"You never should have let me bloom, Brother...!!"

"..."

"You are the light of life, Brother. You awaken everything you touch to its full, terrifying potential. The beautiful…and the ugly alike. Even those like me, with darkness lurking in our hearts."

"Are you sayin' that toxic mushrooms shouldn't exist?"

"…"

Bisco looked down at Shishi, kneeling tearstained on the floor, and smiled.

"All life deserves to live, Shishi."

A breeze from the tunnel ruffled his hair as Bisco awkwardly pieced together what he wanted to say.

"Just bein' in this world, that's somethin' we gotta protect. It don't matter what kinda mushroom you are. It don't matter what path you walk…

"I'm just happy you're alive, Shishi."

Then Bisco twitched his nose and sniffed nonchalantly, before crouching down and peering into Shishi's tearstained eyes.

"If your soul is steeped in darkness, like you say it is, then that's totally fine by me. It means we fight, until one of us falls by the wayside. That's just the way life works; I don't got a problem with that. But, Shishi…I don't fight people while they're cryin'. The way I see it, you don't belong in the darkness at all; you're a soul of light. And if that's the case…we gotta make you bloom again, facin' the sun."

Bisco slowly held out his hand.

And Shishi faltered.

She wasn't sure she was allowed to take that hand. After much hesitation, she reached out…

…and just as she took it…

"Gaagh?!"

Shishi suddenly shivered violently and wrapped her arms around herself, clenching her teeth in pain. Bisco looked around to see the camellia flowers approach Shishi and enter her body through the skin.

"Shishi!"

"Brother…run… The camellia… It wants me back…"

"Like hell! I came here to get you! That's what I've been sayin'! Shishi! Hey, wake up! Shishi!"

Shishi only sobbed loudly, head hung. Then…

"Heh-heh… Hee-hee-hee-hee-hee!!"

…the crying transformed into uproarious laughter.

"Shishi?!"

Bisco walked back over to her, confused, and just at that moment…

Shng!

…the camellia grinned. Wearing Shishi's skin, it brought the blade of the Lion's Crimson Sword to her neck.

"That was a close one. I should keep the mulch nearer at all times."

"Camellia! It's you! What have you done?!"

"Ho-ho-ho-ho! You have done well, to come so far and to touch the heart of poor, withered Shishi. However, you are too late. Shishi is mine. There shall be no discussion."

The camellia pressed the blade into Shishi's flesh, drawing a line of crimson blood.

"Such a tragic performance. I continue to be surprised by your kind's empathy. Yet that is precisely your weakness. Observe. Lift a finger against me, and your precious Shishi will be sliced to ribbons. Ho-ho-ho-ho-ho…"

"You dirty, backstabbin' piece of—!"

"Hissss!!"

Upon seeing the hostaged Shishi, Bisco hesitated, and that moment of hesitation was all that was required for the camellia to strike.

"Gh…hhh?!"

"Ah-ha-ha-ha-ha!!"

Bisco looked down at the sword, its point embedded deep in his chest, piercing his heart. An uncontainable torrent of blood spilled forth, both from the chest wound and his mouth as well.

"How foolish. How very very foolish! See how your sympathy ensures your own defeat? Now, I always intended to discard this pathetic plant pot sooner or later. Ho-ho-ho… I think you shall replace her quite nicely. The power of the divine mushroom will soon be in my grasp…!!"

"…You bad guys all get the same idea."

"…*What?!*"

"Once you get up close, you think you can take a stab."

Blood spilled from the corners of his lips, but the glint in his eyes was as strong as ever. The camellia trembled at the sight.

"You want to know how many times Shishi cut me? Thirty-two. And each of them was worth a hundred of yours."

"Wh-what?! You…you don't mean…? Impossible!! Whaaaagh?!"

As the purifying light worked its way up Shishi's blade, the camellia figured out its mistake. Starting from the point, the sword began dissolving into white petals. Each vigorous beat of Bisco's heart filled him with the power of Hokkaido, of the Ghost Hail, which he then channeled into the camellia.

"Whaah…? Wh-whaaah?! Aaaagh! Aah! Aaaaagh?!"

There was no trace of any scornful derision in the flower's voice now. Only fear.

"My… My flowers! L-let go! Let me go! Let go of meee!!"

Bisco clutched the blade of Shishi's sword, holding it in place so tightly that blood dribbled between his fingers. As the camellia tried in vain to retract it, he spat blood in its face and glared into Shishi's crimson eyes.

"Get the hell outta her," he said, jade-green sparks in his gaze. "And then fuck off and die."

"Ee…ee…eeeeee…"

"You fucked with the wrong kid, asshole. There ain't no savin' you now."

"Gyaaaaghhh!"

Shishi's sword was fastened to her wrist by thick vines, so it was impossible for the camellia to release it before the purification reached Shishi's body. It swept across her crimson skin, returning it to its normal pale-white tone in a flash. At first, it seemed like the Ghost Hail spores would destroy the camellia completely, but at the last moment, the flower behind Shishi's ear detached itself. It fell to the floor and wriggled, slick with blood, lacking any trace of its former dignity.

"Wraaagh! Aaah! Aaargh!!"

It shrieked a pathetic shriek in an old woman's voice, and began burrowing into the ground to hide itself.

"Help me! I don't want to die! I don't want to die…," it cried.

"Huh?! It's makin' a break for it!!"

Bisco swung his Ghost Hail fist at the fleeing flower, but the struggling camellia detached one of its trailing vines like a lizard's tail and escaped into the sky flower's bulk.

Shit. I let it get away. Good thing Milo's not here or he'd slap me silly.

Bisco couldn't deny that the thought of stamping out a newly independent life, even an evil one, caused him to hesitate. He stared, silently, at the spot where the flower had been, before turning at last to the girl shivering and cowering on the floor.

"…"

"…"

Shishi stared up into Bisco's face. Her crimson eyes wobbled with tears, yet she didn't look away. Bisco took a single step toward her, and though she recoiled slightly, she remained transfixed by his jade-green gaze.

"Shishi!"

"Ah…!"

A sound escaped Shishi's lips at the look of that roguish, bad-boy smile. Their crimson and jade eyes seemed to pull on each other magnetically, until finally their foreheads touched.

"Let's go, Shishi."

"…"

"It's been…"

"…"

"It's been tough…I bet."

It was that moment of understanding, Bisco's unconditional validation, that unsealed the floodgates. There in his arms, Shishi decided she would hold it back no longer, and like an avalanche, it all came flooding forth.

"…Brother.

"Brother.

"Brotheeer!"

All restraint came loose. Shishi hugged Bisco back as strongly as she could, burrowing her face in his neck and crying into his shoulder. Bisco simply held her, feeling the teardrops stain his clothes. At this moment, there were no words of comfort or wisdom for him to offer. He could only warm her with the heat of his blood and the heat of his soul. For what seemed like an eternity, he sat there, listening to Shishi's tears.

Then, all of a sudden, the sky flower began to rumble, and Bisco and Shishi both cast their eyes upward.

"What the hell is it this time?!"

"The sky flower is set to burst and scatter its pollen all across Japan," explained Shishi with resolution, wiping her crimson eyes and rising to her feet. "You must run, Brother. The flower grows from me; this is my burden to bear. The very last thing I can do...to atone for my— Owww!!"

Bisco poked her sharply in the forehead and hauled her up into one arm. Then he set off down the tunnel, where he ran into his partner again.

"Bisco...! And Shishi, too! Looks like everything went well! I knew you could do it!"

"Dude, you're covered in blood! Guess those swords did a real number on you!"

"As if you can talk, Bisco. I can barely see a clean spot on you! Anyway, look who I found!"

It was Amli, who rested in Milo's arms, but for some reason, she looked quite displeased.

"Amli!" Bisco cried. "Damn, I forgot you were here! Good to see you're okay!"

"You forgot?! I get the feeling I've just been an afterthought to you lately!"

"Can we do this later?" asked Milo. "Right now we need to get out of here!"

"Our normal mushrooms ain't gonna work inside a flower," said Bisco. "I'm gonna use the Ghost Hail!"

Milo nodded and tossed his staff like a javelin at the ceiling. The Ghost Hail Staff tore through the layers of petals, boring a hole to the outside world.

Meanwhile, Bisco took the upset and struggling Amli in his other arm and waited for Milo to latch on to his back. Then he put all his energy into one leg, which glowed with the silver light of the Ghost Hail spores and cast a shimmer on the dark interior walls.

"I got no idea how strong this is gonna be!" shouted Bisco. "Hold on tight!"

"Roger that, Bisco!"

"Okay, Brother!"

"Fine, do as you must!"

"Right! Here we go!"

Gaboom!

Bisco trod his heel into the floor, and a Ghost Hail mushroom sprouted from his body with incredible force, catapulting him into the air even harder than a King Trumpet. Clad in the Ghost Hail spores, Bisco tore through the petals surrounding the flower and flew into the twilight sky above Hokkaido.

"Eeek! M-Mr. Bisco, sir! I daresay…this is too high!" shrieked Amli, her hair flapping wildly in the wind.

"I told ya, I didn't know how strong it was gonna be! Why don't you come up with some mantra thingy, like always?"

"Some of us are limited in what we can do, Mr. Bisco, sir! From this height, the four of us shall certainly go splat against the floor!"

"That does not bother me," said Shishi. "So long as I can die alongside Brother…"

"Grrr! I'm afraid there's a line, Miss Shishi, ma'am! If you wish to go to Hell with Mr. Bisco, you must take your place behind me!"

"Wait!" said Milo. "I think it's going to be okay! We get to live today, after all!"

"Huh?"

Shishi cast a puzzled look at Milo, who pointed over to the horizon. There, in the distance, was a glimmering orange object, blasting its way toward the quartet and their morbid quarrel on a set of rocket thrusters.

""Actagawa!!""

The loyal steelcrab caught all four plummeting compatriots mere meters off the ground, with the two girls landing in the luggage compartment and the two boys neatly in the saddles. Taking a glance at his unruffled partner, Milo picked up the reins and breathed a ragged sigh of relief.

"That was close," he said. "I actually thought we were going to die that time!"

"Yeah? What about all the other times you said that today and it didn't happen?"

"That just goes to show we've had a particularly high probability of fatality today, Bisco."

"I'm startin' to think Hell ain't lettin' me in for some reason. Can't think why."

After Bisco's flippant reply, he paused, and the two boys took in the sight of each other's bloodied forms, before breaking into smiles. It was a pleasant scene, swiftly interrupted by…

"Akaboshiii!!"

A bellowing voice echoed up from the surface of Hokkaido, audible even over the rocket boosters fastened to Actagawa's rear.

"Make haste, Akaboshi! The sky flower is set to bloom without delay! Fire your newfangled Ghost Hail thingamajigs its way at once!"

"He's right, Bisco!"

Heeding Satahabaki's advice, Milo turned to Bisco, who flashed his usual cheeky grin and glared skyward, at a flower on the verge of Florescent meltdown.

"So we just gotta shoot that leftover before it bursts!"

But all of a sudden, the sky shook, and the camellia's voice emanated from the flower itself.

"All…Benibishi. All…humans… Give way… Give way to us! We are flowers. We are the true victors. We shall supplant you as this world's dominant life-form!"

"Ha! I gotta hand it to you, you're almost as bad at admittin' defeat as me! Milo, the Mantra Bow!"

"Right, Bisco!"

Standing atop the airborne Actagawa, Bisco plucked a few of his spiky red hairs from his head. They quickly became wreathed in white spores, transforming into a sheaf of arrows shining with Hokkaido's silver light.

"Mr. Milo, sir! I shall assist!"

"Thanks, Amli! Let's do it!"

""Won/shad/viviki/snew!""

The two mantra users began their chant, and Milo's cube flew from his hand and into Bisco's. Bisco swept his arm in a half-circle, leaving a silver trail that manifested as a shimmering moonlight bow.

"This is it…the Ghost Hail Bow!"

"Wow, it's turned white! What is that, Mr. Milo, sir?!"

"It's the crystallization of Hokkaido's power. This should let Bisco take that thing down!"

After hearing Milo's words, Bisco suddenly poked his face into Actagawa's luggage rack, extending his hand to Shishi.

"Come on!"

"B-Brother…?!"

"Let's put an end to this…together!"

Bisco guided Shishi into his arms, allowing her to grasp the Ghost Hail Bow. Meanwhile, he took the silver arrows and nocked them to the bow, placing his arrow hand over Shishi's tiny fist.

"Put an end…to this…"

Shishi repeated Bisco's words without even realizing it. Milo and Amli simply watched Bisco's unexpected behavior, funneling their mantra power into the bow without uttering a word. At first, Shishi allowed Bisco to pull her into place, but then she focused her strength, and the flower behind her ear reappeared, more brilliantly than ever. She took the bow in both hands and pulled the bowstring as tight as she could, with Bisco making up the rest. Then she aimed it directly at the flower up in the sky, which looked ready to scatter its maleficent pollen at any moment.

"Akaboshiii!! There's not much time!" came Satahabaki's distant voice. "FIVE! FOUR!"

Then Bisco heard Shishi's hushed tones. "Brother…," she said. "What is that?"

"Just a massive eyesore, as far as I'm concerned. How about you?"

"…"

"…"

"To me…it's my past. It's half of me."

"Still wanna shoot?"

"I do."

Shishi's crimson eyes remained transfixed by the flower—her past—which was ready to open at any moment.

"It's my darkness, Brother, and I should like to see it destroyed."

"THREE! TWOOO!!"

"So please, Brother…lend me your strength!"

"Sure. Just watch closely. Watch your target…and yourself. Then believe. As hard as you can…"

Believe…in myself!!

"OOONE!"

"Bisco!"

"Miss Shishi, ma'am!"

""Take this! Ghost Hail Bow! Cataclysm Shot!!""

Ka-chew!!

A peal of thunder split the twilight sky, and a shard of moonlight crossed the stars. For one brief moment, the whole surface of Hokkaido was lit up by a silver flash.

"ZER—O-ooohh?!"

Satahabaki concluded his countdown, and a moment later…

*   *   *

"*Im…possible…*"

…the camellia's booming voice shook the land.

"*My power…*"

Boom.

"*My evolution…*"

Boom. Boom!

"*…It was meant to be unstoppable…*"

Boom! Boom! Gaboom! Ka-gaboom!!

Sprays of silver spores spurted forth all over the sky flower, twinkling in the sky above Hokkaido like snowflakes. When these spores touched the camellia, it turned pure-white, slowly dissolving into clouds of tiny petals that the wind carried away.

And everyone, the two boys, the two girls…

…Satahabaki, the Mushroom Keepers, and the Benibishi—even Tirol, in the middle of trying to evacuate herself from the area as quickly as possible—all life turned and stared, entranced by the magical sight.

It was Amli who spoke first, as if suddenly waking from a dream.

"Y-you did it…! Mr. Bisco, sir, you actually did it! With just one arrow! Mr. Milo, sir, did you see that?!"

"Biscooo!!"

"Aaagh!"

As the flower in the distance fell apart, Milo leaped upon his partner, wrapping his arms around him. This broke Bisco out of his trance, and he lost his balance, very nearly falling off Actagawa's back.

"Whaaah?! You tryin' to kill me, asshole?! Wh-whoa, easy!"

"You won again, Bisco!! I always knew you could do it! Even turning into a child isn't enough to get you down! You see now, don't you? Nobody believes in you more than I do!"

"Urk. Well, what if I'd turned into a frog or a grasshopper?"

"Or a flea! I'd still believe in you!"

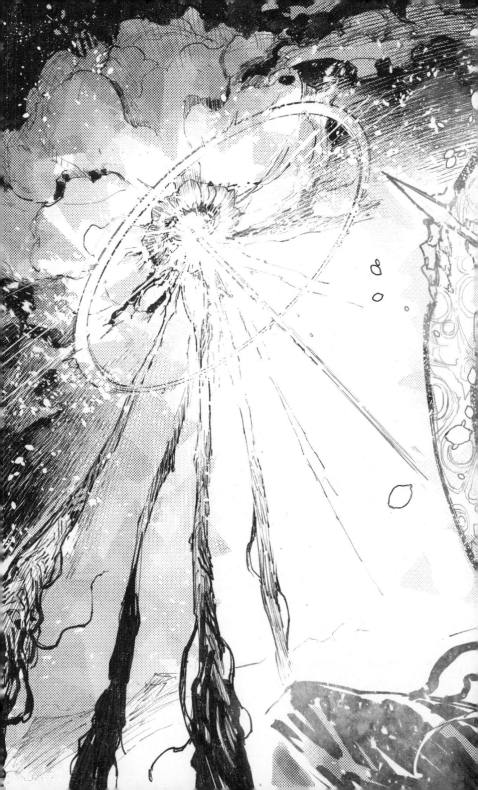

"Whoa!! All right, all right, I get it already! Just keep your hands on the reins! Actagawa's never flown before!!"

With a fed-up look at Milo's usual clingy behavior, Amli suddenly felt her hand fall on Shishi, and she turned to see her hiding in the luggage bags again.

"Miss Shishi, ma'am. I'd have thought you'd like to see the flower disperse for a while longer. It's very beautiful, you know, and I doubt you'll get another chance."

"No," Shishi replied, her long eyelashes quivering. "It's fine." She turned to face Amli and traced her finger across her scars.

"It was my sword that did this…"

"Miss Shishi, ma'am! That tickles!"

"I'm sorry, Amli. I'm so, so sorry…"

"…"

Amli stared at Shishi's trembling lips for a moment, and then, all of a sudden, she threw herself forward and wrapped her arms around her. Shishi's eyes went wide with shock, but it was Amli, more than anyone else, who struggled to come up with an explanation for what she'd just done.

Wh-what's come over me? I've never met the girl before, for crying out loud!

However, as spur-of-the-moment as it was, the hug seemed to reassure young Shishi greatly, and she gradually relaxed, settling into the warmth of Amli's arms. Amli, meanwhile, could hardly take back what she had done, and so remained locked in an embrace, with a brightly reddening color to her cheeks.

Hokkaido, the Island Whale. The ravenous beast that threatened the whole of Japan.

In the end, what put a stop to its devastating rampage was a single arrow, nothing more.

All that remained of the camellia's sky flower was a snow of white petals that fell across Hokkaido and purified the land. Infused with the lingering effects of the Ghost Hail Bow, they purified the fields of camellia flowers that grew across Hokkaido's back, as well as the vines beneath the earth that infested the creature's many organs and brain.

Thus, the beast's cognitive faculties were returned, and in accordance with the words of the oracle of the *sporko*—the Mushroom Keepers of the north—Hokkaido released its jaws from Japan's southernmost isle and set off across the Sea of Japan, journeying back to its original position just north of Aomori.

"Milooo!!"

"Chaika!!"

The young tribal daughter sprinted down from a hilltop and all but leaped into Milo's arms, whirling merrily, a bright smile across her whole face.

"You saved him! You saved Hokkaido! The flowers have all gone, and he's listening to what I say again! It's all thanks to you! Oh, how can I ever thank you enough?"

"Thank us? It's Bisco and I who should be thanking you, Chaika. Without your help, we'd never have saved our friend!"

"Oh, Bisco!" Chaika exclaimed, her eyes suddenly widening. She pressed Milo for an answer. "Where is he? That child lit a flame of courage in my heart that will never go out! I must see him and say my thanks!"

"Heh-heh. If it's Bisco you want…"

"Yo. Nice to see you safe and sound, Princess."

"Oh, come on, you know I'm not—"

But when Chaika turned and saw the person standing there, she froze, blinking in shock. She had to lift her gaze upward to see his bright-red hair and wild canine teeth. There was a resemblance, surely, but the cute little boy she remembered had well and truly grown up into a fine, stouthearted man. Still, when she looked up into his clear, jade-green eyes, she saw the same fierce glint from her memories.

"…I-is that really you, Bisco?!"

"Who else would I be?" replied Bisco, flashing a roguish smirk, before crouching down to meet Chaika's gaze. "You made fun of me for lookin' like a kid, but you gotta believe I'm the real deal now, don't ya?"

"…"

"…Hey, Chaika?"

"I always believed you, silly. Still…"

Chaika's face grew steadily redder, and all of a sudden, she threw her arms around Bisco's neck.

"Wha—?! Hey!"

"You are…rather *ravikal* now, I must say…"

"Hmm? What does that mean?!"

"I shan't tell!"

With that, Chaika planted a kiss on Bisco's cheek, before exploding into a full-flushed glow. She spun around in an attempt to hide her embarrassment, before pointing out a distant hilltop to the two boys.

"The *sporko* and the Benibishi are assisting each other now," she said. "I guess your arrow even purified the relations between our peoples."

The two boys looked over at the hill…to see the remnants of the sky flower, a pile of tiny, pure-white petals. The Mushroom Keepers and Benibishi alike were sifting through the debris, pulling their compatriots free.

"*Ouya!* Hang in there! We're getting these petals moved as quickly as we can!"

"Please. We are a race of slaves. Do what you must to us, but please spare our children…"

"Hauld ye tonge. We *sporko* de nae keep slaves. Aul leife be equal in our eyes. Reight noe, we be two seedes, each aidin te grouth o t'other. An' whenne that be donne, we ken choose te feight or allie as ye wishe… Fer noe, keep it up, me people! Take te man te safety!"

"*Ouya!* Come, proud warriors, assist the chief!"

"Bring the injured this way! We of the Kusabira sect will heal your wounds!"

"Men of the Benibishi, with me! There are still women and children trapped beneath the petals! Let us assist the Mushroom Keepers in rescuing them!"

"Got it!"

Leading the rescue efforts was the Hand of the Ghost Hail himself, Elder Cavillacan, who had managed to survive the whole ordeal. It seemed that because the flowering had been interrupted, many of the Mushroom Keepers and Benibishi sucked up by the sky flower were still alive.

Furthermore, the Benibishi were seemingly free of the camellia's wicked influence, losing the brutal vines that both marred their pale bodies and had the power to command them. Even with this loss, however, the Benibishi were back to their old gentle nature, and they worked hard to assist the Mushroom Keepers with the rescue, despite the fact that they had been at war only a few hours earlier.

"It looks like the Benibishi are back to their old selves again," said Milo. "And since the Mushroom Keepers don't keep slaves, I think this could be the beginning of a wonderful partnership!"

"All's well that ends well, huh…? Somethin' about that rubs me the wrong way."

"You'll grow wrinkles if you keep frowning like that. What did you expect? This always happens whenever we show up."

There was no change in Bisco's sullen look. Milo sighed and went on.

"I understand you don't like to poke your nose into other people's conflicts," he said, "but as a doctor, I can tell you we did the right thing. Just think about all the lives we saved."

"Ha. Listen to you. Such a good panda, ain't ya?"

All of a sudden, Tirol sat up and stretched deeply, gazing into the sunset. Her hair was all messy from Actagawa's maneuvering, and dark bags sat under her eyes.

"Geez Louise! *Yawn...!*"

"Wow, Tirol, you look beat. Haven't you just been asleep?"

"Well, yeah, but I was workin' round the clock to finish Actagawa's jets."

"About that!" Bisco roared. "Who do you think you are, meddlin' with my crab?!"

It was evident that after the sky flower's demise, the Ghost Hail had returned to dormancy within Bisco's bloodstream, alongside the Rust-Eater. No longer did he possess its signature silver glow.

"You're gonna anger the gods, makin' a crab fly! It's blasphemy! Enbiten's gonna be pissed! You better take them off as soon as we're done, you hear?!"

"Geez, a bit of thanks would be nice! You know how hard I worked my butt off for you, Akaboshi?!"

Bisco glanced sideways at Tirol, and at Milo trying to keep her from tearing his head off, and then walked over to Shishi, who was gazing at the distant remnants of the sky flower.

"Shishi, you okay?"

"...Brother."

Instead of answering Bisco's question, Shishi turned to him and smiled. Bisco wasn't quite sure how to respond to the mixture of sorrow and relief she displayed.

"That flower's a pretty sight," he said. "Look at the petals; they're just like snow."

"…Yes. It is pretty, Brother," Shishi whispered, taking in the sight. *"And the people look at peace now. No longer are they forced to march under the standard of my Florescent sword."*

"…"

"This… This is all they ever wanted. I never needed to do the things I did to secure happiness for my people. I bound myself with needless thoughts of vengeance and freedom, and somewhere along the way, they consumed me."

"It's all right, Shishi. It's easy to say so, lookin' back. But you didn't do nothin' wrong."

"Brother. I have a request to ask of you."

Shishi clung to Bisco's front, peering up into his bewildered face with bright, crimson eyes.

"I want… I want you to deflower me, Bisco. Take the camellia…and crush it!"

"Wh-what are you sayin'?!"

Shishi nodded, showing him the flower behind her ear. Though Bisco remembered it detaching from her earlier, it had somehow grown back in the meantime, displaying a terrifying regenerative capability.

"As of right now, the camellia has expended its rage, but eventually it will build up again, and the darkness within will drive my people to violence once more."

Shishi drew so close to Bisco their noses almost touched, and he could feel her hot breath as she spoke.

"Before that happens, Brother, you must destroy it. With that Ghost Hail power of yours."

"But…if I do that, you'll lose your powers!"

"A fate I accept readily and willingly, Brother. I shall lead my people anew, as a naked king without the flower to cloud my mind."

Shishi spoke without hesitation or reservation, such that there was little Bisco could say in the way of protest.

"Brother, even as a powerless child, you never gave up. You are the complete opposite of me, a weakling who yielded to temptation. Yours is the path of the bare soul, which stands on its own merits."

Shishi pressed her head into Bisco's chest.

"If you allow it, I should like the opportunity to flower anew. I wish to follow your path, even if I must do it with my past trailing behind me. So please…use your power to…"

Shishi didn't move. Head buried in Bisco's chest, she remained motionless, as if in prayer. Bisco looked down at her, then turned his eyes on the people around him.

Milo, Amli, Chaika. Everyone was watching, silently awaiting Bisco's next words. (Except Tirol, who didn't seem too bothered one way or the other.) Even Satahabaki, standing off in the distance, nodded as if in support of Bisco's decision, whatever it may have turned out to be.

"…You won't regret this, will you?"

Bisco steeled his resolve and focused on his right arm. Though he had lost the silver tattoos that marked him as the Ghost Hail deity, and the spores had retreated into his body, he managed to make his hand glow white once more.

"…Okay, here I go, Shishi."

"Yes, Brother…"

"…You're a great king, by the way. I think your old man would be proud."

Then Bisco brought his hand close to the flower behind Shishi's ear, and…

…just at that moment.

Crakk!

Out of nowhere, a whip lashed at Bisco's arm, knocking it away and pulling the camellia, roots and all, from Shishi's head.

"Aaaagh?!"

"Shishi!!"

While Bisco swiftly stood in front of Shishi to protect her, the bearer of the bright-green whip lashed out once more, dexterously scooping up the flower and catching it in their hand.

"Hee-hee-hee… I hate to break up this touching final scene…"

A mocking voice rang out in the dusk as the figure tossed the flower idly.

"But it's such a shame to see this gorgeous flower go to waste. After all, there's still so much it can be used for."

"Bisco!" cried Milo.

"Who are you?!" yelled Bisco.

Despite the unexpected attack, the two boys took up positions in front of Shishi and glared at the mysterious figure hidden by the evening gloom.

"I must admit, you've caught me on the back foot yet again, Akaboshi. I suppose it just goes to show I should have researched those white mushrooms beforehand."

"It's you...!!"

"But that's precisely why we villains always have another plan or two up our sleeves...or three or four, even. You see, to be quite honest...I'm a coward."

""""Mepaosha!!"""""

Bisco, Milo, and Satahabaki all cried out at once.

"So that whip of yours was not granted by Shishi's powers," said the ex-warden. "Tell me how a human such as yourself possesses it!"

"Oh, put a sock in it, fatso. I'm done taking your orders as of right now. Actually, you want to know something? The truth is, I was never being brainwashed in the first place. Not by this little squirt, and certainly not by you."

"What?!"

"All I needed to do was extract the power of the camellia from that kid over there. The ultimate power of evolution, having gorged itself on the power of the Rust."

"You mean...you've been after my flower this whole time? Right from the beginning, that was your only goal?"

Bleeding profusely from the head, Shishi glared daggers at Mepaosha, who only returned a toothy grin.

"But it is evil! That flower brings only destruction!"

"Ah-ha-ha-ha-ha!!!"

Mepaosha threw her head back and laughed, crushing the flower in her grip.

"That's exactly what I'm after, brat. Just shut up and watch. Bottoms up!"

She opened her shark-teeth grin wide and, before everyone's eyes, downed Shishi's flower in a single gulp. The flower proved more difficult to swallow than she had expected, and she immediately began coughing, but when that passed, she turned to face the others at last, mucus running from her nose.

"Guh. Awful. Tastes like mashed giraffe brains."

"That's all you have to say after eatin' Shishi's flower?"

Bisco flew into a rage. His eyes lit up with fire, and he shot Mepaosha a deadly, jade-green glare.

"And what are you gonna do with Shishi's powers, huh?! What can you possibly do?!"

"…What, you ask? Hmm. You're asking *me* what I want to do?"

Mepaosha flipped Bisco's question around and turned her pitch-black eyes on him. In them, Bisco sensed a window into a dark abyss that he'd seen only once before.

"Don't you even know the answer to that, Akaboshi? That makes me sad. So sad… Yes, sadder even than Keanu Reeves after his dog was killed in *John Wick*."

…Hmm? Something's strange. Where have I…?!

"All I want, Akaboshi, is to play with you once more. To try out my new toy…and to play with you to my heart's content. You understand, don't you? Akaboshi…"

Bisco sensed the Mepaosha before him turning darker and darker, like an ink stain seeping into the paper. When Bisco and Milo detected the terrifying aura emanating from her every pore, they felt a deep dread that made them shiver.

"I've been waiting so long, you know. Biding my time, waiting for the perfect moment. I've toadied up to fools, bowed down to children…abstained from the wonderful manga and exciting movies I love so much. Nothing to do to pass the time except grope my own breasts, and they aren't even that big."

"B-Bisco! That's…! Mepaosha is…!"

"I was right under your nose, yearning for you, and yet you never even noticed me. Now I know what it's like to be a woman in a soap opera... Though I suppose I *am* a woman right now, aren't I?"

Mepaosha took off her spectacles and replaced them with a pair of sunglasses from her pocket.

"Last hint. You got it yet?"

She grinned, and the smile on her face brought a memory flooding back. A man the two boys could never forget.

"Remember me now, Akaboshi?"

"It's you..."

""Kurokawa!!""

At the sound of her—of *his*—name from their mouths, a sinister smile crept across Kurokawa's lips.

"...Ahh, you don't know how happy that makes me..."

Behind the sunglasses and the glint of her teeth, the look in her eyes was just that of an old friend, brought to reunion after a long, long journey, only far more sinister.

"I'm so happy to see you both again. Akaboshi, Nekoyana—"

Shishi pressed her foot into the snow and shot toward Kurokawa before she could even finish speaking. She scraped together what little Florescence remained in her system and focused it in her arms.

"Oh, come now. You wouldn't disturb my touching reunion scene... would you?"

"Come to me, Lion's Crimson Sword!!"

Shishi swung her shining ivy blade down toward Mepaosha's head, but at the very last moment...

Boom! Boom! Boom!!

...three hollow gunshots rang out, and Shishi lurched three times in the air.

"Urgh... Ghah!"

"Shishi!!"

"I'm afraid your time in the spotlight is over, young lady. Eat your lunch and go home... Ah, perfect timing. I guess this means I get to unveil my newest toy. Watch this, Akaboshi."

Mepaosha…or rather, Kurokawa reborn, pursed her lips and muttered…

"Boom!"

Boom! Boom!

From where she was shot, huge clumps of Rust burst out of Shishi's body. She writhed on the ground, clutching the earth and expelling blood from her mouth.

"Aaah! Shishi!"

"Stop! This is between you and me! Leave Shishi out of it!"

"Between you and me, you say? Ooh, I like the sound of that. But just sit and watch, Akaboshi. Watch what grows out of this girl…"

"Wh-what the…?"

Milo ran over to aid Shishi, but what he found on her body was no ordinary clump of Rust. It was shaped like a rose, as if beautifully sculpted out of the deadly substance.

"A Rust…flower?!"

"A new breed of weapon, combining the qualities of the flower *and* the Rust. Rather beautiful for a clump of Rust, isn't it? Just like an obsidian carving… Of course, it performs beautifully as well."

While everyone else stared, wondering what to make of this strange development, Bisco leaped into action, firing an arrow toward Kurokawa at once. However, with frightening reflexes, Kurokawa constructed a wall of ivy to block the blow, though the force of the exploding mushroom still knocked her off her feet. She went rolling along the ground with a grin on her face.

"Ah-ha-ha-ha! That's the spirit, Akaboshi! But I have one more trick up my sleeve. And it looks like you can't just fire those white arrows whenever you want!"

"Shut your freakin' mouth! You're gonna tell me your plans, one way or another!"

"Ho-ho. Big words, for a man who couldn't even protect one child."

"You…"

"Oh no! Bisco, watch out!"

Milo wrapped his furious partner in his arms and swiftly leaped out

of the way, moments before there was a great fiery explosion in the spot
where Bisco had stood, blasting the snow-covered land bare.

"Wh-what was that? An explosion?!"

"Oh, but this is no ordinary explosion, Akaboshi. There's an added
feature!"

Sure enough, the explosion scattered some sort of rust-colored seeds
outward from the point of impact, which exploded to life in the soil
of the newly cleansed landscape of Hokkaido, producing brand-new
rust-colored flowers.

"H-he's already turned Shishi's power into a new weapon?!"

"Ahh... Aaaahhh!"

"Milo, what's wrong?!"

"Up there, Bisco!"

Bisco followed Milo's gaze, and when he saw what his partner saw,
he became lost for words.

For the sky was filled with...

...a fleet of jet-black escargot planes, each emblazoned with the sign
of the old Imihama government. Out of each and every one of them
descended squadrons upon squadrons of black-suited Immies, the
secret police force of Kurokawa's reign.

"*Ouya!* Who on earth are they?!"

"Fire! Fire! Don't let them land!"

The Mushroom Keepers of Hokkaido fired their bows, loosing a
hail of arrows at the descending Immies. However, their bunny masks
somehow instantly devoured the mushrooms without a trace.

"Aaah-ha-ha-ha!!"

Then the planes began their bombing runs, each explosion spreading
the Rust flowers farther. Soon the air was thick with the screams of the
Benibishi, those of the Mushroom Keepers, and Kurokawa's howling
laughter.

"Oh, don't worry," she cackled. "This is merely the prelude. There's
so much more I have in store! Enough to keep you entertained for a
feature-length, I assure you."

Beneath darkened skies, the two boys stood in front of their friends, eyeing their archnemesis with rage. Already, she was protected by a crowd of Immies who had dropped from the sky and circled around her, pointing the barrels of their Salamander machine guns squarely at the two young Mushroom Keepers.

"Come to think of it, thanks to you tearing my throat out, I never got to say *I'll be back...*"

One of the Immies handed Kurokawa her black coat, and she placed her arms through the sleeves.

"So instead, I'll change it to *I'm back now*, Akaboshi."

Then she took her trademark hat...

"And it's so good to see you again."

...and placed it back atop her head.

AFTERWORD

From the moment I popped into this world, I've been (almost) exclusively a Saitama kid. But lately, my hometown has grown rather busy, mostly due to the new railway line that opened up nearby.

Apartment blocks have been cropping up in places that were once nothing but fields, and in front of the station there are gigantic malls and buildings I don't even know the purpose of. It's a far cry from the town I used to know. In fact, if I were to show what the place looked like to my old elementary school student self, he probably wouldn't recognize it at all.

Developments bring money into the region, which are funneled into more developments... I suppose, from the viewpoint of Saitama's finances, I ought to be happy.

But I wonder what Saitama itself thinks of all this?

Let's say, for example, that I were Saitama. I should think I would be quite angry, and probably react along the lines of: "Hey, who the hell do you think you are? Get your damn buildings off my back!!"

And if that happened, there would be no more to say. After all, I (Saitama) could simply roll over onto my back and bring the entire urban development scheme to a catastrophic end. All the residents would be left without warmth or shelter, with no recourse but to build temples and shrines to me (Saitama) in the hopes of quelling my anger.

Humans feel as though they have conquered the land, but that is not the case. The land merely lets us live here, and we would do well to remember that.

It was about one part this reverent image and nine parts "Wouldn't it be cool if Hokkaido was actually alive?" that inspired this fifth volume.

Well, I've already filled half the page with my grumbling, so to return to the book, the primary theme, in this author's humble opinion, was "searching for a way of life."

So far, the series villains have all embraced the darkness from start to finish, but Shishi is constantly doubting her own path, searching for her own soul. She's a conflicted, more true-to-life villain who wants to do the right thing, and when she consequently strays from her own path, Bisco, our hero, takes responsibility (in his own way) and allows her to start over.

Choosing your own path, which Bisco describes as "blooming," is not as easy a thing to do as Bisco makes it sound. Without the benefit of hindsight, it is very often impossible to know whether your choice is the correct one.

When you bloom in a certain direction, with all your heart, and it just doesn't work out, that can be greatly disheartening. And I think it's at times like those that Bisco says to bloom again, facing the sun this time.

For me, it was only after a few "rebloomings" that I came to write *Sabikui Bisco*. If a flower cries because it blooms in the darkness, one choice may be to try blooming somewhere else.

And there would be no greater pleasure for myself as an author if the words and actions of those in this volume inspire any of my readers.

Now, as I have filled the page, I shall say good-bye. Well then, until next time.

—*Shinji Cobkubo*